Five Star English for
Restaurants and Hotels

五星級

★ ★ ★ ★ ★

餐旅英語

免訂位馬上享用

林昭菁、Jeri Fay Maynard（梅潔理）◎著

★ 100%完全符合**餐廳＋旅館**工作英語對談的需要

★ 適用於高中職、大專院校餐旅系學生、餐廳旅館從業人員

★ 三大篇「**資訊社交表達**」、「**餐廳英語**」、「**旅館英語**」英語應答OK!

★ 停不住**對話**+一點點**文法**解析+必備**單字**+職場補給站=五星級的英語力

★ **Update**你的職場英語**溝通能力**，成為**國際化超級優質餐旅人**!!

作者序

Preface

There is an old joke. It goes like this, "How do I get to Carnegie Hall (a famous performance Hall in NYC)?" The answer? "Practice, Practice, Practice!" Learning a language has the same response. You have to practice speaking it. The goal of this book is to give you an organized and simple approach for practicing English in all areas of hospitality. You can use it alone or with a friend and you can open it to the section you need to know and start practicing the dialogues. By the end of the book, you will know most of the vocabulary needed in the field of hospitality and should be able to understand the requests of your English speaking guests.

English is a tricky language full of inconsistencies and odd slang, but it shouldn't be scary to learn to speak it. By providing practical and realistic conversations to practice, the reader should be able to hone his or her skills so that she speaks with a natural fluid voice. We hope you enjoy practicing it and that your hard work pays off! And when we come into your hotel or restaurant, show off your English! We'll be delighted to hear it!

*Special thanks to David Goorskey and Morris Maynard for their editing effort.

林昭菁

Jennay maynard

在美國有一個老笑話是這樣的，「我如何進入卡內基音樂廳表演呢（在紐約市著名的表演廳）？」答案呢？「練習，練習，再練習！」學習語言也有同樣的答案。

你要不斷地練習說英語。這本書的目的就是提供你一個有組織但簡單的方式來練習所有餐旅領域的英語。你可以自己用這本書，或者和朋友一起用這本書，你可以打開書內你需要知道的單元，並開始練習對話的部分。在看完這本書後，你就會學習到餐旅領域裡最需要用到的詞彙，也應該能夠理解講英語的客人的要求。

英語是一個棘手的語言，這個語言充滿矛盾和奇怪的俚語，但你不應該對學說英文感到害怕。這本書有提供實用和現實的對話練習，這樣你就能夠磨練自己的基礎，最後你可以用自然流利的方式來說英文。我們希望你會喜歡使用這本書來練習英文，有一天你一定會成功的！而當我們進入你的飯店或餐廳，你可以炫耀你的英文！我們會很高興聽到你所說的英文喔！

* 感謝 David Goorskey 和 Morris Maynard 在校稿上的幫忙。

林昭菁
Jeri Fay Maynard
（梅潔理）

編者序

《五星級餐旅英語》一書是依照餐廳、旅館等工作需求而設計的英語學習書。

從地點、方位、時間等資訊的說明到餐桌服務、與旅館服務的英文使用方法上，都有很詳盡的說明。

本書有幾大特點：

第一點：由外籍與中籍作者共同撰寫，英語簡明正確。中文解說符合中文讀者的學習需求。

第二點：對話全部模擬實際可能會發生的情況，藉此學習聽與說。

第三點：大量句子建立句庫，可方便您向顧客用英語解說。

第四點：對話附有簡單文法說明，用簡單的英文可以表達得很清楚。

第五點：小對話練習，供讀者與同伴角色扮演練習口說，或是讀者也可以自己練習。

第六點：職場補給站，附註職場工作的心法，剛入此行業需要注意的地方。中英文撰寫，加強自身的英文閱讀能力。

第七點：融入西式餐廳與旅館的服務內容知識，讓您在應對西方顧客時更有信心。

希望此書可以幫助對餐旅英文有興趣的讀者，在此行業的英文能力上有所提升。

倍斯特編輯部

Contents 目次

Part 3　Hotel English
旅館英語

附錄

常見單字

Part I

Expressing Clearly

清楚表達

Unit 01 **Information** 表達資訊

1.1.1 Ordinals and Numbers 序數和數字

不停住對話 MP3 001

At restaurant, greeting a guest without reservations.
在餐廳接待沒有預約的客人。

Maître	Welcome. Is this your first time **dining** with us today?	歡迎您,這是您今天第一次在我們這裡用餐嗎?
Guest	Yes. How long is the **wait**?	是的。請問需要等多久?
Maître	I hope you enjoy it. It's about twenty minutes. How many are in your party?	我希望您會喜歡這裡,大概要等 20 分鐘,請問您有幾位?
Guest	There are eight of us. The rest should be here in a second.	有我們八個人。其餘人一會兒就會到。
Maître	Is this a special occasion? I see you brought a cake.	這是一個特殊的聚會嗎?我看你帶了蛋糕。
Guest	It's my younger brother's twelfth birthday. Can you put twelve candles on it for us?	這是我弟弟的 12 歲生日。你可以幫我們把 12 蠟燭插上去嗎?

Maître	Certainly! Do you want to be seated first or wait for <u>the rest of</u> your party?	當然！您要先坐下呢？還是要等其他人呢？
Guest	Please seat me first.	請讓我先坐下。
Maître	Are there any children in your party?	你們有小孩參加嗎？
Guest	There are two **children** and six adults.	有兩個小孩，六個大人。
Maître	Perfect. Do you need high chairs or children's menus?	沒問題的，你需要高腳椅或兒童菜單嗎？
Guest	No high chairs, but <u>we would like</u> two children's menus.	不需要高腳椅了，但是我們希望有兩個兒童菜單。
Maître	You're next. Would you like to wait in the **bar**? I will find you when <u>the table is ready</u>.	下一個空位就是您的，你想在酒吧等待嗎？如果桌子已準備就緒，我會去跟您說。

Part I 清楚表達

Words

單　字

* dining /ˈdaɪnɪŋ/　*n.* 吃飯；用餐
* wait /wet/　*n.* 等候；埋伏
* candle /ˈkændəl/　*n.* 蠟燭
* children /ˈtʃɪldrən/　*n.* 孩子們（複數）
* bar /bɑr/　*n.* 橫木；酒吧

Grammar

文法片語

1. **put twelve candles on it for us** 幫我們把 12 蠟燭插上去
   ★小提點：〈on it〉在上面，這裡的〈it〉代名詞指的是前面句子所説的蛋糕，因為在説的是一樣的名詞所以第二個用代名詞〈it〉。
   > 例一：The truck has a scooter on it. 那個卡車上面有一輛機車。〈it〉指的是〈truck〉。
   ★小提點： 另一種〈on it〉也可以解釋為「正在進行，在掌握中」
   > 例二：〈I am on it.〉我這就去辦。或是，我已經正在辦。

2. **the rest of...** 剩下的 ...
   ★小提點：這個名詞〈rest〉是「剩下，其餘」，句型用法是〈the rest of + N〉其餘的, 剩下的。
   > 例一：類似用法有很多，比如〈the rest of the world〉世界其他國家，〈the rest of them〉其他人 ,〈the rest of my family〉我的其他家人，〈the rest of my...〉我的其他……
   > 例一：I live here but the rest of my family lives in Kaohsiung. 我住這裡但是其他家人住在高雄。
   > 例二：Please finish the rest of your food. 請吃完剩下的食物

3. **we would like ...** 我們想要……
   ★小提點：〈would like〉想要，後面可以直接加名詞。這是比較有禮貌的表達一種「意願或希望」。
   > 例一：I would like the soup first. 我想要先喝湯。
   ★小提點：〈would like〉也可以直接請某人做某件事，但是語氣是比較委婉。
   > 例二： I would like you show me the room. 我很希望你能帶我去看看房間
   > 例三：另外一個句型也很實用〈would like to〉後面要馬上接原形動詞，記得記得！！〈He would like to take the train tomorrow to Taipei.〉他明天想要坐火車到臺北。

4. the table is ready 桌子已經準備好了

★小提點：〈 ready 〉是形容詞，是準備好的意思，這是很好用和簡單的
　表達方式如〈I am ready.〉我準備好了，〈Are you ready?〉你準備好了
　嗎？

★小提點：〈 ready 〉後面可加〈for+ 名詞〉。

例一：Are you ready for the trip to Taiwan？你準備好要去台灣了嗎？

例二：Sir, the coffee is ready for you. 先生，咖啡已經為您準備好了。

例三：I am sorry. The shop is not ready yet. 哎，很對不起，這個商店還沒準
　　　備好開門。

Part I 清楚表達

Short Sentences

不尷尬短句

❶ The cafe was officially opened on the 23rd of March 2010.
那家咖啡館在 2010 年 3 月 23 日正式開業。

❷ The Hotel Tainan has 333 elegant guest rooms.
台南飯店擁有 333 間優雅的客房。

❸ The Japanese noodle shop is located right in front of Tainan Train Station,
near the Shin Kong Mitsukoshi Department Store.
那家日本拉麵店就坐落在台南火車站對面，是在新光三越百貨公司附近。

❹ Taiwan is a small island but there are 368 zip codes.
台灣是一個小島，但有 368 個郵政編碼。

❺ Under the effective management, our restaurant has received the
"Excellent Award" 4 times in the past 5 years.
在有效的管理下，我們的餐廳在過去的 5 年有得到 4 次的 “ 優秀獎 ”。

❻ There are at least 4 or 5 B&Bs near the Guan-Zi-Ling Labor Recreation
Center.
在關子嶺勞工育樂中心的附近至少有 4 或 5 家的民宿。

❼ Some of the old trees on the National Cheng Kung University campus
were planted at least 4 decades ago.
在成功大學校園裡有一些老樹是在四十年前種植的。

❽ The famous De Yi Shrimp Cracker was established in 1971 in Anping, Tainan.
著名的德義蝦餅在台南安平成立於 1971 年。

❾ There are hundreds of night markets in the cities and counties of Taiwan.
在台灣有好幾百個夜市。

❿ The menu at the famous restaurant is not really impressive because they only have a few dishes.
那家有名餐廳的菜單其實不怎麼樣，因為他們只有幾樣菜而已。

⓫ At the party, the receptionist put many special candles on the cake.
在那個慶祝會，接待人員會放很多特別的蠟燭在蛋糕上。

⓬ If you have a chance to tour around Taiwan, you will see at least more than 30 types of sweet potato products.
如果你有機會遊台灣，你至少會發現有超過 30 多種的蕃薯產品。

Speak Up!
說出來！   MP3 002

Dialogue 01 對話

Guest: Why doesn't the elevator in Taiwan have the number "4"?
顧客：為什麼台灣的電梯都沒有號碼 "4" 呢？

Staff: Well, culturally in Taiwan, the number "4" is an unlucky number so we don't use the number in some public places like hotel and hospital.
工作人員：是這樣的，就台灣的文化來說，號碼 "4" 是很不吉利的，所以在一些公眾場所如飯店與醫院的電梯都沒有這一個號碼。

Dialogue 02 對話

Guest: What's the weather like in Tainan now?
顧客：台南現在的天氣是如何？

Hotel Staff: It is 14.2° Celsius and is misty with light winds and clouds.
飯店工作人員：現在是攝氏 14.2 度，有霧，微風和多雲。

Dialogue 03 對話

Guest: Do you have any special discount?

顧客：你們有特別的折扣嗎？

Staff: Yes, we do. If you order two main dishes, you will get the second dish for half price.

服務員：是的，我們有折扣，如果你點兩道主餐，第二道主餐會是半價。

Job Wisdom 職業補給站

One of the frequent questions an American will ask is for you translate into Fahrenheit when you tell them the temperature in Celsius. This will happen when you tell them the beach weather (30℃ which is 86 ℉), room temperature (21℃ is 70 ℉) or talking about body temperature (The average normal is 37　℃ which is 98.6 ℉). One formula is to multiple by nine, then divide by five, and add thirty-two. A quick, but not always accurate way (close enough most of the time) to teach your guests is to double it and add thirty.

當你用攝氏告訴美國人天氣的溫度時，他們會請你把攝氏轉換成華氏的溫度。幾個例子，如海灘的天氣 30℃（就是 86 ℉華氏），室溫是 21℃（就是 70 ℉華氏）或談論有關體溫（平均正常溫度是 37℃，就是 98.6 ℉華氏）。這個算法的公式是把攝氏乘以 9，總數除以 5 之後再加 32。還有一個更快速的算法，但並不是很準確的方法（大部分時候算出來是很接近），你可以這樣教你的顧客這個算法，就是攝氏溫度乘以 2，然後總數再加 30。

Unit 01 **Information** 表達資訊

1.1.2　Time 時間

Conversations
不停住對話 MP3 003

A person working at the Reservation Desk in the restaurant talks to the customer.
在餐廳櫃檯的工作人員正在跟顧客說話。

Employee	How may I help you today?	需要協助嗎？
Customer	I need to make **reservations** for a party of 12 for Friday, March 13th.	我需要訂位。我們有 12 個人，日期在 3 月 13 日星期五。
Employee	We have seats for a party that large at 5 o'clock or at 9 o'clock on that date. Does either of those times work for you?	我們在那天的 5 點或 9 點有空位可以容納這麼多人。這兩個時間哪一個可以呢？
Customer	No. How about Saturday evening?	都不行，星期六晚上如何？
Employee	We are **fully** booked on Saturday, March 14th. We do have **openings** on Tuesday and Wednesday though.	我們 3 月 14 日星期六的定位都客滿了。我們在週二和週三有空位。
Customer	Is there any way you could **squeeze** us on the 13th at 8:30?	你們有沒有可能在 13 日儘量騰出 8:30 的時間？

Employee	Let me recheck. I'm sorry but the large room that is **available** for parties has been reserved already and we need to clean the space before we can seat your party.	讓我再重新確認一下。真的很對不起，但是可以容納多人的大型房間都已經被預定了，而且在你們開始之前，我們也需要把房間清理乾淨。
Customer	Ok. <u>Go ahead and book</u> us for 9 o'clock on the 13th.	好吧。請幫我們預定 13 日的 9 點鐘。

Words
單　字

* reservation /rɛzəˋveʃən/　*n.* 預訂
* fully /ˋfuli/　*adv.* 十分地；完全地
* opening /ˋopənɪŋ/　*n.* 空間；空擋
* squeeze /skwiz/　*v.* 擠；榨取
* available /əˋveləbəl/　*adj.* 可用的

Grammar
文法片語

1. a party of... 一群……
   ★小提點：一般我們知道的〈party〉是名詞「派對或聚會」，〈party〉當名詞也可以是「夥伴，同類」，這個片語〈 a party of 〉就是「一群」，片語之後要馬上加上名詞或數字〈 a party of ＋N 〉。
   例一：Can you prepare food for a party of 60? 你們可以準備 60 個人聚會的食物嗎？
   例二：A party of school children is taking a trip to Taipei. 一群小學生要去臺北旅遊。

例三：The tour leader is taking a party of retirees to Kenting for three nights. 導遊要帶一群退休人士到墾丁玩三個晚上。

2. We are fully booked on Saturday. 我們星期六都訂滿了

★小提點：句子可長可短，這個句子其實就是〈We are booked〉〈S+V〉，但是要強調「客滿」，所以加了副詞來強調〈fully booked〉，再加上後面的時間。

例一：That afternoon train is fully booked already. 下午那班火車都已經全部訂滿了。

例二：Our travel agency's schedule to visit the Central Mountain on Friday is fully booked. 我們旅行社的中央山脈之旅已經全部排滿了。

3. We do have openings on Tuesday. 我們在星期二有幾個空位

★小提點：〈We do+ 原形動詞〉，do 在這裡是助動詞，後面要接原形動詞，這裡的助動詞有加強動詞的功能，這句可以簡單的說〈We have openings.〉，因為加了助動詞〈do〉，語氣上比較強調意即「我們確實有空位。」

例一：這句 We do have wireless in the lobby. 「我們的大廳確實可以無線上網」比這一句 We have wireless in the lobby. 「我們的大廳可以無線上網」的語氣堅定多了。

例二：We do have a special on fried fish tonight. 我們今天晚上確實有一道特殊的炸魚。

4. Go ahead and book us for 9 o'clock. 請幫我們訂 9 點的位子

★小提點：〈Go ahead.〉「就是這樣做」，這可以就算一個完整的句子。如果加個〈Please〉會變成有禮貌。

例一：Please go ahead. 請繼續。

例二：Please go ahead and start the drink. 請不要客氣的開始喝飲料。

例三：Please go ahead and I will come later. 請先去，我隨後到。

不尷尬短句

❶ Do you want me to make a dinner reservation for 2 on December 25 at 7:00 in the evening?
您要預約 12 月 25 日晚上 7:00 的兩個人晚餐嗎？

❷ Can you give us a few more minutes?
可否請你給我們幾分鐘的時間？

❸ It is no problem. We can give you a table for four.
沒問題的，我們可以給你四個人的桌子。

❹ Would you like to try one of today's specials?
你想要試試今天特別餐點之一嗎？

❺ Can you do 8:20 instead of 8:30 on Sunday the 16th?
可以在 16 號星期日的時間從 8:30 改到 8:20 嗎？

❻ Would you prefer a round table?
你們希望有圓桌的嗎？

❼ We will be expecting you this Tuesday at 7:00. Thank you.
我們會在這個星期二 7:00 等你來，謝謝你。

❽ It's no problem if you need to cancel the reservation.
如果你需要取消預約，我們是沒有問題的。

❾ Do you need to postpone the party?
您的慶祝會需要延後日期嗎？

❿ Our cafe is open on weekday afternoon.
我們的咖啡店在平日下午是有開的。

⓫ We are usually very busy on Sunday night.
我們通常在週日晚上是非常忙碌的。

⓬ Our chef usually makes some special desserts on Thursday night.
我們的主廚通常會在週四晚做一些特殊的甜點。

Part I　清楚表達

Speak Up!
說出來！ MP3 004

Dialogue 01 對話

Staff: How many people will you need the reservation for on Monday?
工作人員：你們星期一預約是多少人？

Guest: There are six of us, plus two babies.
顧客：我們有六個人外加兩個嬰兒。

Dialogue 02 對話

Staff: What time are you coming to the restaurant?
工作人員：你們幾點會來餐廳呢？

Guest: It will be about 7:00, or perhaps 7:30.
顧客：大概是 7:00 或者是 7:30。

Dialogue 03 對話

Visitor: I heard 7-11 in Taiwan is open all year around.
訪客：我聽說台灣的 7-11 全年都開著的。

Staff: Yes, 7-11 in Taiwan is open 24 hours a day and 7 days a week. It has everything you need.
工作人員：是的，台灣的 7-11 一天開 24 小時，一個星期 7 天都開著，你要的東西他們都有賣。

Think of how you use numbers at your place of employment currently. Would you be able to be effective at your job without them? Numbers and ordinals are used frequently in all kinds of conversations with customers. They will want to know how much something, how many are in a package, what time something starts, what their room number is, and how much money do they owe you for your services. Since they are a critical component of communicating, it is important that you are fluent and can use them with ease. Being able to tell the guests that they are the first or the next will help them wait patiently. Since the months have specific names in English, your guests will make reservations using their names (such as April 9th) frequently as well. Knowing the days of the week, telling time as well as concepts such as either/or will increase your communication abilities quickly.

　　想想看你現在工作的地方是如何使用數字的。你覺得在工作上沒有用數字可以讓你有效的工作嗎？數字和序號常用於各種與顧客的對話。他們都會想知道東西的價格，一個包裝裡有多少東西，什麼時間需要開始做什麼事，他們的房間號碼是幾號，還有他們需要付你多少的服務費。因為數字和序號是溝通時一個重要組成的部分，所以在這方面很流利的運用是很重要的，常常使用這些數字和序號也會讓你覺得越來越容易。如果能夠告訴顧客，在排隊時他們是第一個或下一個，這將可以幫助他們耐心等待。月份在英文裡有特定的名稱，你的顧客在預約上會很頻繁使用這些月份（如，4月9日）。如果你知道英文裡的星期，也會說明時間以及一些概念如（如，兩者其中一個），這些基本的英文可以迅速提高你的溝通能力。

Unit 01 Information
表達資訊

1.1.3 Directions 方向

不停住對話   MP3 005

Employee greets a customer who looks lost.
員工迎接看起來像迷失方向的顧客。

Employee	May I help you? You look **confused**.	我可以幫你嗎?你看起來很困惑的樣子。
Customer	They told me the Seafood Restaurant was <u>up here</u> on the tenth floor.	他們跟我説海鮮餐廳是在這上面的十樓。
Employee	This is the eleventh floor. You need to take the **escalator** down one floor and <u>turn left</u>.	這是十一樓。你需要坐電梯再往下一層樓然後左轉。
Customer	<u>Turn left?</u>	左轉?
Employee	Yes and it will be on your right. You can't miss it.	是的,餐廳就在您的右邊。你不會錯過的。
Customer	What about the watch shop? Is it **nearby** as well?	那手錶店呢?就是這附近嗎?

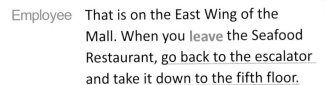

Employee	That is on the East Wing of the Mall. When you **leave** the Seafood Restaurant, go back to the escalator and take it down to the fifth floor.	那是在商圈的東區。當你離開海鮮餐廳時，走到手扶梯然後往下到五樓。
Customer	Is there a map of the **mall** anywhere?	有沒有任何地方提供這個商圈的地圖？
Employee	When you get off the escalator on the fifth floor, you will see a stand with a map. The East Wing is purple.	當您在五樓走下電梯，你會看到有地圖的站點。東區的資訊是用紫色區分。

Part I 清楚表達

Words
單 字

* confused /kənˋfjuzd/　*adj.* 困惑的；煩惱的
* escalator /ˋɛskəˏletə/　*n.* 電扶梯
* nearby /ˋnɪrˏbaɪ/　*adj.* 附近
* leave /liv/　*v.* 離開
* mall /mɔl/　*n.* 商圈；購物中心

Grammar
文法片語

1. The restaurant is up here. 餐廳是在這上面。
    ★小提點：〈 Up here 〉在這上面，這是副詞的使用，是指一個特定的區域或地方。
    例一：The swimming pool is up here on the tenth floor. 游泳池是在這上面的十樓。

★小提點：也可以用類似的〈Over here+on+ 地名〉。

例二：The gift shop should be over there on North Street. 禮品店應該是在北街那裡。

例三：Please ask the manager come over here right away. 請經理馬上來這裡。

2. Turn left. 左轉

★小提點：Turn left 左轉，〈turn〉這個字在動詞是「轉」的動作，通常用在方向的說明。

例一：Turn left when you see the park. 當你看到公園時要左轉

例二：Turn right at the end of the hall way. 在走廊底右轉。

★小提點：很多方向都可以用〈Turn〉來當動詞

例三：〈Turn right〉向右轉，〈Turn to the east〉轉到東的方向，〈Turn around〉回頭

3. The elevator is at the front and you take it down to the fourth floor.
直走就可以到電梯，然後坐到第四層。

★小提點：〈and〉是連接詞，我們對〈and〉是很熟悉，要記得的是〈and〉是用來連接兩個以上的同類詞性，如連接名詞和名詞〈the floor and the wall〉，連接形容詞和形容詞〈delicious and tasty〉，連接動詞和動詞〈come and see〉，一定要記得連接的是同等詞性，下面這個句子看起來很長，可是也就只是〈S+V and S+V〉而已。

例一：I am going to the night market and I will buy some delicious fried chicken. 我現在要去夜市，我會買一些好吃的炸雞給你吃。

4. When you ..., you will ... 當你……，你就會……

★小提點：When 在這裡是連接詞，在連接兩個完整的句子。用來解釋一個動作完成了，接著另一個動作就發生了。就是〈When+S+V, S+V〉用 When 把兩個句子連起來。

例一：When it stops raining, I will go to the store. 當雨馬上停了後，我就會去商店。

例二：　When the weather is good, we can visit the park.　當天氣好的時候，我們可以去公園。

例三：When we visit Taiwan, we will take the train. 當我們去拜訪台灣時，我們會坐火車。

Short Sentences
不尷尬短句

❶ Tainan Catholic Church is located in the West Central District in Tainan City.
台南天主教會是在臺南市的西區。

❷ If you continue straight on and go past some traffic lights, you will see Tainan Canal.
如果你繼續直走，過了紅綠燈，你就會看到台南運河。

❸ You'd better take the Tainan Tour Shuttle Bus because Anping District is very far from here.
你最好是搭乘台南觀光公車，因為安平區離這裡很遠。

❹ If you want to go to the Tainan Story House, you're going the wrong way.
如果你要去台南故事館，你是走錯路了。

❺ You're going in the wrong direction.
你走錯方向了。

❻ Please continue straight ahead for about a mile and you will see Tainan Astronomical Education Area.
再繼續直走約一英里，你就會看到台南天文教育園區。

❼ The easiest way to get to Wufei Temple is to go right on Wufei Street.
到五妃廟最簡單的方式就是直接到五妃街。

❽ It's about a five minute walk to Tainan City Government.
這裡走到臺南市政府約五分鐘的路程。

❾ I'm afraid I can't help you because I don't know where Shen-nong Street is.
我可能無法幫你，因為我不知道神農街在哪裡。

⑩ When you see Klim Supermarket, you will soon see the Tainan Confucius Temple.
當你看到克林超市，你就會看到孔子廟。

⑪ If you go down two more blocks, you will see Yue-jin Old Port on your left.
如果你再走兩條街，你就會在左手邊看到月津舊港。

⑫ You can walk to the night market in ten minutes.
十分鐘你就可以走到夜市。

Speak Up!
說出來！   MP3 006

Dialogue 01 對話

Visitor: What's the best way to get to the Tainan Train Station?
訪客：到台南火車站最好是怎麼走？

Front Desk: You can walk from here. It is not too far. Go straight until you come to an intersection and it is on your right.
櫃檯人員：你可以從這裡走，不會很遠，直走到十字路口，就在右手邊。

Dialogue 02 對話

Guest: Is Tainan National University of the Arts far from here?
顧客：台南藝術大學離這裡很遠嗎？

Staff: Yes, it is very far. You'd better take the Tainan Tour Shuttle Bus.
工作人員：是的，非常的遠，你最好是搭乘台南觀光巴士。

Dialogue 03 對話

Visitor: Can you help me with the directions to the park?
訪客：你可以告訴我到公園怎麼去嗎？

Staff: Yes, let me write down clear and precise directions for you so you don't get confused with the busy traffic.
工作人員：可以的，我把方向很清晰和精確的寫下來給你，這樣你才不會因忙碌的交通而搞亂方向。

"Where is the _____" and "How do I get to _____" are two frequently asked questions by customers. Even if they know where they are, they may not know how to get to their next place. For many foreign guests, this is the first time they are visiting Taiwan and they will spend a lot of their time disoriented and lost. Even when they think they followed someone's directions exactly, they will end up in the wrong place, at the wrong restaurant, in the wrong store. When giving directions to foreigners, they may not understand you and will appreciate the time you take showing them directly to the elevator or starting point. Drawing a map or jotting down the directions on paper will help ease their sense of confusion and frustration. By going the extra mile and making sure they can find their way around, they will be left with a good impression not only of you and your establishment, but the country as well.

〈 _____ 在哪〉和〈我要怎麼去 _____ 〉是顧客最經常問的兩個問題。即使他們知道他們現在所在位置，他們可能不知道下一個要去的地方在哪裏。對於許多外國顧客來說，這是他們第一次到台灣玩，他們會常常搞錯地方和迷失方向。就算是他們覺得他們是完全按照別人給他們的說明，他們還是會到錯誤的地方、錯誤的餐廳、或錯誤的店。當你要給外國人方向的說明時，他們可能不會了解你說的，所以會很感激如果你能花一點時間把他們帶到電梯或明顯起點的地方。畫個地圖或把方向說明寫下來，都可以幫助緩解他們的困惑和挫敗感。帶他們走一點距離，確定他們可以找到他們要找的地方，這樣他們對你和你的公司會有很好的印象，甚至對這個國家會有很好的印象。

Unit 01 Information 表達資訊

1.1.4 Indoor Facility and Locations 室內設備和位置

At the Front Desk of the Hotel, helping a guest.
在飯店的櫃檯前幫助一位顧客

Guest	Can you tell me where the pool is?	你能告訴我游泳池在那裡嗎？
Desk Clerk	The **pool** is on the sixth floor. When you get off the elevator, it will be down the hall on your left.	游泳池在是在六樓。當您走下電梯後走廊直走就在你的左手邊。
Guest	And which elevator is closest?	哪一個電梯是最近的？
Desk Clerk	Go straight down this **hall** and the elevators on the right will take you there.	這個走廊直走，用右手邊的電梯就可以到達。
Guest	Is the **exercise room** close by it?	附近有健身室嗎？
Desk Clerk	The exercise room is across the hall from the pool on the right. You can't **miss** it when you find the pool.	健身室在穿過走廊後的游泳池的右邊。您如果看到游泳池就不會錯過的。

Guest	Is the formal restaurant on that floor as well?	那層樓有沒有正式的餐廳呢？
Desk Clerk	That is on the twelfth floor. <u>Would you like me to</u> make reservations for it for tonight since the view of the city is **stunning** from it?	那是在 12 樓。您需要讓我幫您預訂今天晚上的位子嗎？從餐廳看到這個城市景色是極好的！

Words 單字

* pool /pul/　*n.* 游泳池
* hall /hɔl/　*n.* 走廊；大廳
* exercise room /ˈɛksɚˌsaɪz/ /rum/　*n.* 健身室
* miss /mɪs/　*v.* 遺漏；錯過
* stunning /ˈstʌnɪŋ/　*adj.* 極好的

Grammar 文法片語

1. on the sixth floor　在第六樓
   ★小提點：〈on〉是介係詞，在這裏是表示位置在……上。
   例一：He put the American dollars on the counter. 他把美金放在櫃檯上。
   例二：Please pick up the trash on the floor. 請把地上的垃圾撿起來。
   ★小提點：on 也可以表示什麼東西帶在……身上。
   例三：I did not have any Taiwanese money on me. 我身上沒有台幣。

2. get off the elevator　走出電梯
   ★小提點：〈get off〉是動詞片語，〈get off + 受詞〉這裡的受詞可以是

任何的交通工具，〈get off the car〉下車，〈get off the scooter〉下摩托車，〈get off the plane〉下飛機，〈get off the train〉下火車，還有啊，加上了〈Please〉會顯得更有禮貌。

例一：Please get off the bus after it comes to a stop. 當車子停了下來後，請下車。

3. The exercise room is across the hall from the pool. 健身室在穿過走廊後的游泳池的右邊。

★小提點：〈across〉 當介係詞是指「與……交叉；在……對面」。

例一：The park is just across from our house. 公園就在我們的房子對面。

例二：There's also a bank across from the drug store. 這個藥店的對面還有一家銀行。

4. Would you like me to... 你想不想要我……

★小提點：〈Would you ...〉是一種禮貌的請求或建議。

例一：Would you like me to help you? 你想不想要我幫你呢？

例二：Would you like me to tell you about the big news? 你要不要我跟你說那則大新聞呢？

★小提點：也可以直接把〈me〉省掉。〈Would you like to + V〉你要不要，您想要不要？

例三：What you like some water? 你想要喝水嗎？

Short Sentences
不尷尬短句

❶ There are many theme based B&Bs in Taitung.
台東有很多主題式的民宿。

❷ In our hotel, there is a heated pool, two game rooms and an outdoor play area for children.
在我們的飯店裡，有一個溫水游泳池，兩個遊戲室和一個兒童戶外遊樂區。

❸ From the entrance hall, there is a door leading to the ballroom.
從入口大廳，就有一扇門可以通到宴會廳。

❹ Each room in our hotel is furnished with original antique furniture.
我們飯店的每一間客房均配備原有的古董家具。

❺ Each hotel room is furnished with a three-seater sofa, matching comfy armchair, a flat screen TV and a coffee table.
每一個房間都配有一個三人座沙發，配套舒適的扶手椅、平板電視和一個茶几。

❻ You will be able to have your breakfast on the balcony in the morning sun.
你可以在美好晨光的陪襯下，在陽台享受你的早餐。

❼ Most hotels in Taiwan have wireless internet connection in the rooms and in the public areas.
台灣的飯店大部分在客房和公共區都有無線上網。

❽ Our guests can use the business services and the well-equipped meeting rooms.
我們的客人可以使用商務服務和設備齊全的會議室。

❾ In our Bed & Breakfast, we have two well-stocked bookcases where you are welcome to borrow books during your stay.
在我們的民宿裡，我們有兩個藏書豐富的書櫃，歡迎您在入住期間借閱圖書。

❿ National Martyrs' Shrine is down this street on the left.
忠烈祠就在這條街的左邊。

⓫ Shilin Night Market is located in Shilin district about a mile and a half from here.
士林夜市位於士林區離這裡約一英里半的距離。

⓬ The Youth Hostel is very close to Taipei Train Station.
那個青年旅館非常靠近台北火車站。

Part I 清楚表達

Speak Up!
說出來！ MP3 008

Dialogue 01 對話

Guest: The online review says that your bathroom is very nice.
顧客：網路評價說，你們的浴室是非常好的。

Staff: Yes, we have a marble bathroom and stained glass ceiling in every room.
工作人員：是的，我們每間客房都有一個大理石的浴室和彩色玻璃屋頂。

Dialogue 02 對話

Guest: Do you have a cabin available for six people?
顧客：你們是否有六人的小木屋？

Staff: Yes, we have one cabin that offers 1 double bedroom, 2 twin bedded rooms, a bathroom, a comfortable living area and a well-equipped kitchen.
工作人員：是的，我們有一個小木屋是有一間雙人臥室，兩間有兩張單人床的房間，還有浴室，舒適的起居區和一個設備齊全的廚房。

Dialogue 03 對話

Visitor: Is City Garden Cafe located on a busy street?
訪客：城市花園咖啡廳是位在繁忙的大街上嗎？

Staff: No. It is not. It is actually located on an alley. It is hard to find it but once you find it, you will be surprised by how suitable the location is for such a charming cafe.
工作人員：不是，不是在大街上。這個咖啡廳實際上是位於一條小巷內。很難找到的地方，但一旦你找到了這個地方，你會很驚訝這樣迷人的咖啡館的所在位置是非常合適的。

There are plenty of housing choices for the tourist visiting Taiwan- everything from high end hotels to bed and breakfast places, but your guest chose your place of business and you want them to come back next time they need a place to stay as well. Repeat business boosts sales and profitability because there are no marketing or advertising costs for that return guest. They are a walking advertisement for it as well and tend to leave glowing reviews online or when asked about where they are staying. The first thing a hotel can do to get return guests is to hire the right person- and that's YOU! Stay positive, friendly, concerned, and knowledgeable. Offer professionalism with a smile and be prepared to help your guests find their way around the hotel and the city. Being on the front desk is critical for encouraging guests to stay at your hotel again. Prove to management that you are the right person repeatedly with every guest interaction and you'll make a difference.

在台灣旅遊的遊客有很多的住宿選擇，從高級酒店到民宿的地方都有，但你的客人選擇你的工作的地方，你也希望他們下次需要住宿時還會再來這個地方。回流的客戶可以提升銷售額和盈利，因為對這個回流的客戶是不需要用到營銷或廣告費用。他們就是一個活廣告，而且在離開後或者當被問到有關他們的住宿經驗時，他們往往會在網上留好評。飯店能做到保留回流客人的第一件事就是僱用合適的人——那就是你！你要保持積極的態度，友好，關心，也要很有知識。提供專業服務時要面帶微笑，並準備好可以幫助你的客人在飯店和城市內找到他們要去的地方。對於鼓勵客人再度光臨，在前台工作是很有關鍵性的。利用與每一位客人互動的機會來不斷地證明，讓你的上級知道你是這個工作的合適人選，你也會做出很多的貢獻。

Part I 清楚表達

Unit 01 **Information** 表達資訊

1.1.5 Dimensions and Sizes 尺寸和大小

不停住對話 MP3 009

In the Gift Shop, a sales clerk helps a guest make purchases.
在禮品店，一名銷售人員在幫助客人進行採購。

Guest	I want to get a cute dress for my **granddaughter** but I don't know what size to get her.	我想買一件可愛的衣服給我的孫女，但我不知道要買什麼尺寸給她。
Sales Clerk	How big is she?	她有多大？

(Guest **measures** from the floor.)（顧客用手從地板指了身高的高度）

Guest	About this tall.	大概這麼高。
Sales Clerk	How old is she?	她幾歲呢？
Guest	She turns five years old in November and she wears a 4T in the states.	她在十一月就 5 歲了，她現在在美國穿的是 4T 號碼。
Sales Clerk	I think a size six or seven would work perfectly for her.	我覺得六或七的尺寸會很適合她。

Guest	This one looks too big. Do you have it in a smaller size?	這個看起來太長了，你有沒有比這件更小一號的呢？
Sales Clerk	Not that **model**, but this one is a size 5. Does it look like it would work?	這個款式的沒有你要的尺寸，但是這件是 5 號，看起來會合適嗎？
Guest	Perfectly. Now, I would like a box of pineapple cakes for her parents.	這個很棒，還有，我想要買一盒鳳梨酥給她的父母。
Sales Clerk	Do you want a large one or a smaller more **compact** one? Both boxes are beautiful.	你想要一個大盒子的還是小一點放的比較擠的呢？兩個盒子都很美的。
Guest	The smaller one takes up less space in my suitcase. I'll take it.	小的盒子在我的手提箱裡會佔少一點的空間。我買小盒的。

Part I 清楚表達

Words 單 字

* granddaughter /ˈɡrændˌdɔtɚ/   *n.* 孫女
* measure /ˈmɛʒɚ/   *v.* 測量；衡量
* model /ˈmɑdəl/   *n.* 模型；模特兒；型號
* compact /ˈkɑmpækt/   *adj.* 緊密的
* suitcase /ˈsutkes/   *n.* 手提箱

Grammar
文法片語

1. How old is she? 她幾歲呢？

　★小提點：一般人所熟悉的 How old 就是，多大，多大年紀。

　　例一：How old is your daughter？你女兒有多大年紀？

　★小提點：這個 How old 其實用法很廣，可以指建築物的年歲，也可以問一個城市有多久的歷史。

　　例二：How old is the Eternal Golden Fort? 億載金城蓋有多久了？

2. It would work perfectly for her. 這對她來說百分之百的適合

　★小提點：would 是助動詞，後面動詞一定要原形動詞，在這裡是「將要；將會」。

　　例一：I would strongly advise against going out on your own to the night market. 我會強烈的建議你晚上不要自己出去逛夜市。

　★小提點：〈would〉也通常用於疑問句中，表示禮貌的請求某人做某事〈Would + S+V〉。

　　例二：Would you come in here for a moment, please? 請進來一下好嗎？

3. A box of pineapple cake 一盒鳳梨酥

　★小提點：〈A box of _____〉一盒，後面直接加食物，可以說 one box of chocolate「一盒的巧克力」，或 two boxes of sweet red bean dessert「兩盒的羊羹」。

　　例一：I can eat 10 boxes of Anping shrimp rolls by myself. 我可以自己一次吃十盒的安平蝦卷。

　　例二：I bought three boxes of mangoes at Yujing Mango Market and the price was really cheap. 我在玉井芒果市場買了三箱的芒果，價格很便宜。

4. takes up less space in my suitcase 可以在我的行李箱占用比較少的空間

　★小提點：〈take up〉「佔用空間」，〈takes up less space〉占用比較少的空間，〈takes up too much space〉占用很多的空間

例一：Backpack usually will take up less space on the plane. 背包在飛機上比較不占空間。

例二：The souvenirs you bought at the Taiwan Taoyuan International Airport take up too much space in the luggage. 你在臺灣桃園國際機場所買的紀念品占用太多行李的空間。

★小提點：〈take up〉也可以解釋為「佔用時間」。

例三：Please don't take up any more of my time. 請不要再浪費我的時間了。

Short Sentences

不尷尬短句

❶ We have various saddles in different sizes.
我們有大小不同尺寸的車座 (自行車、腳踏車的車座)。

❷ I am sorry. I'm not familiar with American sizes.
對不起。我不熟悉美國人用的尺寸。

❸ You are welcome to try this special size on.
歡迎您試試這個特殊的尺寸。

❹ We don't have the swimming suit in an extra small size.
我們沒有額外的小尺寸的泳衣。

❺ Would you rather have a full-size table in the conference room?
您是不是比較希望在會議室有一個完整長度的桌子？

❻ It looks like the jacket is just your size.
這個看起來就是你的尺寸的外套。

❼ Do you want a large size or a medium size?
您是想要一個大尺寸或中等尺寸？

❽ The design of these shoes is too wide.
這雙鞋的設計太寬。

❾ The gift shop in the hotel has a wide selection of merchandise.
飯店裡的禮品店有多種選擇的商品。

⑩ Did it fit when you tried it on?
您試穿的時候合適嗎？

⑪ Do you need an extra-large bag for these gifts?
您需要一個額外大的袋子來裝這些禮物嗎？

⑫ We don't carry the extra-large size of this color.
我們沒有進這種顏色的超大尺寸。

Speak Up! 說出來！ MP3 010

Dialogue 01 對話

Guest: Do you carry some kind of blue color handbag?
顧客：你們有進類似像藍色的手提包嗎？

Staff: Well, we have a dark blue, medium-sized hang bag. Do you want to take a look?
工作人員：嗯，我們是有一個深藍色，中等尺寸的手提包。你想看看嗎？

Dialogue 02 對話

Guest: Do you have a gift shop inside this hotel?
顧客：你們這家飯店裡是否有禮品店？

Front Desk: Yes, we have a large gift shop with a wide selection of merchandise. It is next to the cafe around the corner.
櫃檯人員：有的，我們有一個很大的禮品店賣各種各樣的商品。禮品店就在轉角處咖啡廳的旁邊。

Dialogue 03 對話

Guest: Excuse me. I like this dress very much but I can't find the right size.
顧客：對不起。我很喜歡這件衣服，但我找不到合適的尺碼。

Staff: Let me check. I might be able to find the right size for you in the storage.
工作人員：讓我看看。我也許在倉庫能找到適合您的尺寸。

Who would think that you would encounter dimension so frequently while working? But it's everywhere from the size of a meeting to the amount of coffee in a cup. While most of the world uses the metric system of measurement, Americans still cling to a system that uses feet, inches, and ounces, pints, and gallons for most things. There are no easy conversion tricks but there are plenty of apps that make the conversion in seconds. If you have a favorite, you may want to share it with your guests who ask for help making conversions. Another interesting thing is that words such as small, medium, and large are imprecise words with a huge variation from place to place. It helps if you keep samples of the sizes available to show the guest who isn't sure which one he or she wants.

誰會想到在你的工作中會這麼頻繁的用到尺寸呢？但是尺寸是無處不在，從會議的規模到一杯咖啡的量都是和尺寸有關。雖然世界上大多數國家使用公制計量法制度，美國人仍然堅持對大部分的東西使用英尺、英寸、還有盎司、品脫和加侖的衡量制度。雖然沒有簡單的轉換技巧，但也有很多的 App（應用程式）可以在幾秒鐘內就轉換單位。如果你有一種你最喜歡的轉換方式，當你的客人要求幫助轉換衡量單位時，你可以與客人分享你的方式。另一個有趣的事情是，如小型、中型和大型這樣不精確的字（相對比較出來的），這些字在不同的地方就會有巨大的變化。如果隨時持有不同尺寸的樣本可以讓客戶參考，這樣對不確定要選擇哪一個尺寸的客戶來說是很有幫助的。

Unit 01 **Information**
表達資訊

1.1.6 Road Directions 指路

不停住對話 MP3 011

At the Front Desk, the desk clerk is giving driving directions to a guest.
櫃檯前在提供開車方向給一名顧客。

Guest	Can you help me get to Kenting National Park <u>by car</u>?	你能不能跟我說開車去墾丁國家公園怎麼去？
Desk Clerk	It's about two hours and twenty minutes from here if you drive. Do you know how to get to the toll road?	如果你開車的話，從這裡大約 2 小時 20 分鐘。你知道怎麼去高速公路？
Guest	Yes, but do I go right or left at the **ramp**?	是的，但我在匝道是到左邊或右邊呢？
Desk Clerk	<u>Let me draw you a map</u>. At the Kaohsiung **Interchange**, take the ramp and follow the signs for 1.	讓我畫一張地圖給你。在高雄交流道，上匝道，並順著 1 號路的指標。
Guest	I know that interchange.	我知道那個交流道。

Desk Clerk	At the Wujia System Interchange take the right ramp for 88 **towards** Pingtung. Stay on that road for a little over thirteen miles.	在五甲系統交流道走右邊的匝道到 88 號往屏東。在那條路上再開約 13 公里。
Guest	Is there an easier way?	有沒有更簡單的方法？
Desk Clerk	Sure. You can take Route 17 <u>along the coast right to Kenting</u> but it is a longer drive.	當然有。你可以開 17 號公路沿著海岸直接到墾丁，但是這是比較長的車程。
Guest	How much longer?	比較起來是多久呢？
Desk Clerk	Another twenty or thirty minutes, but it is very **scenic**! It <u>follows the coast line.</u>	會多了二、三十分鐘，但是這條路沿路景色非常優美！它是沿著海岸線的。

Part I 清楚表達

Words

單 字

* ramp /ræmp/ *n.* 斜面；坡道；匝道
* interchange /ɪntɚˋtʃendʒ/ *n.* 交流道
* towards /təˋwɔrdz/ *prep.* 向；對於
* scenic /ˋsinɪk/ *adj.* 風景好的
* follow /ˋfɑlo/ *v.* 跟隨；接著

Grammar
文法片語

1. by car 坐汽車

★小提點：by 是副詞。從某個地方到某個地方所使用的任何交通工具在前面都可以加〈by〉。

例一：〈by train〉坐火車，〈by airplane〉坐飛機，〈by bus〉坐公車，〈by ship〉坐船

例二：Many tourists like to tour the island by train. 很多遊客喜歡坐火車環島。

例三：The tiny island is accessible only by boat. 那個小島上只有乘船才能到。

2. Let me draw you a map 讓我畫一張地圖給你

★小提點：Let me「讓我」，Let her 讓她，Let us 讓我們，這些後面要加原形動詞，此外〈Let's go.〉其實就是〈Let us go.〉的縮寫版喔。

例一：Please let him help you. 請讓他幫你。

例二：Let her try the fried stinky tofu. 讓他試試吃臭豆腐。

例三：Let me see, what date are they leaving Taitung? 我看看，他們哪一天離開台東？

3. along the coast right to ... 隨著海岸邊到……

★小提點：〈along〉這個字是當介係詞，是「沿著，順著」的意思。

例一：They walked slowly along the country road. 他們沿著鄉間小路慢慢得走。

★小提點：類似的片語如〈along the way〉沿路上。

例二：The shuttle bus from the hotel to the airport does not stop along the way. 從飯店到機場的接駁車沿路上是都不會停站的。

★小提點：〈along the way〉不只侷限在實際的「沿著」，也可以用在抽象的情況。

例三：He is learning to be a better manager along the way. 這樣一路走來，他也在學著當一個比較好的經理。

4. It follows the coast line. 順著海岸

★小提點：〈 follow 〉「跟在某人的後面」。

例一：Please follow me, Sir. 請跟我來，先生。

★小提點：〈 follow 〉還有「很仔細聽或看的意思」。

例二：The teacher followed every movement of the student. 老師觀看那一個學生的每一個動作。

Short Sentences
不尷尬短句

❶ You are going to pass three traffic lights before you see Eslite Xinyi Store.
你會經過三個紅綠燈才會看到誠品信義店。

❷ If you see Taipei Fine Arts Museum, you have gone too far.
如果你看到台北市立美術館，你就是超過了。

❸ The lane is going to merge before the turn.
車道在轉彎前合併。

❹ Miramar Entertainment Park is on your left.
美麗華百樂園就在你的左邊。

❺ The drive is about thirty minutes on the country road.
走鄉間小路的車程大約是三十分鐘。

❻ Let's take the shortcut.
我們來抄近路。

❼ I took a wrong turn and we got lost in Wanhua District.
我走錯轉彎的地方結果在在萬華區迷失了。

❽ If you take a shortcut, you can walk to Manka Qingshan Temple in only five minutes.
如果你走近路，你步行到艋舺青山寺就只有五分鐘的時間。

❿ Which is the best route to take?
最佳路線是什麼？

Speak Up!
說出來！ MP3 012

Dialogue 01 對話

Visitor: Is Taipei City Mall near here?

訪客：台北城購物中心離這裡很近嗎？

Staff: No. Taipei City Mall is very far from here. The best way to get there is by MRT.

工作人員：沒有，台北城購物中心離這裡很遠，到那裡最好的方式是坐捷運。

Dialogue 02 對話

Visitor: I made a wrong turn. What do I do now?

訪客：我轉錯地方了，怎麼辦呢？

Staff: Well, I am not sure but I can pull up directions using Google Maps to help you.

工作人員：哎啊，我不太確定，但我可以用谷歌地圖來幫助你。

Dialogue 03 對話

Visitor: What's the best way to walk to the night market?

訪客：到夜市最好的方向怎麼走？

Staff: There is a shortcut behind the hotel that connects to the same street as the night market.

工作人員：飯店後面有一條近路直接可以走到夜市那條路。

Have you ever gotten lost in a new place and found yourself in the wrong place? Usually you are late for something or frustrated by the experience. It is a difficult time and is one that you'd rather forget. Yet, it is one of those memories that refuse to fade away and it pops up in conversation with people saying, "Remember when we got lost going to..." If you have had that kind of experience, then you can empathize with your guests as they adventure out. If you can help them get to their end location safely without too many mishaps, they will have a different story to tell when they get home. Draw them a map or print out directions using the Internet and give them the address of the hotel in Chinese so they can show it to Chinese speaking people when they need to get back. A taxi driver will know where to take them instantly after reading their slip of paper. Who knows, maybe someday someone will do the same for you!

你有沒有在一個新的地方迷路過，也同時發現自己在錯誤的地方？通常你是遲到了，或因為迷路而感到沮喪。這是艱難的時刻，也是你寧願忘掉的時刻。然而，這又是那些不肯消失的回憶之一，當你在和別人講話時，這個經驗就會出現在你的腦海裡，"還記得我們要去 ... 迷路了 "，如果你有過這樣的經歷，當你的客人遇到迷路這樣冒險的事時，你就會同情他們。如果你能在沒有太多的失誤下幫助他們安全到達他們的最終地點，當他們回到家後，他們將講述的是一個不同的故事。你可以畫地圖給他們，或者透過電腦印出路線，給他們飯店中文的地址，這樣當他們需要回到飯店時，他們可以把地址拿給講中文的人看。計程車司機在看到中文的紙條後就會會馬上知道要載他們去哪裡。誰知道，說不定哪一天有人也會為你做同樣的事！

1.1.7 Weight and Capacity 重量和容量

Conversations

不停住對話 MP3 013

A Guest is booking a reservation for a conference with meeting rooms and Coffee Service.
一位客人在做有關會議室和咖啡服務的預約。

Employee	How many people do you plan on having for the meeting room?	你計劃有多少人會在會議室裡？
Guest	I'm not sure how many people will <u>register</u> to attend yet.	我不知道有多少人會報名參加呢。
Employee	Our large conference room <u>holds 600 people</u> and you can open the side doors to add another 200 if you need too.	我們的大會議室可以容納 600 人，如果你需要更多的空間的話，你可以打開側門還可以添加 200 人。
Guest	Do you have a smaller conference room that holds about 400 people?	你們有沒有較小的會議室可以容納約 400 人？

Employee	We have one that holds 500 people, but you will find the extra space helpful if you are planning to have tables for sales materials. Our smallest conference room holds 250.	我們有一個會議室可容納500 人，如果你計劃有桌子擺設銷售資料的話，你會覺得有額外的空間會有所幫助。我們最小的會議室可容納 250 人。
Guest	How many people do your small meeting rooms hold?	你們的小型會議房間可以容納多少人？
Employee	We have ten meeting rooms that hold between 40 – 60 people easily.	我們有 10 間會議房間，每間可以很容易的容納 40 - 60 人。
Guest	Let's reserve the medium-sized conference room and five each of the meeting rooms. Will we need a room for registration?	我們就預約中型會議室和五個會議房間。我們需要一個房間來做登記的地方嗎？
Employee	No Ma'am. We offer tables outside the conference room for registration.	不需要的，女士。我們在會議室外面有提供桌子可以做登記。

清楚表達 Part I

Words 單字

* conference /ˈkɑnfərəns/　*n.* 會議；討論會
* register /ˈrɛdʒɪstər/　*v.* 登記；註冊
* extra /ˈɛkstrə/　*adj.* 額外的
* reserve /rɪˈzəv/　*v.* 預備；保留
* registration /ˌrɛdʒɪˈstreʃən/　*n.* 登記；掛號

Grammar
文法片語

1. register to attend 報名參加

★小提點：〈register〉動詞，報名的意思。也可以表示登記結婚、出生等意思。

例一：Have you registered for the training course? 你報名訓練課程了嗎？

例二：The baby's birth was registered yesterday. 昨天登記小嬰兒的出生。

2. The room holds 600 people. 那個房間可以容納 600 人

★小提點：〈hold〉這個動詞是「容納」，後面直接加受詞，可以用很簡單的〈S+V+O〉造句。

例一：The conference room can hold one hundred people. 那個會議室可以容納 100 人。

例二：The room can only hold one queen size bed. 那個房間只能容納一張大號床。

★小提點：〈hold〉這個動詞也可解釋為「持有」。

例三：We hold different views. 我們持有不同的觀點。

3. You will find the extra space helpful if you are planning to have.... 如果你計劃……，你會覺得有額外的空間會有所幫助

★小提點：我們一般所知道的〈find〉是「找到」的意思，但是用在樣的句子，〈find〉有「認為」的意思，後面不用加介係詞。

例一：You will find the room very comfortable. 你會覺得那個房間很舒適。

★小提點：否定句〈You will not find...〉「你不會認為……」，〈I will not find...〉「我不會認為……」。

例二：I am sure I will not find it interesting. 我很確定我不會覺得這是有趣的。

4. medium-sized 中等尺寸，中型

★小提點：〈medium-sized〉其實是很口語化的用法，這個和〈medium size〉有完全一樣的意思。類似的用法有〈large size〉大號，〈small size〉小號，〈average size〉一般尺寸，〈wrong size〉錯的尺寸。

例一：Taichung is not a medium size town. 台中不是中型的城市。

例二：This is a medium sized hotel. 這是一個中型的飯店。

例三：I have two large size luggage. 我有兩個大型的行李箱。

Short Sentences
不尷尬短句

❶ Please tell us where, when and what type of room capacity you'll need for your conference in April.
請告訴我們您在四月的會議要在哪裡辦，何時以及需要何種類型的房間。

❷ At this moment, the banquet room is almost filled with guests to its capacity.
就目前來說，宴會的房間是幾乎坐滿了客人並達到了房間容量的極限。

❸ Our seating capacity for an outdoor banquet is 200 people.
我們在戶外宴會的座位是 200 人。

❹ Our conference room includes a large screen and a projector and it can be seated up to 25 people.
我們的會議室是有包括一個大螢幕和投影機，其限制客人的數量為 25 人。

❺ The conference room on the second floor has 1,496 has Sq. Ft. and the maximum capacity is 30.
在二樓的會議室有 1,496 平方英尺，和最大容量為 30 人。

❻ What is the weight limit for the escalator nearby the cafeteria?
自助餐附近的電梯重量限制是多少？

❼ A reservation is necessary in the winter because we have a limited space in the winter.
在冬天做預約是必要的，因為我們在冬天的空間是有限的。

❽ Here is our floor plans and capacity charts for your planning of your next special event.
這是我們的樓層平面圖和容納人數表，你可以參考這個資料以為你的下一個特殊活動做策劃。

Part I 清楚表達

Speak Up!
說出來！ MP3 014

Dialogue 01 對話

Guest: How big is your hotel?
顧客：你的飯店有多大？

Front Desk: Our hotel can accommodate up to 350 people. We have a variety of rooms and suites for the need of our guests.
櫃檯人員：我們的酒店可容納 350 人。我們有不同的客房和套房可以讓我們的客人做選擇。

Dialogue 02 對話

Guest: The online review said that it is hard to get a room at your hotel in the summer. Is it true?
顧客：網上的評論說，你們的酒店在夏季很難訂到房位。是真的嗎？

Staff: Yes. The occupancy rate of our hotel is very high in the spring. Also, the hotel is filled to capacity in the summer.
工作人員：是的。我們飯店在春天的入住率是非常高的。還有，在夏天都是住滿的。

Dialogue 03 對話

Guest: Do you have a scale?
顧客：你有重磅嗎？

Front Desk: Yes. We have a scale right here. Do you want me to help you weigh your luggage just in case it won't exceed the weight limit?
櫃檯人員：有的，這裡就有一個，要不要我幫你稱看看你的行李重量，以防萬一超過重量限制？

The key to helping someone plan a successful conference is to remind them of details that may have slipped their mind. Make sure you know what your conference center provides as far as specific technology and meal plans as well as the cost of each so that you appear knowledgeable and helpful. Have a planning guide available that shows the location of the rooms and the costs per day for the rental of the space to show the guest. It will assist them in making wise decisions. If there are good reasons for reserving the larger spaces, make sure you point those out so that the guest can decide if it's worth the extra cost. Once you have confirmed all the details, it's critical to make the reservation as soon as possible so that there are no disappointments later if the space is booked by someone else.

幫助別人策劃一個成功的會議的關鍵是要提醒他們有可能沒有想到的細節。你要確定說明你的會議中心所提供的特定的科技設備和膳食計劃，以及每項的成本，這樣會讓你看起來很有專業知識，也會對對方很有幫助。你也要提供規劃指南可以讓對方明顯地看到房間位置和每天空間租用的費用。這些資料將幫助他們做出明智的決定。如果你覺得有充分的理由可以預定較大的空間，確保指出這樣的意見，這樣可以讓客人可以決定是否值得付額外費用。一旦你有確認所有的細節，馬上做預約是很重要的，這樣可以避免空間已被他人預訂而造成客人的失望。

Conversations
不停住對話　　MP3 015

At the Front Desk, helping a guest plan for a trip.
在櫃檯前幫助一名顧客策劃旅行。

Guest	We are thinking about spending a few days in Kenting. Is this a good time to go there?	我們正在考慮要去墾丁玩幾天。這個時候去那裡好不好？
Desk Clerk	Kenting is a hot tropical climate with a lot of rainy days so late April is the perfect time to go there.	墾丁是炎熱的熱帶氣候，有很多的陰雨天，4 月下旬去那裡是最好的。
Guest	How warm will it get?	天氣會多熱呢？
Desk Clerk	It should be about 29℃ during the day and 21℃ at night on the average.	白天應該是在約 29℃，晚上平均在 21℃。
Guest	What temperature is that in **Fahrenheit**?	這樣的溫度轉換華氏是多少度？
Desk Clerk	I think it's 84 ℉ and 73 ℉ . You will need to take an umbrella just in case it rains.	我覺得是 84 ℉和 73 ℉。你需要帶雨傘以防萬一有下雨。

Guest	Do you think it will be **humid**?	你覺得會很潮濕嗎？
Desk Clerk	Not as **humid** as it will be in May, June, and July. It might be windy or cloudy this early in the season though.	跟五月、六月、七月比起來還不算很潮濕。可是在季節初期可能會刮風或陰天。
Guest	So we need to take **light jackets**?	所以我們需要帶薄外套？
Desk Clerk	And **sunscreen**. You can get **burned** even on cloudy days.	還有防曬油。你在陰天還是有可能會曬傷。

Words 單 字

* Fahrenheit /ˈfɛrənˌhaɪt/　*n.* 華氏溫度
* humid /ˈhjumɪd/　*adj.* 潮濕的
* light jacket /laɪt/ /ˈdʒækɪt/　*n.* 薄外套
* sunscreen /sənˈskrin/　*n.* 防曬油
* burn /bɝn/　*v.* 曬傷

Grammar 文法片語

1. Is this a good time to...? 這是去……的好時機嗎？
   ★小提點：此為強調句型的用法，it 為虛主詞，真正的主詞是後面的不定詞片語或子句。
   例一：It is a good time to take a nap now. 現在是睡個覺的時候。
   例二： Is this a good time to visit Taiwan? 這是去台灣玩的好時機嗎？

例三：Is this a good time to take a rest? 這個時間可以休息嗎？

2. on the average 通常，一般來說

★小提點：〈average〉是平均，加上介係詞 on，形成介係詞片語。

例一： On the average, it rains a lot in spring time in Taiwan. 一般來說，台灣的春天下很多雨。

★小提點：另外一個相似意思的副詞是 typically「典型地；通常」。

例一：The workers of the factory are typically middle-aged women. 這工廠的工人們通常是中年婦女。

例二：They have a typically Taiwanese lifestyle. 他們過著典型的台灣人生活。

3. just in case 以防萬一

★小提點：just「只是」，介係詞片語 in case「一旦」，合起來 just in case 就是「以防萬一」，是這句片語的用法很彈性，可以在句首 (加逗號)，也可以在句尾，不會影響意思。

例一： Just in case, please bring the umbrella with you. 以防萬一，請帶你的雨傘。

4. It might be... 可能是……，可能會……

★小提點：〈might〉是助動詞，其後直接加「原形動詞」，表示你對答案不是很確定。〈 The weather is sunny. 〉這句是肯定的語氣「天氣很晴朗。」如果說〈The weather might be sunny〉「天氣可能會是晴朗的。」就是有點不確定，也因為〈might〉是助動詞所以後面要加「原形動詞」，所以〈is〉就要用〈be〉。

例一： I am not sure but you might be right. 我不確定，但是你有可能是對的。

例二：The train might be late due to the rain. 因為下雨的關係，火車可能會遲到。

Short Sentences
不尷尬短句

1 It is possible that the weather might turn chilly at night.
晚上的天氣是可能轉為寒冷。

2 I am not sure about the average temperature in Taichung in May?
我不知道台中的天氣在五月平均溫度是多少。

3 It might get cold in Taipei at night.
台北的夜晚可能會變冷。

4 The cabin is on top of the mountain and it can be freezing at night.
小木屋是在山頂上，晚上可能會很冰冷。

5 The weather in Hualien was bright and breezy last Sunday.
上星期日花蓮的天氣是風和日麗。

6 The weather here by the ocean can be cloudy and drizzly for days.
靠近海岸地方的天氣有時會一直都是陰濛濛的天氣。

7 The forecast said it would be sunny in Kenting.
天氣預報說墾丁會是陽光明媚的。

8 Do you know how to convert from Fahrenheit to Celsius?
你知道要如何從華氏轉換為攝氏嗎？

9 The temperature now is 38 Celsius and it is burning up.
現在的溫度為攝氏 38 度，真的是要燒起來了。

10 The cottage on top of the mountain was cold and damp.
在山頂的小屋是寒冷和潮濕的。

11 Please drive carefully because the weather is foggy.
請開車小心，因為有很多的霧。

12 That late afternoon in Tainan was dark and stormy.
那天台南傍晚真是月黑風高。

Speak Up!
說出來！  MP3 016

Dialogue 01 對話

Visitor: Should I bring sunscreen to the beach?
訪客：我需要帶防曬油去海灘嗎？

Staff: Yes, you should. The scorching sun will burn you!
工作人員：是的，你應該要帶。烈日炎炎真的會曬傷！

Dialogue 02 對話

Visitor: Does it rain a lot in the mountain?
訪客：在山上會下很多雨嗎？

Staff: The rainfall can be plentiful. You need to be very careful when you travel in the mountains.
工作人員：雨量可能會很豐沛。你去山上旅行時仍然需要非常小心。

Dialogue 03 對話

Guest: Is your patio open?
顧客：你的戶外用餐區有開放使用嗎？

Waiter: Well, it is usually open but we had to close it today because of the storm.
服務員：嗯，通常是開放的，可是今天我們需要關起來因為有暴風。

Since the Tropic of Cancer runs through the middle of Taiwan, it has tropical and subtropical weather, making it pleasant most of the time, but there are times when it's more extreme. Dressing inappropriately for the weather or not having the right equipment with you can turn a pleasurable experience into a nightmare. Knowing that it can get very cold in the mountains and that not all Bed and Breakfast places have heat means that your guest will be better prepared for their time spent there. Remind them to pack heavy coats, hats, and gloves if they are going to Alishan to ride the train up the mountain to see the sunrise. They will be very grateful when they return! It's the same about their time at the beach. You can get seriously burned even on a gray overcast day at the beach and should wear sunscreen when you go outside. In Taiwan, one can experience all kinds of weather in one trip and not every guest will be aware of the variations or extremes. Giving guests advice about the weather and what they should take with them will help them have a pleasant time.

　　由於北迴歸線貫穿台灣中部，所以台灣有熱帶和亞熱帶氣候，這樣的天氣大部分都是很宜人的，但有些時候會比較極端。穿著不當或者沒有合適的設備，這些都會讓應該是愉快的經驗變成一場噩夢。你要知道在山區可能會變得非常寒冷，而不是所有民宿都會有暖氣，也就是說你的客人要對自己的行程做更好的準備。如果他們要去阿里山坐小火車上山看日出，你要提醒他們要帶厚厚的大衣、帽子和手套。當他們返回後，他們會對你的建議感到很感激！對於他們要去沙灘玩，你也可以做同樣的意見。陰天時一整天在沙灘上還是會有嚴重的曬傷，到外面去就應塗抹防曬油。在台灣，遊客在一次的旅行就可以體驗各種天氣，但不是每一位客人都知道天氣變化或極端的天氣。提供給客人有關天氣的意見以及他們應該帶什麼來幫助他們即使下雨天也可以度過愉快的時間。

Unit 02 Social Talks 基本社交

1.2.1 Self-Introduction 自我介紹

Conversations
不停住對話　　MP3 017

At the Front Desk in the Hotel, greeting a guest.
在飯店的櫃檯前歡迎一位顧客。

Desk Clerk	Welcome to our hotel. My name is Jane Lee. I am the **Concierge**. How may I help you?	歡迎光臨我們的飯店。我的名字叫簡恩・李。我是禮賓專員。我如何幫助您呢？
Guest	Have you worked here long?	你在這裡工作了多久了呢？
Desk Clerk	I have been **employed** here for three years, but I am studying Business **Management** at school. It is a challenging program and I am in year 2.	我一直在這裡工作有三年了，我目前在念商業管理學校。這是一個具有挑戰性的課程，現在是二年級。
Guest	Do you like it?	你喜歡這樣的工作嗎？

Desk Clerk	I love working here. I love meeting people from <u>all over the world</u> and helping them **discover** how wonderful my country is. Are you enjoying your visit?	我很喜歡在這裡工作。我喜歡認識來自世界各地的人，也可以有機會幫助他們發現我的國家是多麼的棒。您喜歡您在這裡的時光嗎？
Guest	I am. Everyone is so helpful and kind.	喜歡，每個人都很幫忙也很親切。
Desk Clerk	You can't learn how to be kind in school, can you? It has to come <u>from your heart.</u>	你無法在學校學到如何親切待人，不是嗎？這是發自內心的。
Guest	<u>What do you want to do when you</u> **<u>graduate</u>**?	當你畢業後你想要做什麼呢？
Desk Clerk	I want to be the general manager of a major hotel chain someday. But I still have a lot to learn.	我想成為一個有名氣的飯店的總經理，但我仍然有很多東西需要學習。

清楚表達 Part I

Words
單 字

* concierge /ˌkɑnsiˈɛrʒ/ *n.* 飯店禮賓人員
* employ /ɛmˈplɔɪ/ *v.* 僱用
* management /ˈmænədʒmənt/ *n.* 管理；處理；經營
* discover /dɪsˈkʌvɚ/ *v.* 發現；找到
* graduate /ˈɡrædʒəwət/ *v.* 畢業

Grammar
文法片語

1. I am studying … 我在念 (+ 學科)

★小提點：studying 是「動詞進行式」，在這裡可以是「在唸書」後面可以加任何的學位。

例一：I am studying Mathematics and Science at college. 我在大學念數學和科學。

例二：I am studying at a national university. 我在一所國立大學唸書。

★小提點：〈studying+for〉也可以用來當做「準備」

例三：I am busy studying for my final exam. 我忙著準備我的期末考試。

2. all over the world 全世界

★小提點：〈all over〉是「各地，到處」的意思，在後面加上地名，用法會很廣泛。

例一：〈all over Taiwan 〉台灣整個島，〈all over Taipei City 〉正個台北市，〈all over America 〉全美國，〈all over the countryside 〉整個鄉下地方。

例二：There are good places to visit all over the country. 全國各地都有很棒的地方可以參觀。

例三：The fried stinky tofu is known all over Taiwan. 全台灣的人都知道什麼是臭豆腐。

3. from your heart 發自內心

★小提點：介係詞 from 有「來自」的意思，這個片語的直接意思就是「來自內心」當然可以更加強調不只是發自內心，而是發自內心深處〈from the bottom of my heart 〉，不錯的片語吧？

例一：If you don't love this job from your heart, you will not last long. 如果你不是從內心喜歡這份工作，你不會做太久的啦。

例二：I love Taiwan from the bottom of my heart. 我是真心真意的愛台灣。

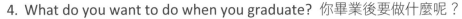

4. What do you want to do when you graduate? 你畢業後要做什麼呢？

　★小提點：〈What do you want to do when S+V〉「當你 ＿＿＿，你要做什麼？」，因為有〈when〉當連接詞，所以後面要加另一個完整的句子，別緊張，真的不難，就是兩個句子用〈when〉接起來而已。而完整句子就是一個句子有主詞有動詞。

　　例一：What do you want to do when you grow up? 你長大後想要做什麼？

　　例二：What do you want to do when the school is closed? 學校沒開時你要做什麼？

Short Sentences

不尷尬短句

❶ I have been an employee here for six months.
我已經在這裡工作 6 個月了。

❷ I want to become the Concierge and help our guests with their needs.
我想成為禮賓服務人員，並幫助我們的顧客滿足他們的需要。

❸ I am studying hospitality in college.
我在大學念餐旅系。

❹ It is fun to discover new places to share with our guests.
與我們的客人一起分享發現新的地方是很有趣的。

❺ I will graduate next month and will apply for a full-time position here then.
我下個月就要畢業也將申請在這裡全職的職位。

❻ I am a student but I will work here full-time soon.
我現在是學生，但我很快就會在這裡做全職的工作。

❼ I am the newest employee here, but I learn quickly.
我是這裡最新進的員工，但我學得很快。

❽ I started out as a janitor but now I am the Concierge.
我一開始是清潔人員但現在我是禮賓人員。

❾ I like working the front desk because I meet so many new people.
我喜歡做櫃檯的工作，因為我可以認識很多新朋友。

⑩ The manager said he will hire me full-time when I graduate from school.
那位經理說，當我從學校畢業後他將僱用我為正職。

Speak Up! 說出來！ MP3 018

Dialogue 01 對話

Guest: Have you worked here long?
顧客：你在這裡工作多久了？

Staff: I am the oldest employee here and have worked here for twenty years.
工作人員：我在這裡是資歷最深的員工，在這裡已經工作了二十多年。

Dialogue 02 對話

Guest: Do you like being the Concierge?
顧客：你喜歡當禮賓人員嗎？

Staff: My favorite part is helping our guests find new places to visit in our country.
工作人員：我最喜歡的部分是幫助我們的客人在我們的國家尋找新的地點去玩。

Dialogue 03 對話

Guest: Will you be still working here next summer?
顧客：你明年夏天還會在這裡工作嗎？

Intern: I am not sure. I am just an intern this summer. If I am offered a full-time position after I graduate next summer, I will stay and work here.
實習人員：我不確定，我這個暑假只是實習生，如果我明年暑假畢業後他們有提供全職的職位給我，我會留下來在這裡工作。

When introducing yourself to a guest, make sure you speak your name and position clearly so they can identify you later. It's important to develop a sense of trust with your clients so that they feel they can come to you with their problems. It will leave them with a good feeling about your company even if they have problems. Don't share private information with them but feel free to ask them about their family and jobs back home. By developing a personal connection with your guests, they will feel more comfortable and more at home.

當跟客人做自我介紹時，一定要清楚地說出你的名字和職位，這樣他們以後可以識別你的身份。與你的客戶建立信任感是很重要的，這樣當他們有問題時，他們覺得可以來找你。即使你工作的地方出現一些小問題，他們也還會對你的公司有一個良好的感覺。你最好不要與他們分享私人資料，但是可以隨意問問有關他們的家庭和工作。與你的客人建立一些私人關係，他們會覺得住在這裡很舒適也很自在。

1.2.2　Greetings 小小寒暄

Conversations
不停住對話 　MP3 019

Front Desk Employee is greeting a new Guest who arrived late the night before and is still tired and a bit disoriented.
櫃檯人員迎接昨天晚上深夜到達的顧客，這個顧客還是感覺很累，也有一點暈頭轉向。

Employee	Good morning. Did you sleep well?	早，昨天睡得好嗎？
Guest	Good morning. My body is still on US time though.	早。我的身體仍然是在美國時間呢。
Employee	Then I should say Good evening to you instead. Is it 9 pm back home?	那這樣的話我應該要說晚安，你家鄉的時間現在是晚上 9 點嗎？
Guest	I think so but my body doesn't know if you should say Good afternoon or Good evening!	應該是吧，我的身體不知道應該說是午安還是晚安！
Employee	The jet lag won't last if you drink a lot of water and try to stay on the current time schedule. Have you been to Taiwan before or is this your first trip?	如果你喝了大量的水，並盡量配合當地的時間，這樣的話你的時差不會持續太久。以前有來過台灣嗎，或者這是第一次來？

Guest	I've been to Japan before but this is my first time here. <u>Is it too late for breakfast?</u>	我之前去過日本，但這是我第一次來這裡。這個時間還有早餐嗎？
Employee	**Breakfast** is still being served in the dining room for another thirty minutes. Do you know where it is?	餐廳還有三十分鐘的時間會供應早餐，你知道在哪裡嗎？
Guest	Down the hall?	走廊到底嗎？
Employee	Let me show you where it is. Follow me. Even though your body feels ready for dinner, you should serve it breakfast today.	我跟你講在哪裡。請跟我來，雖然你的身體感覺是要吃晚餐但是你今天還是吃早餐會比較好。
Guest	Thank you. I might not find it today by myself without your help.	謝謝。沒有你的幫忙，我可能自己沒有辦法找到餐廳。
Employee	I hope your visit is **enjoyable**. <u>Have a good day</u>, Ma'am.	小姐，希望你玩地愉快也有一個美好的一天。

Part I 清楚表達

Words 單字

* disoriented /dɪsˈɔrɪɛntɪd/　*a.* 失神的
* instead /ɪnˈstɛd/　*adv.* 反而；卻
* current /ˈkɝənt/　*adj.* 當前的；目前的
* breakfast /ˈbrɛkfəst/　*n.* 早餐
* enjoyable /ɛnˈdʒɔɪəbəl/　*adj.* 享受的；令人愉快的

Grammar
文法片語

1. I think so. 我認為是這樣的

★小提點：〈so〉是副詞「如此」〈I think so.〉是非常口語化的句子，表示認同對方的說法，也可以這樣說〈I believe so.〉「我相信是如此的。」

例一：I think so but I am not sure. 我認為是這樣，可是我不是很確定。

例二：If you say so, I will have to believe it. 如果你這樣說，我就會相信是這樣的。

2. Jet lag 時差

★小提點：〈jet〉是「噴射機」，〈lag〉當名詞有「停滯，時間間隔」，基本上，飛機在飛行上非常有可能飛過不同的時區，也造成旅客身體上對時間調適的問題，所以這兩個字合起來的片語就是「時差」的意思。

例一：It is possible to have jet lag for days! 時差有可能會持續很多天！

例二：Are you over your jet lag yet? 你的時差調好了沒有？

例三：I always have a big problem with jet lag. 時差對我來說一直都是一個大問題。

3. Is it too late for...? 太遲來做某件事？

★小提點：〈too〉副詞「太或非常」，這個副詞形容的是後面的〈late〉，不只是晚，而是太晚。

例一：If you don't go now, you will be too late for the train. 如果你現在不馬上走，你坐火車會太晚。

例二：It is not too late for you to check-out for today. 今天退房還不會太晚。

★小提點：〈It is never too late.〉「永遠不會太晚。」這句是在鼓勵人，只要有心，做什麼都不會太晚。

4. Have a good day. 希望你有美好的一天

★小提點：〈Have〉是動詞「有」的意思，這個句子原本是〈You have a good day.〉但是口語化就把〈You〉給省略掉了，幾乎任何一般說再見的

時候，可以跟對方這樣說〈 Have a good day. 〉。

例一：Have a good trip. 祝你旅程愉快。

例二：Have a good time. 祝你玩的愉快。

例三：Have fun. 中文可以解釋為「好好的玩」，這也是很常用到的口語話。

Short Sentences
不尷尬短句

❶ Which state are you from in America?
您是來自美國哪一州？

❷ Thank you for coming!
謝謝您的光臨！

❸ It's so nice to see you again!
真的很高興再次見到你！

❹ Thank you for staying with us.
感謝您住在我們這裡。

❺ How have you been?
你過得如何？

❻ How's it going?
你好嗎？

❼ How is everything?
一切都好嗎？

❽ How are things with you?
你過的好嗎？

❾ We are so excited to see you again.
我們很高興再次見到你。

❿ It is nice talking to you.
很高興能與你交談。

⓫ Good to see you.
很高興見到你。

Part I 清楚表達

⓬ It has been a long time. How are you?
已經過了很長的一段時間了。你好嗎？

⓭ We are so happy to see you tomorrow.
我們很高興明天會看到你。

Speak Up!
說出來！ MP3 020

Dialogue 01 對話

Guest: Thank you for your help finding the store today.
顧客：很感謝你今天幫我找到這家店。

Staff: I am happy to have met you and am eager to be of assistance to you so please let me know what you need.
工作人員：我很高興能遇見你，也很希望幫助你，所以請讓我知道你需要什麼幫忙的地方。

Dialogue 02 對話

Guest: Are you Ms. Lin? We met last year here at the hotel.
顧客：你是林小姐嗎？我們去年在這家飯店有見過面。

Staff: Yes, Mr. Smith. What a surprise. How have you been?
工作人員：是的，史密斯先生。很驚訝看到你。你好嗎？

Dialogue 03 對話

Guest: I really enjoy being here. The hotel staff are so attentive.
顧客：我真的很喜歡這裡。飯店的工作人員是如此周到。

Staff: Thank you so much. We try to be friendly and do our best for our guests.
工作人員：非常感謝你。我們會盡量做到很友善，也要對我們的客人做到最好的服務。

Many foreigners tend to be informal by nature and use short cuts and slang when talking. They may come across as brash and rude because they are so informal, but they don't mean it like that. Many have no difficulty in approaching a stranger to ask for advice or to get directions, and will introduce themselves to you if you don't approach them first. Others will be very shy and hesitant when they are faced with a new situation. But nearly all of them have an individualistic personality and will give direct answers when people ask them questions. They will expect the same from employees they encounter so expect to be challenged by their questions and be prepared to answer them with simple and sincere replies. They will look you directly in the eye and expect a firm handshake when they shake hands. Almost all greetings include a handshake when you are first introduced as well. Some overly exuberant guests may even give you a bear hug or slap on the back as a sign of appreciation for your hard work.

許多外國人天生就是比較隨和的個性，也喜歡在交談時使用捷徑和俚語。因為他們是如此不拘束，所以他們可能會讓人感到傲慢和粗魯的，但他們往往沒有這個意思。很多美國人對於請教陌生人有關方向的問題是沒有多大的困難，如果你沒有先接近他們，他們也會把自己介紹給你。有些美國人遇到新的狀況還是會感到很害羞和猶豫。但是幾乎大部分的美國人都有個人主義的個性，如果你問他們問題，他們都會給予直接的回答。他們對所遇到的工作人員也會有這樣的期望，所以你對他們的問題也要做好心理準備來給予簡單而真誠的回答。他們會直視你的眼睛，當他們和你握手時，也會期待你在握手時會用一些力量。幾乎所有的第一次見面的介紹一開始都包括握手。有一些比較過於熱情的客人甚至可能給你一個擁抱，或拍拍你的背面來表現他們對你們的辛勤工作的感謝。

Conversations
不停住對話 MP3 021

A customer is reguesting some services.
一位顧客正在要求一些服務。

Desk Clerk	We have you staying with us for four nights in a room with two queen sized beds. Is that ok with you?	我們為你們準備有兩個大號床的房間四個晚上。這樣可以嗎？
Customer	I would prefer two king size.	我比較希望兩張特大號的床。
Desk Clerk	Let me check and see what we have available. There is one room like that left but it will cost you another $30 a night. Is that acceptable to you?	讓我看一下我們有什麼空的房間。是有這樣的一個房間，但是需要額外付 30 美元一個晚上。你可以接受嗎？
Customer	That's fine. I'll take it. What kind of pillow is on the bed?	可以。就這樣安排吧。床上是什麼樣的枕頭？

Desk Clerk	We have goose down pillows in that room but we can bring you something different. What would you like to have hospitality bring you?	我們在那個房間裡有鵝絨枕頭，但我們可以給您提供不一樣枕頭。您希望我們提供什麼服務呢？
Customer	I need a hard pillow that doesn't have feathers.	我需要一個沒有羽毛的硬枕頭。
Desk Clerk	We have hypoallergenic pillows in housekeeping. Would you like to try one? If it doesn't work, call me and I will send up an **assortment** for you to try.	我們的客房清潔部是有防過敏的枕頭。您想試試嗎？如果您覺得不適合，請打電話給我，我會請人送另一個類型的給您試用。
Customer	My **luggage** is still at the airport. Can you have it sent to my room when it arrives?	我的行李還在機場。當行李到達時，可否麻煩你將行李送到我的房間？
Desk Clerk	Certainly, and would you like some toothpaste and a toothbrush to use while you are waiting for its arrival?	當然了，在您等待行李到來之前，您會需要一些牙膏和牙刷？
Customer	Yes please. Do you have shaving supplies and a comb <u>as well</u>?	是的，麻煩你。你有刮鬍鬚的東西和梳子嗎？
Desk Clerk	I have those as well, but may I recommend that you visit the hotel's **barber** shop for a shave? <u>I can give you a coupon for a free shave</u> and you will feel very **refreshed** afterwards.	我們是有這些，但我想建議您可以到飯店的理髮店請他們幫你剔鬍鬚？我可以給你一個免費刮鬍鬚的優惠券，刮完鬍鬚後你會覺得很清爽的。

Words
單 字

* acceptable /ək`sɛptəbəl/   *adj.* 可以接受的
* assortment /ə`sɔrtmənt/   *n.* 不同類型的同一種物品
* luggage /`lʌgədʒ/   *n.* 行李
* barber /`bɑrbə/   *n.* 理髮師
* refreshed /ri`frɛʃt/   *adj.* 恢復精神的；清爽的

Grammar
文法片語

1. Is that ok with you? 你覺得這樣可以嗎？

    ★小提點：這樣的句子可以從簡單的句子〈Is that ok?〉，加上〈with you〉你覺得，甚至加上子句，讓句子越來越長。要記得，所有很長的句子都可以用〈S+V〉來看到最基本的意思喔！

    例一：Is it ok? 這樣好嗎？

    例二：Is it ok with you? 你覺得這樣好嗎？

    例三：Is it ok with you that I cancel the reservation? 你覺得我取消預約可以嗎？

2. I would prefer… 我比較願意……；我比較希望……

    ★小提點：一般我們所學的〈would〉是〈will〉的過去式，但也可以用來當做「意願」，〈prefer〉動詞「較喜歡」，後面可接不定詞或動名詞。

    例一：He would prefer to meet the manager in the hotel lobby. 他希望和經理在飯店的大廳見。

    例二：I would prefer paying the bill by my credit card. 我是希望用我的信用卡付賬。

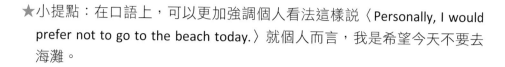

★小提點：在口語上，可以更加強調個人看法這樣説〈Personally, I would prefer not to go to the beach today.〉就個人而言，我是希望今天不要去海灘。

3. as well 也；還有

　★小提點：副詞片語，通常放在句子的最後面。語氣有點在説「不止有某種，也有另一種」。

　　例一：The hotel manager speaks English and Chinese as well. 那個飯店經理會説英文和中文。

　★小提點：類似這個副詞還有〈too〉或〈also〉。

　　例二：She speaks Chinese and Taiwanese dialect too. 她會講中文也會講台語。

　　例三：The hotel has a gift shop also. 這個飯店也有一個禮品部。

4. I can give you a coupon for … 我可以給你一個……的優惠券〈coupon〉優惠券，可以有比較優惠的價格或者是免費，另外〈giveaway〉是贈品的意思。

　　例一：The coupon entitles you to NT$100 off your next purchase. 這個優惠券可以讓你在下一次消費時折 100 元。

Short Sentences

不尷尬短句

❶ They made a request for housekeeping for room 121.
他們要求對房間 121 做清潔。

❷ Please don't worry about it. I have no problem with your requests.
請不用擔心，我不會覺得你的請求很麻煩。

❸ Please let the visitor come in.
請讓訪客進來。

❹ I will ask the manager to call you back when she's back.
當經理回來時，我會請她給您回電。

❺ Would you mind repeating that? I didn't quite catch it.
你可否重複一次嗎？我沒有聽的太明白。

❻ Would you mind changing shifts with me?
你願意和我換班嗎？

❼ Would you mind giving him a message for me?
你可以幫我給他留言嗎？

❽ Would you please forward this letter to his new address?
可否請你將此信轉轉發到他的新地址？

❾ Would you prefer the table near the window?
你會比較喜歡靠窗的桌子嗎？

❿ Please keep your voices down.
請將你的音量降低。

Speak Up!
說出來！　MP3 022

Dialogue 01 對話

Guest: I would like another blanket. It is colder here in the mountain than I expected.
顧客：我需要另外一個毯子。這裡的山上比我的預期還冷。

Staff: I will get one blanket for you. You can turn the heater up in your room as well.
工作人員：我會去幫你拿一條毯子。你可以把你的房間的暖氣調高一點。

Dialogue 02 對話

Front Desk Staff: Room 111 made a request for more big towels.
櫃檯工作人員：111 房間請求我們提供更多的大毛巾。

Housekeeping: Yes, no problem.
房務部：好的，沒問題。

Many times your foreign hotel guests are arriving after long flights and a couple of transfers. They have made a great effort to arrive in Taiwan, but they won't always be happy about the process of getting there. All they want is to check into their room and crash for a while before they start their visit. Anything you can do to help them feel at home and refreshed will be appreciated. Efficient and concerned employees can change the mood of a guest quickly. Know your job thoroughly and learn what you can do to ease the process for the tired guest. If you can give them a small discount or extra coupon, they will appreciate it later. Those little touches of kindness can diffuse anger and frustration. Remember that you don't know what kind of day they've had before they got to your establishment.

很多時候，你的外國客人都是經過長途飛行和幾次的轉機才抵達。他們是做出很大的精力才抵達台灣，但每個人對到那裡的過程並不是全然都很愉快的。所以在他們開始玩之前，他們最想要的是趕快進入房間到他們的房間躺下來好好的休息。任何你可以幫助他們有賓至如歸和舒服的感覺，他們都會不勝感激。工作人員的高效率和關懷都可以迅速改變一個客人的心情。工作人員應該要徹底了解本身的工作，並學習如何為疲憊的客人簡化飯店的手續。如果你可以給他們一個小小的折扣或額外的優惠券，他們之後都會很感激的。這些親切的小細節可以化解憤怒和沮喪。你要銘記在心的是，他們來到你工作的地方之前，你並不知道他們之前有什麼樣的經歷。

Unit 02 Social Talks 基本社交

Conversations

不停住對話   MP3 023

The Concierge at the hotel is recommending a Tour Bus Trip to a couple of Foreign Visitors.
飯店的禮賓人員在建議觀光巴士之旅給一對外遊客夫婦。

Concierge	One of the best ways to see the city is to take a tour bus. They have half-day and full day tour itineraries.	要看這個城市最好的方式之一是坐遊覽車。他們有半天和全天旅遊行程。
Guest	Where will the bus meet us?	要在哪裡坐遊覽車呢？
Concierge	It will come directly to the hotel as long as you make a reservation first.	只要你先做預約，遊覽車就會直接到飯店來接你們。
Guest	Which tour do you suggest?	你會建議哪一個旅遊行程呢？
Concierge	How about a day trip to the North Coast? It is the perfect way to spend a day.	北海岸一日遊如何？用這樣的方式來玩一天是很完美的。
Guest	Are you sure it will be fun?	你真的認為這會是很有趣的嗎？

Concierge	The rock **formations** at Yeliou are **incredible** to see while the art work at Juming Museum has Ju Ming's sculptures, one of our greatest living artists. On the way back, it will stop for a snack at a roadside restaurant.
Guest	<u>It must be **expensive**</u>!
Concierge	That trip is NT$1,500 which is about $50US each and includes **admission** tickets to Yeliou and the Juming Museum. It leaves the hotel at 9 am and returns to Taipei around 6 pm.

能看到野柳的岩層你會覺得很不可思議，而且朱銘美術館可以看到朱銘的雕塑藝術作品，朱銘是我們台灣最偉大的當代藝術家之一。在回來的路上，遊覽車會停在路邊的餐廳讓你們有機會吃到一些小吃。

這樣的行程很貴吧？

這樣的行程是新台幣 1,500 元，一個人約是美金 50 元，這有包括野柳及朱銘美術館的入場券。遊覽車會在早上 9 點從飯店啟程，會在下午 6 點左右返回台北。

Words 單字

* itinerary /aɪˋtɪnəˏrɛri/ *n.* 旅程；行程
* formation /fɔrˋmeʃən/ *n.* 形成；構成
* incredible /ɪnˋkrɛdəbəl/ *adj.* 難以置信的
* expensive /ɪkˋspɛnsɪv/ *adj.* 很貴的；奢華的
* admission /ædˋmɪʃən/ *n.* 入場卷；入學申請

Grammar
文法片語

1. as long as 只要，如果

★小提點：〈as long as〉當連接詞是「只要」，同等於〈while〉，可以連接兩個句子。

例一：We can't go anywhere as long as it is still raining. 如果一直在下雨的話，我們什麼地方都不能去。

★小提點：〈as long as〉表示有條件的「如果」，同等於〈if〉，也是可以連接兩個句子。

例二：You may stay here as long as you keep the noise down. 如果你可以把聲音降低，你可以一直待在這裡。

★小提點：這句名言可以學起來喔，〈As long as there is life there is hope.〉「只要活著，就有希望」。

2. How about..? 做……如何？

★小提點：〈How about..?〉和〈What about...?〉的意思完全一樣，都是要向對方提出請求，或向對方提出看法。

例一：How about taking the train to Tainan? 坐火車去台南如何？

例二：What about renting a car? 租車如何？

★小提點：〈How about you?〉和〈What about you?〉也可以用在寒暄的句子，在反問對方「你呢？」。

例三：I am from Taiwan. How about you? 我來自台灣，你呢？

3. Are you sure? 你確定嗎？

★小提點：〈sure〉是形容詞「確定」，這個句子也可以這樣說〈Are you sure about that?〉「你確定這件事嗎？」，也可以在後面加子句。

例一：Are you sure this is the right order? 你確定這是正確的訂單？

例二：Are you sure you made the reservation online? 你確定你有在網路上預約？

★小提點：〈be sure to do something〉務必要做的事

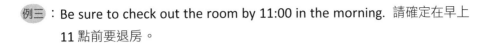

例三：Be sure to check out the room by 11:00 in the morning. 請確定在早上 11 點前要退房。

4. It must be expensive! 那一定很貴！

★小提點：〈must〉是助動詞「一定」，說話者用這個〈must〉時是在表達對事情有很肯定的看法，〈It must be + 形容詞或名詞〉，如果雙方知道彼此在講的內容，也可以這樣說〈It must be.〉意思是「一定是這樣的。」。

例一：You must be back by 10:00 at night. 你一定要在晚上 10 點前回來。

例二：You must try Bubble Tea while you are in Taiwan. 你在台灣時一定要試試珍珠奶茶。

★小提點：〈It must be.〉的相反是〈It can't be!〉「不可能」。

Short Sentences
不尷尬短句

❶ Why don't you try the Pig Blood Cake?
你要不要試試看豬血糕？

❷ I would say to stay away from fried food.
我覺得不要吃炸的東西。

❸ What would you like to eat for your dinner?
你晚餐想要吃什麼？

❹ We prefer to serve local food.
我們希望能提供當地的食物。

❺ Would you like to try the special pizza seafood topping?
你想試試特殊的海鮮比薩嗎？

❻ Staff members at the visitor center can help you purchase tickets once you get there.
一旦你到達那裡，遊客中心的工作人員可以幫您購買車票。

❼ I believe the Taipei City Night Tour includes English speaking guides.
我相信台北市夜遊有包括英語導遊。

❽ If you want to experience the culture and essence of the traditional Taiwanese Arts, I would recommend the one day tour of Yunlin.
如果您想體驗台灣傳統藝術文化和精髓，我會建議做雲林一日遊。

❾ Since you are talking about visiting the off shore islands, why don't you book a tour of the Green Island for a day trip?
既然你正在談論有關參觀離島，你為什麼不預訂綠島一日遊呢？

❿ I think you would love the tour of Yanmingshan National Park because it includes time at the Hot Springs.
我想你會喜歡陽明山國家公園之旅，因為這個行程有包含溫泉。

⓫ My favorite half day trip is to Sanxia since it includes the Yingge Pottery Arts.
我最喜歡的半天行程是到三峽，因為這個行程有包含鶯歌陶器藝術。

⓬ You should try to fit in at least a half day visit to see Wulai Aboriginal Culture.
你應該考慮至少半天的行程參觀烏來的原住民文化。

Speak Up! 說出來！ MP3 024

Dialogue 01 對話

Guest: What could you recommend for the dessert?
顧客：有什麼你可以推薦的甜點呢？

Waiter: You should try tofu pudding with syrup. The texture is very soft and it is sweet with syrup. It is served cold. It is a very popular dessert in the summer in Taiwan.
服務員：您可以試試有加糖水的豆花。這個口感很柔軟，因為有加糖水所以是甜的。這是冰品。這是在台灣的夏天一個非常受歡迎的甜點。

Part I 清楚表達

When you are recommending places for tourists to visit, try to find out what they are interested in. Do they like taking scenic photographs? Are they in to hiking and nature or are they curious about the traditions and cultures of Taiwan? Some love museums while others want to shop at high-end stores. Maybe they love the movies and dramas and would like to visit some of the places where their favorite drama was filmed. Take the time to figure out what they want to see before you make a recommendation. If you can match the guest's interests with a tour perfectly, they will create memories that will last a lifetime. Everyone is different and what appeals to one will not work with another guest.

當你在建議給遊客有關參觀的地方，盡量找出他們對什麼較感興趣，他們喜歡在有風景的地方照照片？他們喜歡健行或大自然的地方，還是他們對台灣的傳統和文化很好奇？有些人喜歡參觀博物館，有些人則希望在高價位的地方買東西。也許他們會喜歡電影和電視劇，並想參觀一些他們喜愛的電視劇所拍攝的地方。在你提出建議之前，花一些時間去了解他們所希望參觀的地方。如果你能把客人的興趣與旅遊完美的結合，他們將創造一生難忘的回憶。每個人都不一樣，有些人喜歡的東西對另一個人來說就不一定有興趣。

Conversations
不停住對話 MP3 025

The Desk Clerk is talking to a Newly Arrived Guest who <u>arrived early</u> and whose room won't be ready for another hour.
櫃台服務員正在跟一個剛到的顧客講話，這位顧客提早到來，他的房間還沒有準備，還要一個小時才會好。

Desk Clerk	Thank you for choosing our hotel but <u>I am afraid</u> your room isn't ready for your **occupancy** yet. It will be another hour.	非常感謝您選擇我們的飯店，但您的房間還沒有準備好。我們需要再一個小時的時間整理。
Guest	I thought we could check in at 2 o'clock.	我以為我們可以在 2 點辦理入住手續。
Desk Clerk	I'm sorry if you **misunderstood** but our check-in time is 3 o'clock and our check-out is 11 am.	對不起，您誤會了，我們的入住時間是 3 點鐘，我們的退房時間是上午 11 點。
Guest	Can you check us in early?	你可以早一點讓我們住入嗎？

Desk Clerk	I can go ahead and **register** you if you like. I can let you in the room as soon as I get word that it is ready for you.	如果您需要的話，我可以讓你您先註冊。只要我得到消息說您的房間已經準備好，就可以馬上讓您入房。
Guest	Please do. Do you think <u>it might be</u> ready early?	是的，請讓我們辦理住房，你覺得房間可能早一點準備好嗎？
Desk Clerk	I don't know. I'm sorry, but why don't you leave your bags in our bag room and use this **voucher** for tea in the tea room. I will send for you <u>as soon as</u> the room is ready. Once again, I **apologize** that your room isn't prepared yet.	我不知道呢。我感到很抱歉，但是您可以把您的行李放在我們的包房內，並使用此券在茶室裡休息一下。當房間準備好後，我會盡快的請人告訴您。我再次地向您的房間還沒有準備好而致歉。

Words

單 字

* occupancy /ˈɑkjəpənsi/   *n.* 佔有；居住
* misunderstand /ˌmɪsəndəˈstænd/   *v.* 誤解
  （misunderstood- 過去式、過去分詞）
* register /ˈrɛdʒɪstə/   *v.* 登記；註冊
* voucher /ˈvaʊtʃə/   *n.* 禮券；憑証
* apologize /əˈpɑləˌdʒaɪz/   *v.* 道歉；認錯

Grammar
文法片語

1. It arrived early. 有點早到。

   ★小提點：〈early〉是副詞「早地」，在這裡是形容前面的動詞。

   例一：The manager arrives early for work every day. 那位經理每天都會早到。

   例二：She always arrives early. 她總是會早到。

   ★小提點：〈early〉的反義詞是〈late〉「晚地」，也是副詞，

   例三：Our schedule got delayed because the bus was really late. 我們的行程都延遲了因為公車很晚才到。

2. I am afraid that... 我是擔心……

   ★小提點：〈afraid〉是形容詞，在這裡的句型是〈S+V+ afraid +that + 子句〉或者可以用〈afraid of〉後面加名詞。

   例一：I am afraid that the food is too spicy for you. 我是擔心那食物對你來説太辣。

   例二：I am afraid of earthquakes. 我很擔心地震。

   例三：當在緊急狀況需要安撫別人，也可以直接説〈Don't be afraid.〉不用害怕。

3. It might be... 有可能……

   ★小提點：〈might〉是助動詞，表「可能」的推測和不確定的意思，〈might〉的後面直接加原形動詞。

   例一：It might be a good idea to take the hotel shuttle bus. 如果可以搭乘飯店接駁車會是很棒的。

   例二：You never know what might happen in the future. 你永遠不知道未來會發生什麼事。

   例三：Don't worry, everything might just work out. 不用擔心啊，船到橋頭自然直。

4. as soon as 一……就……

★小提點：這個片語可以解釋為「一件事情做完後，另外一件事情馬上會發生」，〈as soon as〉是從屬連接詞，用來連接兩個句子。

例一：I will call you as soon as we arrive. 我們到達時，我一定會馬上打電話給你。

例二：Please turn off the light as soon as you leave the room. 當你離開房間時，請馬上關燈。

★小提點：〈as soon as possible〉「儘可能地」，通常加在句子最後面

例三：Please return the room key as soon as possible. 請儘可能快速的還回房間鑰匙。

Short Sentences

不尷尬短句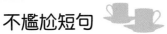

❶ I'm sorry but we are out of rooms with balconies at the moment.
對不起，但是我們目前沒有空出有陽台的房間。

❷ I wish we were able to help you solve this problem but we don't have a solution for you now.
我希望我們能夠幫你解決這個問題，但目前我們沒有答案給你。

❸ I would like to apologize for your wait and tell you thank you for waiting so patiently.
對於你的等待我感到很抱歉，我想告訴你，謝謝你這麼有耐心的等待。

❹ I am sorry that your room isn't as clean as it should be and will send housekeeping up immediately to take care of it.
對不起，你的房間不是很乾淨，房間應該是要很乾淨的，我會請房務部馬上清理乾淨。

❺ I'm sorry for the inconvenience but the hotel restaurant is closed for renovations.
我很抱歉給您帶來不便，但飯店的餐廳目前是關閉在整修中。

❻ Please accept my apologies for your inconvenience.
為您帶來不便，請接受我的道歉。

⑦ I am sorry that your stay wasn't comfortable and I hope we can do better next time.
對不起，讓您住得不舒服，我希望我們下一次能做得更好。

⑧ Please excuse our staff for their mistake and I will try to make it up to you.
請原諒我們的工作人員的錯誤，我會盡量補償給你。

⑨ Please accept my apology.
請接受我的道歉。

⑩ I am awfully sorry about the long wait.
對於漫長的等待，我感到非常的抱歉。

Speak Up!
說出來！　　MP3 026

Dialogue 01 對話

Guest: The lights won't turn on in my room when I enter and I can't figure out how to make them work.
顧客：當我進房時，無法開燈，我不知道該怎麼開燈。

Front Desk: I'm sorry, sir but you have to place your room card in the holder by the door and the lights will turn on automatically.
櫃檯人員：對不起，先生，但你必須把你的房卡放在門上的支架後，燈就會自動打開。

Dialogue 02 對話

Guest: I wanted diet coke but you gave me regular coke.
顧客：我點的是健怡可樂，但你給我是一般的可樂。

Waiter: I'm sorry, ma'am. That was my mistake. Let me fix that right away and there will be no charge for your coke on the bill.
服務員：對不起，小姐。這是我的錯誤。我馬上處理，而且在賬單上不會收取可樂的費用。

Everyone makes mistakes and it is a wise employee that knows how to apologize and express regret to the client so that they feel respected and listened to when they have a problem. Saying you're sorry without emotion, like a robot, doesn't help the client at all. Anything you can do to help them feel at ease while you solve the problem will help resolve their anxiety. Give them viable solutions and let them feel your concern and care. Express your knowledge that they are valuable to you and that you will do whatever it takes to solve the problem. Let them know that you understand how they are feeling and allow them to vent some of their frustration without taking it personally.

　　每個人都會有犯錯的時候，一個聰明的員工會知道如何道歉，並對顧客表示遺憾，讓他們感覺被尊重，也覺得當他們有問題時，你會傾聽這些問題。說你很抱歉時卻沒有帶感情，就會像一個機器人一樣，這樣對顧客是沒有幫助的。所有你認為可以幫助他們的方式都可以減輕他們的焦慮。給他們可行的解決方案，讓他們感受到你的關心和愛護。表現出他們對你來說是有價值的顧客，你會盡一切力量來解決這個問題。讓他們知道你了解他們的感受，並讓他們發洩他們的挫折感而不要覺得他們是衝著你來的。

1.2.6 Expressing Gratitude 表達感謝

Conversations
不停住對話 MP3 027

A guest returns the next day with a gift for the Concierge who had helped her earlier.
一位顧客隔天返回到飯店要送給禮賓人員一個禮物，因為這個禮賓人員在先前有幫助她。

Guest	Thank you for your help yesterday.	昨天很謝謝你的幫助。
Concierge	It was my pleasure. I hope you had a fun time at the play last night.	這是我的榮幸。我希望你昨晚看的那場戲看得很開心。
Guest	We wouldn't have seen it without your help getting tickets.	沒有你的幫忙拿到門票，我們是沒有機會看到的。
Concierge	I'm glad you able to attend it. Do you need my assistance today with anything else?	我很高興你有去看。你今天需要我幫你做別的事嗎？
Guest	No, No, No. I know you don't tip in Taiwan, but I wanted to show my appreciation for your extra effort. (Hands a small gift to the Concierge)	沒有，沒有，沒有 我知道在台灣是沒有給小費，但是我想表達我對你的額外努力的感謝。（雙手拿給禮賓人員一個小禮物）

Concierge	Wow! Thank you very much. But you didn't have to do that. Helping people is part of my job.	哇！非常感謝你。但是你不需要這樣做。我的工作的一部分職責就是幫助別人。
Guest	Please accept it. It's just a small gift.	請接受它。這只是一個小禮物。
Concierge	I am grateful for your **thoughtfulness** but you shouldn't have.	我很感謝你的體貼，但你不需要這樣做的。
Guest	Thank you for going above and beyond what one can expect.	謝謝你額外的努力來幫助我們，也讓我們有意外的收穫。
Concierge	This is a real surprise. I can't tell you thank you enough. It is too much!	這真的很驚喜。真的是太謝謝了。實在是太多禮了！

Part I 清楚表達

Words 單字

* pleasure /ˈplɛʒɚ/   *n.* 快樂；愉快
* attend /əˈtɛnd/   *v.* 出席；參加
* assistance /əˈsɪstəns/   *n.* 援助；幫助
* appreciation /əˌpriʃɪˈeʃən/   *n.* 賞識；感激
* thoughtfulness /ˈθɔtfəlnɪs/   *n.* 沉思；體貼

Grammar
文法片語

1. Thank you for… 謝謝你……

★小提點：〈Thank you.〉「謝謝你」就是一個完整的句子，如果後面要解釋謝謝對方所做的事，一定要先接介係詞的〈for〉有「為了」的意思。

例一：Thank you for your kind hospitality. 謝謝你的盛情款待。

例二：Thank you for being so kind. 謝謝你對我這麼好。

例三：I can never thank you enough for your kindness. 你這麼好真的讓我感激不盡。

2. It was my pleasure. 這是我的榮幸

★小提點：這句有〈was〉所以是過去式，〈pleasure〉是「快樂，高興」，這個句子也可以用現在式〈It is my pleasure.〉後面也可以加不定詞片語 to-V。

例一：It's my pleasure to help you. 我感到很榮幸可以幫助您。

例二：It's my pleasure to know you. 能認識你是我的榮幸。

例三：It's my pleasure to serve you. 為您服務是我的榮幸。

3. I am glad. 我很高興

★小提點：〈glad〉「高興的」是形容詞，和這個字最接近的就是〈happy〉。〈I am glad.〉和〈I am happy.〉有同等的意思。

例一：I am glad to see you again. 我很高興再次看到你。

★小提點：這個句子後面可以加子句，〈I am glad that+S+V〉。

例二：I am glad that you have decided to visit the night market. 我很高興你已經決定去逛夜市。

例三：I am glad to hear that you enjoyed your visit in Taiwan. 我很高興聽到你喜歡在台灣的時光。

4. I am grateful for your thoughtfulness. 我很感謝你的體貼

★小提點：〈grateful〉是形容詞「感激的」，通常會接介係詞〈for〉副詞是〈gratefully〉。

例一：I am grateful for your advice. 我很感謝你的建議。

例二：We gratefully accept the invitation. 我們感激地接受了邀請。

★小提點：〈grateful〉的反義詞是〈ungrateful〉可以解釋為〈沒有感激之心的〉。

例三：I have seen so many ungrateful people. 我見過很多沒有感恩之心的人。

Short Sentences
不尷尬短句

❶ It's been a pleasure to help you.
我感到很高興可以為您服務。

❷ May I have the pleasure of helping you?
我可以有這個榮幸來幫你嗎？

❸ I am very thankful to see you all arrived safely.
我很感恩能看到你們所有人都安全到達。

❹ There are no words to express my gratitude.
沒有任何的字可以表達我的感激之情。

❺ It was very kind of you to say that.
你這麼說真的是很友善。

❻ We really appreciate your cooperation.
我們非常感謝您的合作。

❼ We would like to offer this small souvenir as a token of our appreciation.
我們提供這種小紀念品來表達我們的感謝之意。

❽ We are very thankful for your nice comments.
我們非常感謝您的好評語。

❾ We would like to express our appreciation and thanks to you all for coming.
我們想表達我們的感謝，也謝謝各位的光臨。

❿ I am very happy to have you here with us.
我很高興有你在我們這裡。

Part I 清楚表達

Speak Up!
說出來！   MP3 028

Dialogue 01 對話

Hotel staff: I will pick you up outside the train station on the east side away from all the traffic so it will be easy to spot me.

飯店工作人員：我會去東邊的火車站外接你，這個地方比較遠離所有的車流量，這樣你會很容易看到我。

Guest: Thank you very much for going out of your way to greet me. I appreciate your extra effort.

顧客：非常感謝你繞道來接我。我很感謝你額外的努力。

Dialogue 02 對話

Guest: Your English is fairly good.

顧客：你的英文講得很好。

Staff: Thank you for your kind words. You've been very patient with my English. I still have so much to learn.

工作人員：謝謝你的讚美。你對我的英語聽得很有耐心的。我還有很多要學的。

Many foreigners are used to tipping for every service and find it difficult to not do so when in Taiwan- especially if the service was excellent. They are unsure how to express their gratitude since their usual way isn't acceptable. Occasionally one will insist on tipping and you will need to educate them on the Taiwanese practice of not tipping and tell them saying thank you will suffice. Many times a guest will want to let you know that you have given them an incredible level of service. If you go out of your way for a guest and do something special, they will want to find a way to show their appreciation and may show up with a small gift. If it isn't against your company's policy, accept the gift graciously and tell them how thankful you are that they thought of you. If it is against your company's policies to accept gifts from guests, inform them of that rule and tell them that "it's the thought that counts" - a saying that means the very fact that they thought about you is enough.

很多外國人也很習慣對每一種服務給予小費，他們發現在台灣時不給予小費有點難做到，特別是當如果他們接受到很好的服務。這樣的話他們不知道如何表達自己的感激之情，因為他們通常表現感激的方式在台灣是不能被接受的。偶爾有人會堅持要給你小費，這個時候你需要教育他們有關台灣不收小費的文化，並告訴他們說謝謝就足夠了。很多時候，客人會想讓你知道，你提供給他們的服務是到達令人難以置信的程度。你不怕麻煩地幫客人做一些其它的事，他們會希望表達自己的感謝，並可能會親自給你一個小禮物。如果沒有違背你的公司的政策，你可以大方接受禮物，並告訴他們（顧客）你的感激之情因為他們（顧客）有想到你。如果收禮物有違背公司的政策，這時你要告訴他們有關公司的規則，並告訴他們，"心意最重要"，這樣的説法意味著他們的內心有想到你這樣就足夠了。

Part II

Restaurant English

餐廳英語

Unit 01 **Preparatory Work** 餐前準備

2.1.1 Preparatory Work Before Opening- Front End 外場

Conversations
不停住對話   MP3 029

The Manager is talking with the Waiter and Waitress that <u>came in early</u> to help prepare for a busy day at a restaurant.
一家餐館的經理正在與比較早來工作的男性服務員和女性服務員說明要忙碌的一天的準備工作。

Manager	I'm glad you were able to come in early today. There is a lot of prep work before we can open the restaurant.	我很高興你今天能早點進來。在我們餐廳營業前是有很多準備工作要做。
Waitress	No problem. <u>I was free this morning</u> and could use the **extra** money. Where do you want me to start?	沒問題。我今天上午沒事，所以可以賺取額外的錢。你要我從哪裡開始？
Manager	We have several large reservations today so you need to make sure the tables are set for them.	我們今天有幾個大型的預約，所以你需要確保這些桌子有佈置好。

Waitress	I'll check the reservation book then to see exactly how many tables we need to prepare and for how large the parties will be.	我來查一下預約簿,然後看看我們需要準備多少桌子,也看看這些慶祝會有多大。
Waiter	When you finish that, <u>I could use some help</u> **steaming** the glassware and **vacuuming** the floors.	當你完成那些,我可以請你幫忙蒸汽一下玻璃杯和用吸塵器清理一下地板。
Manager	And the windows are looking dirty as well.	還有窗戶看起來蠻髒的。
Waiter	I have them on my **to-do list**. I want to replace the candles first.	我有把這項列在待辦清單裡。我想先去更換蠟燭。
Manager	The chef is introducing several new specials today so <u>make sure</u> you **review** them with him when you have a minute.	廚師今天推出了幾個新的特色菜,所以當你有時間時,你一定要確保你跟廚師檢查一下這些特色菜。

Part II 餐廳英語

Words 單字

* extra /ˈɛkstrə/　*adj.* 額外的
* steam /stim/　*v.* 蒸
* vacuum /ˈvækjum/　*v.* 吸塵
* to-do list /tu/ /du/ /lɪst/　*ph.* 待辦清單
* review /riˈvju/　*v.* 檢討;復習

Grammar
文法片語

1. came in early 早點進來

★小提點：〈came〉是動詞〈come〉的過去式，有〈來〉的意思，〈come in〉是「進來」，early 是副詞「早地」形容動詞，不只是「來」，而是「早點來」。

例一：〈Please come in.〉請進來。〈Please come in quietly.〉請小聲地進來。

例二：The door was open so I just came in. 那個門是開著的，所以我就進來了。

★小提點：如果加了不一樣的介係詞〈on〉就有完全不一樣的意思。意為「快點啦」、「拜託」。

例三：Come on! Hurry! 快點，趕快啦！

例四：Come on. This is not the end of the world. 拜託好不好，這不是世界末日。

2. I was free this morning. 我今天早上有空

★小提點：〈free〉有「免費、自由」的意思。

例一：Now that I am free, I can enjoy some coffee. 現在我有空，我可以享受一下咖啡。

例二：I am free today. 我今天都有空。

例三：If you free tomorrow afternoon, we can have lunch together. 如果你明天下午有空，我們可以一起吃午餐。

3. I could use some help. 我是需要人手

★小提點：〈could〉是助動詞，後面加原形動詞〈could + V〉，用〈could〉時，語氣會比較委婉。

例一：Could I borrow your table? 我可以借一下你的桌子嗎？

★小提點：〈could〉也可以就現在或將來的動作做推測。

例二：If the schedule allows, we could go to Kenting next week. 如果行程可以的話，我們下星期可以去墾丁。

4. make sure 確定

★小提點：〈make sure〉確定，常用於祈使句，後面加〈that+ 子句〉。

例一：Make sure that you check out by 11:00 in the morning. 請確定在早上 11:00 前退房。

例二：Please make sure all cell phones are turned off. 請確定所有的手機有關機。

★小提點：類似的片語有〈be sure to〉「確定」。

例三：Please be sure not to be loud again. 請確定不要再大聲了。

Short Sentences
不尷尬短句

❶ All the candles need to be removed and replaced with new ones.
所有的蠟燭都需要拿掉並更換新的。

❷ Put fresh flowers in the vases and place one vase on each table.
把鮮花放在花瓶內，同時每張桌子上都要有一個花瓶。

❸ The containers for condiments need to be filled and refreshed.
調味品的容器都需要填滿和換新的調味品。

❹ Don't forget to fold the napkins when you are free.
當你有時間的時候，不要忘了折餐巾紙。

❺ After you sweep the floor, please polish the silver tea sets.
當你掃完地後，請擦亮銀茶具組。

❻ Did you check to make sure that there is enough napkins prepared for tonight?
你有沒有檢查確保今晚有準備好足夠的餐巾紙？

❼ Make sure the silverware is clean and organized properly.
要確保銀器是乾淨的，也要擺設好。

❽ Use the oldest products in storage first and move the newer ingredients to the back.
先使用儲藏室裡最舊的產品和把較新的材料移到最後面。

⑨ Since table six is missing silverware, you will need to reset it.
由於第六桌有缺少銀器，你需要重新擺設。

⑩ If you have some time, please polish the brass door knobs.
如果你有時間，請擦亮黃銅門把。

Speak Up!
說出來！　　MP3 030

Dialogue 01 對話

Waitress: How many tables are reserved for dinner tonight? I need to know so I can set up the right amount of tables.
女服務員：今天晚上有多少預約的桌位呢？我需要知道，這樣我可以把正確的桌子數量準備好。

Waiter: I counted 10 in the reservation book for 7 o'clock and another 6 for 7:30.
男服務員：我在預約簿裡數過了，7 點時有 10 個預約， 7:30 有 6 個預約。

Dialogue 02 對話

Waiter: We are running low on coffee and tea.
男服務員：我們的咖啡和茶的量剩下沒有多少。

Waitress: I will go to the storage room and bring back some. Do we need decaf too or just regular?
女服務員：我會去儲藏室把一些拿出來。也要拿低咖啡因的咖啡嗎？或只要拿一般的咖啡？

Dialogue 03 對話

Manager: After the tables are set for dinner, can you restock the salt and pepper shakers?
經理：桌子在晚餐前擺設好後，你可否把鹽和胡椒瓶加滿？

Waiter: Sure. Let me finish these last two tables first.
服務員：當然。讓我先準備好這最後的兩張桌子。

Job Wisdom
職業補給站

The preparatory work is critical if a restaurant is to be efficient and profitable. It sets the tone for the diner who may be entering the restaurant for the first time. They will judge the quality of the place first with their eyes and then with their nose. If the restaurant is clean and pleasant, then they will expect for the kitchen to be sanitary and health conscious. You may be expected to come in two hours or more before the restaurant opens to help prepare for the day. The tasks are many and varied but they all help the day run smoothly and organized. It is time well-spent, and no matter how many napkins you prepare-you will need more! Look around you when you enter in the morning and see what stands out to you. Are there fingerprints on the glass? Is there anything out place? After you finish doing all the assigned prep work, take a few minutes and do those little things that you spotted first thing in the morning. That kind of extra care makes a big difference.

如果一個餐廳要有效率和有盈利的話，準備工作是至關重要的。這樣對第一次來用餐的客人會無形中立下餐廳的標準。他們首先將會用他們的眼睛來判斷這個地方的品質，然後用鼻子來判斷。如果餐廳是乾淨和舒適，那麼他們就會期望廚房是注重衛生和健康的。你可能會被要求在餐廳開業之前的兩小時或更早的時間就要進來幫忙為一天的營業做好準備。要準備的任務是多種多樣的，但這些準備工作會讓一天的運作更加平穩和有組織。這樣的時間花的是很值得的。 而且，不管你準備了多少的餐巾紙，你還是需要準備更多！當你在早上剛去上班時，看看你的周圍，你就會知道怎麼做。是否玻璃杯上有指紋？有什麼是放在不對的地方？在你完成做所有被分配的準備工作後，你可以花幾分鐘的時間來做那些你在早上所發現的小事情。你所做的額外關心對事情會有很大的貢獻。

Part II 餐廳英語

Conversations
不停住對話 MP3 031

The Kitchen Manager <u>is meeting with</u> his staff before the restaurant opens.
在餐廳開業之前，廚房經理正在與他的工作人員開會。

Kitchen Manager	It's going to be a busy day out front today so <u>let's get started</u>. Since the kitchen is **spotless**, I want the dish washer to work with the **prep** cook.	今天在前台將會是忙碌的一天，所以我們就開始工作吧。廚房現在是一塵不染，所以我要洗碗員工和清理蔬菜員工一起工作。
Prep Cook	I checked my prep sheet and there are a lot of vegetables on the menu today so we could use the extra help.	我已經檢查了我的準備表，今天的菜單上有很多的蔬菜，所以我們會需要額外的幫助。
Dish Washer	I've not prepped the vegetables yet.	我還沒有準備過蔬菜呢。
Kitchen Manager	Today is your lucky day. Teach him everything you know, Prep Cook.	今天是你的幸運日。清理蔬菜員，請你教他你所知道的一切。

Part II 餐廳英語

Prep Cook (to Dish Washer)	First we start by **unloading** the truck and washing the vegetables. <u>Follow me</u>. If we have time, I'll teach you how to make the soup stock.	首先，我們先來卸下卡車上的東西和洗蔬菜。跟我來。如果我們有時間，我會教你如何製作高湯。
Kitchen Manager	After everyone gets their stations set up, I need two people to check the **pantry** for **expiration** dates and throw out anything that's expired.	在每個人對自己的工作做好了之後，我需要兩個人來檢查儲藏室看看是否有到期的東西，也要扔掉過期的東西。
Pastry Chef	I was planning to do that today already. The desserts the chef added to the menu are mostly <u>last minute</u> prep work.	我今天是有打算這樣做。廚師添加到菜單的甜品的準備工作大多是最後再準備就可以。

Words 單字

* spotless /ˈspɑtləs/   *adj.* 無缺點的；無可挑剔的
* prep /prɛp/   *n.* 預備
* unload /ənˈlod/   *v.* 卸下
* pantry /ˈpæntri/   *n.* 餐具室；食品室
* expiration /ˌɛkspəˈreʃən/   *n.* 期滿；截止

Grammar
文法片語

1. be meeting with 和某人有會議，和某人正要會面

★小提點：〈meeting〉是〈meet〉的現在分詞，meet 的三態變化：meet, met, met。

例一：The executive chef will be meeting with the kitchen staff tomorrow. 行政總廚會在明天與廚房工作人員開會。

★小提點：〈meeting〉也直接當可數名詞「會議」，因為是可數，所以前面要加〈a〉或〈the〉。

例二：We will have a meeting with the manager at 9:00. 我們在 9:00 會和經理開會。

2. Let's get started! 我們開始吧！

★小提點：動詞〈get〉取得，後面不能直接加動詞〈start〉開始，所以要用過去分詞〈started〉，這句也可以很簡單的這樣說〈Let's start.〉我們開始吧。

例一：I just can't get him started. 我無法讓他開始著手。

★小提點：如果要詳細解釋「做什麼…」則要加介係詞〈on〉，〈Let's get started+ on...〉。

例二：When can we get started on this special project? 我們什麼時候可以開始這個特別的企劃案？

3. Follow me. 跟著我

★小提點：動詞〈follow〉是跟隨，後面接名詞或代名詞。

例一：Please follow me this way, Sir. 先生這邊請。

例二：Please make sure you follow the instructions carefully. 請確定你有小心的遵守說明。

4. Last minute 最後一分鐘

★小提點：〈last minute〉是有時間的緊迫性的講法，也就是「最後一刻」。

例一：Don't always waits until the last minute to do the cleaning. 不要總是等到最後才做清理。

例二：Please don't change your mind at the last minute. 請不要在最後時刻改變主意。

Short Sentences
不尷尬短句

❶ The Sous chef is second in command and is in charge when the Chef is absent.
當主廚不在，副廚師是第二個負責任的人。

❷ The Sous chef is responsible for training others so inexperienced staff members can be more productive.
副廚師負責培訓別人，這樣沒有經驗的工作人員做事可以比較有成效。

❸ All kitchen employees should have good personal hygiene.
所有廚房的員工都應該有良好的個人衛生習慣。

❹ The chef is trying out several new dishes tomorrow so plan on coming in early to prep for them.
主廚明天要設計幾道新菜，所以你們要早點來工作以做好新菜的準備。

❺ When cutting steaks off the sides of beef, be careful not to ruin the cut or waste the meat.
當你從牛肉兩旁切牛排時，要小心不要破壞或浪費肉。

❻ The chef is trying to decide on the ingredients for today's soup special.
廚師正在決定今日例湯的材料。

❼ The soups and sauces are all prepared and ready to be used in cooking.
湯和醬料都準備好可以用來煮菜了。

❽ The hotel's kitchen is compact but well equipped.
飯店的廚房空間雖小但設施齊全。

❾ The chief chef asked his assistant to take care of cooking the pasta.
主廚要他的助手負責煮義大利麵。

Part II 餐廳英語

說出來！ MP3 032

Dialogue 01 對話

Sous Chef: Do you know how to operate all the equipment in the kitchen yet?

副廚師：你知道如何操作廚房所有設備嗎？

Line Cook: Not yet. I am still learning all the ins and outs of the cold stations.

廚師助手：還沒有，我還在學習冷食區所有裡裡外外的事。

Dialogue 02 對話

Chef: I was not happy with the quality of the plating last night.

主廚：我對昨天晚上擺盤感到很不高興。

Sous Chef: I will review plating with the staff during prep time today to address that issue, Chef.

副廚師：主廚，我會在今天準備工作的時間與工作人員審查擺盤來解決這個問題。

Dialogue 03 對話

Manager: The sous chef called this morning saying he was sick and cannot be here today.

經理：副廚師今天早上打電話來說他生病了，今天無法來上班。

Chef: Okay. Thanks. It will be not easy but we will try to manage it today without the sous chef.

主廚：好的，謝謝你。沒有副廚師會很不容易但是我們還是會試著讓今天運作順利。

Starting as a dishwasher in a kitchen that promotes from within may be a good career move for a beginner. A few tips that will help you get promoted quickly are to work quickly and efficiently and take advantage of slow times to learn new skills. Be sure to always be doing something: wiping down counters, collecting dirty dishes, stacking dishes where they belong, etc. Not only will it make the time go faster, but it will make everyone's job easier. Maintain a good attitude around everyone even when things get tense. By working well with others in a fast-paced situation and learning from constructive criticism, you will be seen as a team player who is valuable.

對一個初學者來説，從廚房開始當洗碗員工可以有機會在內部被提拔升職。有幾個技巧可以幫助你迅速晉升，那就是要快速和高效率的工作，並好好的利用不忙的時間來學習新的技能。你就是要確定讓自己不停的在做事，如清理櫃檯，收集髒盤子，把碗盤堆放在應該放的地方。這樣不僅將讓時間會過得更快，也會讓其他每個人的工作做起來更容易。要對周圍的人保持良好的態度，即使事情在緊張的時刻也要這樣做。在忙碌的時候與別人好好的合作，以及從建設性的批評中學習，這樣別人就會把你看成一名有價值的團隊隊員。

Part II 餐廳英語

2.1.3 Introduce New Staff Member to Crew 介紹新員工

Conversations

不停住對話 MP3 033

The Manager introduces a new Waitress to the rest of the workers during prep time.

經理在餐前準備工作的時間裡介紹一個新進的女服務員給其他員工認識。

Manager	I'd like to take a minute and introduce the newest member of our team, Sue Lee.	我想用一分鐘的時間來介紹我們最新的團隊成員，李淑。
New Waitress	Hello. I am **eager** to join you. I have heard good things about the work **environment** here.	你們好。我很高興能加入你們。我有聽說過這個工作環境很不錯。
Manager	She has eleven years of waitressing experience so I'm sure it won't take long to train her in our procedures.	她有 11 年的服務生經驗，所以我敢肯定，我們不會需要很長時間來訓練她我們的程序。
New Waitress	I have worked in <u>a couple of high-end restaurants</u>, but it's been awhile so thank you for helping me learn the ropes.	我有在幾個高檔餐館工作過，但那已經有一段時間了，感謝你們幫助我學習新的任務。

Maître	Welcome. We will start **training** you tonight. One of our most **competent** waiters will show you how we do things here.	歡迎你。我們將在今晚開始訓練你。我們其中一個最好的服務員會教你我們這裡做事情的方式。
Waiter	I'm sure a lot of what we do will be old hat, but there are a few things that are specific to our restaurant. What is your <u>favorite</u> thing about waiting tables?	我很肯定我們做的有很多是一般的規則，但也有一些事情是我們餐廳的特色。有關於服務餐廳客人你最喜歡的是哪方面？
New Waitress	I love families. <u>It makes me happy to</u> see families eating together.	我很喜歡家庭。我很喜歡看到家人一起吃飯的情景。

Part II 餐廳英語

Words

單　字

* eager /ˈigɚ/   *adj.* 熱切的；渴望的
* environment /ɪnˈvaɪrənmənt/   *n.* 環境；外界
* training /ˈtrenɪŋ/   *n.* 訓練；培養
* competent /ˈkɑmpətɪnt/   *adj.* 能幹的；勝任的
* favorite /ˈfevərɪt/   *n.* 喜歡的事物

Grammar
文法片語

1. a couple of… 幾個……

　★小提點：〈a couple of 〉後面是都要接複數名詞但數量不是很大，和這個片語類似的有〈a small number of〉少數；〈a few〉少數；〈several〉一些。

　　例一：I've only been here a couple of weeks and I don't really know the set-up. 我只有在這裡幾個星期而已，我對擺設還不是很了解。

　　例二：We only visited Taiwan for a few days. 我們只參觀台灣幾天而已。

2. High-end 高檔的；尖端的；挑剔的

　★小提點：形容詞〈High-end〉是非正式的用法，可以形容產品和服務。

　　例一：This is a high-end restaurant. 這是一個高檔的餐廳。

　★小提點：這個片語的相反詞是〈low-end〉較便宜的；較差的。

　　例二：This is a low-end computer system. 這是比較差的電腦系統。

3. What is your favorite…? 你最喜歡的……是什麼？

　★小提點：形容詞〈favorite〉最喜歡的，直接可以加名詞。

　　例一：What's your favorite place in Taiwan? 你最喜歡台灣的哪一個地方？

　　例二：Tainan is my favorite city. 臺南是我最愛的城市。

4. It makes me happy. 讓我感到很高興。

　★小提點：〈It〉代名詞，〈make〉有「讓、使」的意思，為使役動詞。形容詞〈happy〉為補語。

　　例一：The smell of the fried stinky tofu makes me sick. 臭豆腐的味道讓我感到很噁心。

　　例二：The lousy service makes me mad. 這麼爛的服務讓我感到很氣憤。

不尷尬短句

❶ The hours are long, but the pay is good and the coworkers are very nice.
工作時間長，但薪水不錯，同事也都很好。

❷ Our newest employee started last week, but she is very competent.
我們最新的員工上週才開始上班，但她是很能幹的人。

❸ We are hiring for several positions, but you need prior experience to apply for them.
我們正在招聘幾個職位，但你需要有經驗才能申請這些職位。

❹ What did you do before you started working with us?
你在我們這裡工作之前，你以前是做什麼工作呢？

❺ It is nice to work with you here.
能在這裡與你工作是很不錯的。

❻ May I introduce you to our new manager?
我可以向你們介紹我們的新經理嗎？

❼ It's my great pleasure to introduce Chef Wang.
我非常高興可以在這裡介紹王師傅給大家。

❽ Mr. Zheng is a very experienced restaurant manager.
鄭先生是一個非常有經驗的餐廳經理。

❾ She will start work here as a trainee chef.
她將在這裡以實習廚師的身份開始工作。

❿ Let's welcome her as our team member.
讓我們歡迎她成為我們團隊成員。

Speak Up! 說出來！ MP3 034

Dialogue 01 對話

Manager: Have you worked as a waiter before?

經理：你有當過服務生經驗嗎？

New Employee: It's been a while, but I am a quick learner.

新進人員：已經有一段時間了，但是我可以學得很快。

Dialogue 02 對話

Manager: What is your dream position?

經理：你夢想的職位是什麼？

New Employee: Someday I want to own my own restaurant, but in the meantime I am looking forward to learning as much as I can.

新員工：總有一天，我要擁有自己的餐廳，但在此期間，我期待著盡我所能的學習。

Dialogue 03 對話

Waiter: Welcome to our restaurant. I hear you are new at this.

服務員：歡迎加入我們的餐廳。我聽說你在這方面是新手。

New Employee: Yes, I am. I worked in an office, but got tired of sitting all day long.

新員工：是的，我是。我曾在辦公室裡工作，但已經厭倦了一整天都是坐著的工作。

Waiter: I think you will like working here.

服務員：我想你會喜歡在這裡工作的。

Be a team player! What does that mean? It means that you are considerate of others and willing to help out when they get busy or are overworked. It may mean getting drinks or refilling coffee for a coworker's table while they are taking orders at a different table. This kind of behavior is more than being kind. It's making sure the customer has a good experience even if your staff is overworked or understaffed. Your customer won't know you went the extra mile, but your coworker and your boss will! Help the new employee learn how to be efficient and effective at their job and you will have two competent employees on the floor at the same time. As the new employee, you will make mistakes as you learn the routine and the expectations of the other staff members. Be observant and ask questions. When you make a mistake, learn from it. You will quickly learn what is expected and how to do your new position effectively and efficiently.

要當一名團隊成員！這是什麼意思？這個意思是，你要為他人著想，當他們忙碌或勞累過度時，你會願意幫忙。這可能意味著當同事正在忙別桌的時候，你要幫忙同事的桌子倒飲料或咖啡。這種行為不只是仁慈而已。這是為了確保即使你的員工過度勞累或人手不足時，顧客還是有很好的用餐經驗。你的客戶不會知道你有在加倍努力，但你的同事和你的老闆會知道你的努力！幫助新員工了解如何讓他們的工作更為有效率和效果，這樣你在餐廳內的同一時間就會有兩個能幹的員工在工作。就當新員工來說，你在學習工作的例程和達到其他工作人員的期望時，你是會做錯的。所以你要善於觀察，提出問題。當你犯了錯誤，你要從中吸取教訓。你會很快學到什麼是應該做的，以及如何有效果地與有效率地做你的新工作。

2.1.4 Taking Phone Reservations 電話訂位

Conversations
不停住對話   MP3 035

The Reservationist is talking with a customer on the phone who wants to make reservations for dinner.
有一名顧客想要為晚餐做預約,預約員正在用電話與這名顧客談預約的事。

Reserva-tionist	Thank you for calling us. How may I help you?	謝謝您的來電,我可以為你服務嗎?
Guest	I would like reservations for four at 8 o'clock tonight.	我想預約今晚八點四個人。
Reserva-tionist	I'm sorry but we are <u>completely booked</u> tonight and don't have any openings.	對不起,我們今晚全部預約都滿了,沒有任何空位。
Guest	What about next Saturday evening then?	那下星期六晚上呢?
Reserva-tionist	I have two tables **available** for next Saturday. One at 7:30 and one at 9:30 pm. Would you like either of these openings?	我在下星期六有兩個空的桌子,一個在 7:30,一個在 9:30。你要其中一個有空位的時間嗎?

Guest	I would like the 7:30 reservation. It's my mother's birthday. Would it be **possible** for us to sit by the window where she can see the **river**?	我想訂 7:30 的。這是我媽媽的生日。我們可以坐靠窗的座位嗎？這樣她可以看到河流？
Reserva-tionist	I will make notes about that, but I can't **promise** we will be able to seat you there.	我會把這些記下來，但我不能保證我們能夠讓你們坐那裡。
Guest	It would be very special if you could.	如果可以的話就會很特別。
Reserva-tionist	I have a table for four at 7:30 on next Saturday. We will not hold the table for longer than 30 minutes. And the name on that reservation is?	我幫您在下星期六 7:30 做了四個人的預約。我們只保留 30 分鐘。請問預約者的名字？

Part II 餐廳英語

Words
單 字

* booked /bʊkt/　*pp.* 登記
* available /əˋveləbəl/　*adj.* 可用的
* possible /ˋpɑsəbəl/　*adj.* 可能的；潛在的
* river /ˋrɪvə/　*n.* 河流
* promise /ˋprɑməs/　*v.* 允諾；答應

Grammar
文法片語

1. We are completely booked. 我們都被訂滿了。

  ★小提點：動詞〈 book〉預訂，相近詞有〈reserve〉。

    例一：Would you like to book a room for tomorrow? 你想預訂明天的房間嗎？

2. sit by the window 坐在窗戶旁邊

  ★小提點：動詞〈sit〉坐，介係詞〈by〉在側，〈sit by〉後直接加名詞。

    例一：I would like to sit by the sofa. 我想坐在沙發旁邊。

    例二：He likes to sit by the coffee table. 他喜歡坐在咖啡桌旁邊。

  ★小提點：〈Sit by〉也可以用作成語的「袖手旁觀」。

    例三：Don't just sit by and do nothing. 不要袖手旁觀。

3. I can't promise. 我不能保證

  ★小提點：動詞〈promise〉保證，用法有 promise someone (that)+ 子句。

    例一：I promise you that I will come back home before 12pm. 我像妳保證我會在十二點之前回家。

  ★小提點：promise someone the moon 這句的直譯是「保證摘月亮給某人」，但不可能實際上去摘月亮，所以這是誇張的説法，就是所謂的「信口開河」。

    例二：I can't promise you the moon, but I can do everything I can to help you. 我不能答應我辦不到的事情，但我會盡可能的做到我可以做的來幫助你。

4. to seat you 帶你就座

  ★小提點：通常我們所知道的〈seat〉位子，是當名詞。〈seat〉也可以當動詞，就是「就座」。

    例一：The room is not big enough to seat 8 people. 這個房間不夠讓 8 個人就座。

例二：He ran the business by the seat of his pants. 直譯是「用他褲子的座位來做生意」，靠直覺在做事。這個俚語是形容「無頭無腦、沒有計劃地在做事。」

Short Sentences
不尷尬短句

❶ To be fair to our guests we only hold reservations for an hour unless you reserve it with a credit card.
為了公平對待我們的客人，我們對預約只能保留一個小時，除非你是用信用卡做預約。

❷ I am sorry. The wait will be 40 minutes instead of 20 minutes!
對不起。等待時間將是 40 分鐘，而不是 20 分鐘！

❸ Your reservation was for six people, but it looks like you have 8 people.
你是預訂了六個人，但看起來像你有 8 個人。

❹ There will be no fee on your credit card if you cancel the reservation.
如果你取消預約，我們不會在你的信用卡扣款。

❺ There will be a fee of $25 on your credit card if you don't show up for the reservation.
如果你有預訂但沒有來，我們會在你的信用卡收取 25 元的費用。

❻ Normally, there is no refund if you choose to cancel the reservation.
如果你選擇取消預訂，我們通常是不會退款。

❼ There are empty tables, but they are reserved for guests who will be arriving shortly.
我們是還有空桌，但這些是保留給很快就會到達的客人。

❽ There are few cancellations today due to the just announced typhoon warning.
今天有幾個預約被取消，因為剛剛有宣布颱風警報。

❾ We have reserved two round tables for you.
我們有為你準備好兩個圓桌。

Speak Up! 說出來! MP3 036

Dialogue 01 對話

Guest: I am calling to tell you we are stuck in traffic and will be late for our 7:30 reservation. Can you hold our table another 40 minutes or so?

顧客：我現在打電話是想告訴你，我們被卡在擁擠的車流中，我們 7:30 的預訂會遲到。你可否幫我們的餐桌再留 40 分鐘左右？

Reservationist: We usually only hold a table for 30 minutes, but since you called us I will hold it another 45 minutes or so.

接待員：我們通常只能留 30 分鐘的空桌，但既然你有打電話來，我會再幫你們留 45 分鐘左右。

Dialogue 02 對話

Guest: We would like a table for two.

顧客：我們需要有兩張桌子。

Host: I'm sorry, sir, but we are completely booked tonight and have no openings. If you wish to wait, we may have some cancellations.

接待員：對不起，因為我們今天晚上全部都被訂滿了，目前沒有空桌。如果你想要等，我們可能會有人取消的。

Dialogue 03 對話

Guest: We had reservations for 8 and it is 8:30 and we are still waiting for our table.

顧客：我們有 8 個人的預訂，時間是在 8:30，但是我們仍然在等我們的桌子。

Hostess: I'm sorry, sir. Your table is being cleared off immediately. I would like to send one of the Chef's new appetizers to your table free of charge as an apology.

領班：對不起，先生。你的桌子馬上會被清理好。為了向你道歉，我想送給你廚師新的開胃菜之一。

The quicker a server is able to finish up with one party and get another party seated, there will be less of a wait by the guests and the restaurant will increase revenue. That doesn't mean you should sacrifice the quality of the dining experience for your currently seated guests. Good communication between the staff will decrease wait time and insure that your guests leave happy. If there is a reason why the wait time is going to be long, tell the guests when they check in so they can decide if they want to be patient or not. Gentle explanations and an occasionally comped drink or appetizer will leave the guest feeling like you made an effort to meet their needs. When taking phone reservations, make sure you know the reservation system and double check your facts.

　　如果服務生能很快的整理好桌子，並讓新進來的客人儘快坐下，客人等待的時間就會更少，餐廳將會增加收入。這並不意味著你應該犧牲你目前正在用餐的客人用餐經驗的品質。員工之間的良好溝通將減少等待時間，並確保你的客人留下美好的印象。如果你知道會有很長的等待時間，客人來的時候你就應該告訴客人，這樣可以讓他們決定他們是否有耐心要等桌子。溫柔的解釋和偶爾提供飲品或開胃菜，會讓客人感覺你有為他們的需求做出了努力。當在接受電話預約時，你要確保你知道預約系統的使用，並仔細再檢查一次。

Unit 01 **Preparatory Work**
餐前準備

2.1.5 Big Banquet and Convention 宴會 / 會議

The restaurant manager is <u>going through</u> a wedding schedule with the staff.
餐廳經理在和員工檢查婚禮時間表。

Manager	By 9:30 we should have everything in place. The decorations should be done and the multi-media **equipment** should be set up and ready to use. The bride's family will start arriving at 10:00 and the groom's family will come at 10:15. Doing everything at the appropriate time is <u>very **critical** for</u> a wedding. Make sure delays aren't our fault.	在 9:30 前我們就應該一切就緒。裝飾應該都已經做好,多媒體設備也要設置好可以準備使用。在 10:00 的時候新娘的家人會開始抵達,新郎的家人會在 10:15 抵達。對婚禮來説,在什麼時間時候做什麼事是非常關鍵的。如果有延誤要確保不是我們的錯。
Staff 1	The wine and water are on the table for the first part of the wedding **ceremony**.	婚禮儀式第一部分桌上的酒和水都已經準備好了。
Staff 2	The small gifts for guests are on each table.	給客人小禮品也都放在每張桌子上。

Manager	The banquet host and the **photographer** should be here <u>any moment</u>.	宴會主持人和攝影師應該很快就會到了。
Staff 1	The bride and groom's toast is at 12:15 and after the toast, the banquet meal will start.	新郎和新娘的敬酒是在 12:15，在敬酒之後宴會餐就可以開始。
Staff 2	After three dishes, the bride will go back stage and change into a different dress.	在上了三道菜後，新娘將回到後台換不同的禮服。
Manager	What about the **Champagne** toast tower and cake cutting? All these should be ready to go soon after the bride returns from changing her dress.	敬酒香檳塔及切蛋糕呢？所有這些都應該在新娘去後台換衣服時就準備。
Staff 1	I just <u>checked with</u> the bakery and they will be sending the cake by 11:00. We are getting the wine glasses ready.	我剛剛有和烘焙店查過了，他們在 11:00 前把會把蛋糕送過來。我們現在在準備酒杯。

Part II 餐廳英語

Words
單 字

* equipment /ɪˈkwɪpmənt/   *n.* 裝備
* critical /ˈkrɪtɪkəl/   *adj.* 關鍵性的
* ceremony /ˈsɛrəˌmoni/   *n.* 典禮；儀式
* photographer /fəˈtɑgrəfə/   *n.* 攝影師
* Champagne /ʃæmˈpen/   *n.* 香檳酒

Grammar
文法片語

1. going through 檢查一下

★小提點：介係詞〈through〉從……開始至終，有「經歷；通過；討論」等常用的意思。

例一： He went through a very hard time. 他經歷過很艱辛的時光。

例二： The call did not go through. 電話沒有通。

例三： Let's go through the menu again. 我們來討論一下這個菜單。

2. It is very critical for... 對……來說是很有關鍵性的

★小提點：〈critical〉形容詞，後面加介係詞〈for〉。

例一： Good customer service is critical for the success of the restaurant. 對餐廳的成功來說，好的客戶服務是很有關鍵性的。

★小提點：〈critical〉表達批評或反對，後面如果要解釋對什麼表達批評或反對，要用〈of〉。

例二： The customer is very critical of our food. 那個顧客對我們的食物很批評。

★小提點：〈critical thinking〉批判性思維，〈critical moment〉關鍵時刻，〈critical time〉危急時刻，〈critical way〉批判的方式。

3. any moment 任何時候（很快）

★小提點：名詞〈moment〉是「瞬間，片刻」。

例一： The bus will be here at any moment. 巴士就快要來了。

★小提點：〈In a moment〉馬上；〈At the moment〉現在。

例二： I will help you in a moment。我馬上就可以幫你。

例三： There is no table available at the moment. 現在目前沒有桌位。

4. checked with 核實一下

例一： I want to check with my friend before I make the reservation. 在做預約之前，我要和我的朋友核實一下。

★小提點：〈check〉可以當名詞為「支票」，在台灣一般公司行號所發的

支票，英文就是〈check〉，在餐廳用完餐的「賬單」，也是〈check〉
這個名詞，飛機準備入座或飯店住入是用〈check-in〉。

例二：Can I have the check, please? 請你把賬單拿來給我好嗎？

例三：When is the hotel's check-in time? 飯店的住入時間是什麼時候？

Short Sentences
不尷尬短句

❶ All our tables are reserved for several year-end dinner parties on Friday.
我們所有的桌子都在星期五被尾牙所訂完了。

❷ Do we have enough wine and beer for the dinner party?
我們是否有足夠晚宴要用的葡萄酒和啤酒？

❸ A company's year-end party is usually a big feast so we need the
decorations to be very festive.
一個公司的尾牙通常是一個很大的盛宴，所以我們需要的裝飾很有喜氣。

❹ The business owner will invite all the employees for a year-end dinner
party so we need to make sure we have enough seats for everyone.
公司老闆會邀請所有員工參加尾牙，所以我們需要確保我們有足夠的座位
給大家。

❺ Please make sure the lucky drawing box is ready and all the gifts are
displayed.
請確定摸彩箱已經準備好，還有所有的禮物都有陳列出來。

❻ What about the lucky drawing tickets?
摸彩箱的摸彩券呢？

❼ Is the stage set up for the show already?
要表演的舞台搭建好了了嗎？

❽ Is the equipment for the singing for the end-year party ready?
尾牙唱歌用的設備準備好了嗎？

❾ Can someone make sure the company's name is displayed properly at the
event entrance?
有誰可以確保公司的名稱在活動入口處有正確的排列好？

Part II 餐廳英語

Speak Up!
說出來！   MP3 038

Dialogue 01 對話

Company secretary: Do you offer banquet service in your hotel?
公司秘書：你的酒店有提供宴會服務嗎？

Front Desk: Yes. We do. What type of banquet service do you need?
前台人員：有的。我們有提供。你需要什麼類型的宴會服務呢？

Company secretary: This is for the end-of-year company party.
公司秘書：這是公司尾牙的聚會。

Dialogue 02 對話

Guest caller: We are planning a convention next year.
打電話來的客人：我們計劃在明年有一個大型會議。

Resort manager: We specialize in convention food services: large or small. Our Banquet staff is quite large and is well trained to serve at any event. Do you want to make an appointment so we can go over the options?
度假村經理：我們專門做大型或小型的餐飲服務。我們的宴會工作人員是相當多的，他們也都是訓練有素可以在任何宴會做服務。你要不要做一個預約以便我們能夠談談服務的選項？

Dialogue 03 對話

Secretary: We are looking for a banquet service for an international convention.
秘書：我們正在找一個國際會議的宴會服務。

Hotel manager: We are very experienced in international conventions. All our banquet servers are well trained in serving international guests.
飯店經理：我們對國際會議非常有經驗。我們所有的宴會服務人員服務國際客人是訓練有素的。

A good banquet server is more than just a waiter or busboy. The three main job skills as a banquet server are good customer service, physical endurance, and efficiency. First of all, as a banquet server, you need to provide good customer service including greeting guests, making sure they have all the basics on the table, and keeping their glasses filled. You also need to be spotless, with good hygiene, and use good manners, which will help create a great first impression. You need to be courteous and attentive to guests. Good listening and speaking skills are also helpful. Secondly, you also need to have good physical endurance because you will be expected to set up and arrange tables and to deliver heavy trays of food to the tables. The physical demands might also include bending, lifting and carrying trays and possible heavy items. You also need to follow health and safety standards at all times before, during, and after the function. Lastly, because you will serve many tables at the same time, from tens to hundreds of people, you will need to be very efficient and be attentive.

一個好的宴會服務員不僅僅是一個服務員或是打雜的人。宴會服務員的三個主要的工作技能包括有良好的客戶服務，身體耐力和效率。首先，作為宴會的服務員，你需要提供良好的客戶服務，包括招呼客人，確保他們的桌子有基本應有的東西，並要倒滿他們的杯子。你還必須看起來一塵不染，有良好的衛生習慣，並有舉止良好，這將可以幫助創造一個良好的第一印象。你對客人要有禮貌和周到。良好的聽說能力對這樣的工作也是很有幫助的。其次，你還需要有良好的身體耐力，因為你會被要求擺設和陳列桌子，並端上裝有食物很重的盤子到桌上。體力上的需求可能還包括彎腰，抬起和端起盤子和可能的很重的東西。在宴會之前，期間和之後，你也要時時刻刻都要遵循衛生和安全標準。最後，因為你會在同一個時間服務很多桌子，從幾十人到幾百人，所以你需要把工作做的非常有效的，並留意客人的需求。

Unit 02 Dining Services 用餐服務

Conversations
不停住對話 MP3 039

Hostess is taking to a guest who just come in.
女接待員正在接待剛剛進來的客人。

Hostess	Welcome! Thank you for dining with us today. Do you have a reservation?	歡迎！感謝您今天在我們這裡就餐。您有預約嗎？
Guest	We do. It's for 6 o'clock.	我們有的。6 點的預約。
Hostess	What name is it under?	是用什麼名字預約的呢？
Guest	It should be Lin.	應該是林。
Hostess	I see it. Would you like to be seated **immediately** or wait for the rest of your party?	我看到了。您想要立即入座或等您的其他朋友呢？
Guest	Go ahead and seat us. They should be here soon.	就直接讓我們入座。他們應該很快就到這裡。

Hostess	Certainly. Follow me. You **requested** seats <u>by the window</u> and I'm glad to say we can accommodate your wish today.	當然可以。跟我來。您要求靠窗的座位，我很高興地說，我們今天能做到您所希望的。
Guest	Thanks! It's my favorite place in the restaurant.	謝謝啦！這是我在這餐廳最喜歡的地方。
Hostess	May I bring you a drink while you wait for the rest of your group?	在您等其他人的時候，我可以幫您上點飲料嗎？
Guest	I would like to see the wine list now <u>if possible</u>.	如果可能的話我想看看酒單。
Hostess	Of course. We have **several** local wines we are **currently** featuring. I can bring you a <u>taste</u> of them while you check the list.	當然可以。有幾個我們目前推薦的當地葡萄酒。當您在看酒單時，我可以給您一些來品嚐看看。
Guest	That's a good suggestion. Thank you!	這是一個很好的建議。謝謝你！

Part II 餐廳英語

Words 單 字

* immediately /ɪˋmidɪtlɪ/   *adv.* 立即地
* request /rɪˋkwɛst/   *v.* 請求；要求
* several /ˋsɛvrəl/   *adj.* 幾個；一些
* currently /ˋkɚəntlɪ/   *adv.* 目前地
* taste /test/   *n.* 味道；品味

Grammar
文法片語

1. It should be... 應該要⋯⋯

★小提點：助動詞〈should〉應該，〈It should be+p.p.〉是被動語態，動詞用 p.p.。也可以 be 後面直接接形容詞。

例一：It should be done in no time. 應該很快就做好了。

例二：It should be easy. 這應該很簡單。

2. by the window 靠窗邊

★小提點：介係詞〈by〉靠著。

例一：Please set this table by the counter. 請把這個放在櫃檯旁。

★小提點：〈by the way〉雖然符合上述的解釋，但是這個片語是語氣詞，是「順便一提」。

例二：By the way, the guest said she really enjoyed the dessert. 對了，那位客人說她真的很喜歡那個甜點。

3. if possible 如果可能的話

★小提點：〈if〉假如，為連接詞；〈possible〉可能的，〈if〉是連接詞所以應該連接兩個句子，但是，〈if〉可以用省略的形式表現，在這裡就是〈If + 形容詞，S+V〉，〈if possible〉可以在句首或句尾。

例一：If possible, please let us know about the reservation by this afternoon. 如果可能的話，請在今天下午前讓我們知道預約。

例二：I will do my best to help you if possible. 我會儘量做到我可能做到的來幫助你們。

4. a taste of 嚐一點點

★小提點：這個片語可以用的範圍非常地廣，〈of〉後面加名詞。〈a taste of you skill〉領會了你的真功夫〈a taste of your quality〉，試試你們的本領，〈a taste of democracy〉嚐到民主的滋味，〈a taste of Taiwan〉台灣的風味，〈a taste of reality〉體驗現實。

不尷尬短句

1 How many people are in your party?
你們這團有多少人？

2 We always try to seat guests promptly.
我們總是試圖讓客人儘快入座。

3 I'm sorry that I can't find your reservation, but I will be able to find you a table in a few minutes.
我很抱歉，我無法找到您的預約，但我一定能在幾分鐘內找出一個空桌給你。

4 Is this table satisfactory or would you rather sit next to the fireplace?
你對這樣的位子滿意嗎，還是你想要坐在火爐旁邊？

5 Would you like a quiet table?
你想要一個安靜的位置嗎？

6 Do you need a high chair or a booster seat for the children?
你需要讓小孩坐嬰兒椅或加高座椅呢？

7 Let me take your name and add it to the first-come list.
讓我把你的名字加到先到先坐的單子裡。

8 There is currently a 25 minute wait for a table so do you want me to put you on the list?
目前等待的時間需 25 分鐘，你要我把你加在名單內嗎？

9 Do you need to make a new reservation or is this a confirmation?
你需要做新的預約或這是要確認預約？

10 Someone just cancelled the reservation so we have a table available at 7:00.
有人剛剛打電話來取消預訂，所以我們在 7:00 有一個空桌位。

Speak Up!

說出來！ MP3 040

Dialogue 01 對話

Guest: I'm running late so I think the rest of my friends arrived already.
顧客：我來晚了，所以我覺得我的朋友應該都已經到了。

Host: What name was the reservation under? I'll check for you.
接待員：是用什麼名字預約的呢？我可以幫你查查看。

Dialogue 02 對話

Guest: My mother said she made a reservation for our family on Friday night, but we need to cancel it.
顧客：我的母親說她為我們的家庭預約了週五晚上，但我們需要取消預約。

Hostess: I will cancel it immediately. What name did she use to make the reservation?
女接待員：我立即為您取消。她是用什麼名字來做預約的呢？

Dialogue 03 對話

Manager: We are so happy to see you back again.
經理：我們很高興看到你再來這裡。

Guest: Your staff here are all very hospitable and welcoming. We really enjoy dining here.
顧客：你這裡的員工都招待很周到和也讓人感到備受款待。我們真的很喜歡在這裡用餐。

Manager: Thank you for your nice comments. We try to do the best for our guests. Please enjoy your meal tonight.
經理：謝謝你的好意見。我們為我們的客人會儘量努力做到最好。今晚請享用你的晚餐。

The first person the guest meets when they enter your restaurant is the greeter who sets the tone for the entire experience. By being warm and friendly, the Host or Hostess conveys that this is a special place where the guest will feel special and comfortable. Speak with an upbeat tone and wear a smile. Be respectful and use formal titles such as Sir, Ma'am, or Doctor. Listen to the guest and care about what they are saying. If they ask for a specific seat or want to change seats, help them accomplish that with a minimum of fuss. If you are upfront and honest with the customers when there is a problem, they will be more willing to trust your solution. By putting the customer's needs ahead of your own, you will help create a memorable experience that the customer will want repeated in the future.

當客人進入你的餐廳時，第一個所會見到的是接待員，這個接待員在無形中會影響整個用餐經驗的氣氛。男接待員或女接待員如果表現出親切和友善，他們就會傳達給客人這是一個特殊的地方，也會讓客人感到特別的舒服。接待員要用樂觀的説話方式，並要有笑容。接待員也要用尊重和使用正式的稱謂，如先生、女士、或者某某醫生。聽客人講話，關心他們在説什麼。如果他們要求一個特定的座位或想換座位，接待員應該有最少的抱怨來幫助他們實現這個目標。當有問題時，如果你很坦白和誠實面對客戶，他們會更願意相信你的解決方案。把將客戶的需求視為比你自己的需求更重要，你會幫忙創造一個難忘的用餐經驗，客戶在未來還會再來光顧。

Part II 餐廳英語

Unit 02　Dining Services
用餐服務

Conversations

不停住對話 MP3 041

The Host is explaining that the restaurant is full when a guest who's been waiting complains.
接待人員在處理因餐廳客滿而等待過久客人的抱怨。

Host	I'm sorry but it will be a bit of wait for the next table. We are completely full at the moment and the only empty tables are reserved.	對不起，要等下一個空出來的桌子會需要一點時間。我們目前是完全客滿，唯一的空桌已經被預約了。
Guest 1	How long will the wait be?	要等多久呢？
Host	Maybe 45 minutes? We have two large groups and they are having a good time so I don't expect they'll leave any time soon.	可能要 45 分鐘？我們有兩大群人，他們還正在用餐，所以我並不認為他們會很快的就離開。
Guest 1	I've heard good things about this place and really wanted to eat here tonight. Are you sure we have to wait that long?	我聽說這裡很不錯，真的很想今晚在這裡用餐。你確定還要等那麼久嗎？
Guest 2	We've been waiting nearly an hour already!	我們已經等待了近一個小時了呢！

Host	I'm sorry we're so busy tonight. I will get you to a table as soon as one is free. Let me check.	對不起，我們今天晚上很忙。如果有桌子空出來，我就會盡快為你準備。讓我看看。
Guest 2	I hope this place is <u>worth</u> the wait.	我希望這個地方是值得等待的。
Host	I can show you to your table now and let me compensate you an appetizer as an **apology** for your long wait.	我現在可以帶你到你的桌子，讓我招待你們一道開胃菜，以表達我讓你們等這麼久的歉意。

Part II 餐廳英語

Words

單　字

＊ complain /kəmˋplen/　　*v.* 抱怨

＊ completely /kəmˋplitli/　　*adv.* 完全地；十分地

＊ empty /ˋɛmpti/　　*adj.* 空的；空虛的；空腹的

＊ worth /wɝθ/　　*adj.* 值得的

＊ apology /əˋpɑlədʒi/　　*n.* 賠禮；道歉

Grammar

文法片語

1. a bit of⋯　少量的⋯⋯

　　★小提點：名詞〈bit〉一點。這個名詞片語〈a bit of〉直接加名詞。

　　例一：Can you taste that the dessert has a bit of ginger power? 那道甜品你有嚐到一點的薑粉嗎？

　　★小提點：這個片語如果加了〈quite〉「相當」意思就完全不一樣，〈

quite a bit〉相當多。

例二：This jacket cost quite a bit of money. 我花了很多的錢買這個夾克。

2. at the moment 在這一時刻

★小提點：介係詞〈at〉在，名詞〈moment〉時刻，這個片語和〈at this moment〉有同樣的意思，可以放在句尾，也可以放在句子的最前面。

例一：We are cleaning the table at the moment. 我們目前正在清理桌子。

例二：At this moment, the kitchen is very chaotic. 在這個時後，廚房是非常混亂的。

3. I've heard good things about this place 我聽説這裡很不錯

★小提點：〈hear about〉的意思為「聽説過；有……的資訊」。

三態變化：hear、heard、heard。

例一：Have you heard about Cindy, she got married last week. 你知道 Cindy 的事嗎？她上週結婚了。

4. worth the wait 值得等待的

★小提點：形容詞〈worth〉值得的，後面可以接名詞或動名詞。

例一：This restaurant is really worth the wait. 這家餐廳很值得等待的時間。

例二：The mango snow ice is so tasty, and it worth a try. 芒果雪花冰真的太好吃了，值得一試。

★小提點：〈The best things in life are worth waiting for.〉生命中最好的東西是很值得等待的。這句是用在説明生活中最好的事情是需要耐心和時間，如找對適當的對象結婚或等待時機成熟。

Short Sentences
不尷尬短句

❶ The restaurant is very crowded tonight because there are several large groups who made reservations for special events.

餐廳今晚非常擁擠，因為有幾個大團體做了特殊活動的預約。

❷ The customers have been waiting for too long and they are getting impatient.

那些顧客已經等了太久了，他們快要沒有耐心了。

❸ If you wait a minute, we will put two tables together to accommodate your large group.

如果你等一下，我們可以為你們的大團體把兩個桌子併在一起。

❹ Would you like to wait in the bar until your table is ready?

在你的桌子準備好之前你想要在吧台等一下嗎？

❺ I will fetch you from the bar the minute your table is available if you like.

如果你要的話，當你的桌子準備好了之後，我們可以去吧台叫你。

❻ We are always this busy on weekends but it is less crowded mid-week.

我們在週末總是這樣忙碌，但在平時是沒有那麼擁擠。

❼ We will prepare you a table with wheelchair access and a high chair for the baby.

我們可以會為您準備有輪椅通道的桌子，也可以為寶寶準備一個嬰兒椅。

❽ Would you prefer to sit far away from loud guests?

你會比較希望坐遠離吵鬧的客人嗎？

❾ We are really busy right now and it will be hard to combine tables together.

我們現在忙得不可開交，所以這個時候很難併桌。

❿ It is not a problem at all to combine three tables together.

要把三個桌子併在一起不是一個問題。

Speak Up!
說出來！ 🔔 MP3 042

Dialogue 01 對話

Guest: We have been waiting nearly an hour for a table. How much longer will it be?

顧客：我們等空桌已經等了近一個小時。還需要多少時間呢？

Hostess: I'm sorry the wait is so long tonight. There was a sporting event earlier and a lot of people came in right after it ended.

接待員：對不起，今晚讓你等待這麼久。在早一點有一個體育活動，所以之後很多人就進來這裡用餐。

Dialogue 02 對話

Guest: I'm tired of standing here waiting for a table. How much longer will it be?

顧客：我站在這裡等空桌已經等了很煩了。還需要多少時間呢？

Host: I'm sorry for the wait. Would you like to go to the bar for a drink and I will let you know as soon as a table opens up.

接待員：我很抱歉讓你這樣等。你要不要去酒吧喝一杯，如果有空位，我會盡快告訴你。

Dialogue 03 對話

Guest: I have been waiting for the bill. I can't be here all night. (speaking with an unhappy tone)

顧客：我等賬單等了很久了。我不能整晚都在這裡。（非常不高興的語氣）

Host: Oh, I am so sorry for your long wait. I will check with the front desk and will be right back.

接待員：喔，很對不起讓你等這麼久。我會和櫃檯查查看，我會馬上回來。

Guest: Yes, please.

顧客：是的，請這樣做。

Job Wisdom
職業補給站

When a guest is upset, some of them will have the need to vent their frustration before they are willing to let you solve the problem. The best thing to do is to listen to them and respect their feelings. Sometimes you may need to comp something to help them feel better or have them talk to the manager. While you won't be able to resolve every issue, it may make the guest feel better about the problem if you acknowledge it and apologize for it. If you can rectify it, do so immediately. Some things aren't in your control- like crowded restaurants and long waits, but you can always explain why the wait is longer than usual and suggest an alternative. Being polite and friendly goes a long way in diffusing a situation.

當客人生氣時，在他們願意讓你解決問題之前，有些人需要先發洩自己的沮喪。你能夠做到最好的一件事就是聽聽他們的發洩，尊重他們的感受。有時你可能需要用一些東西來彌補以幫助他們能感覺比較好一點，或讓他們跟經理談。當你不能夠解決所有的問題時，如果你承認有錯，並為此道歉時，這樣可能會讓客人對這個問題感覺比較好一點。如果你可以把問題糾正過來，那你就要立即這樣做。有些事情是不能在你的控制範圍內，比如擁擠的餐廳和長時間的等待，但你總是可以解釋為什麼等待時間比平時更長，並提出了替代方案。表現出禮貌和友善都可以讓情況大大改善。

Part II　餐廳英語

Unit 02　Dining Services
用餐服務

2.2.3　Bartender 吧檯人員

不停住對話　　MP3 043

A Bartender is talking to the Front End Manager as she prepares for the day.
一個調酒師正在與外場經理做好今天營業的準備。

Front End Manager	I see you have all the **stools** down already.	我看到你把所有的凳子都放下來了。
Bartender	And I've **stocked** the bar for the day as well. I got here a bit early today.	我也把酒吧這一天所需要的量都準備好了。我今天來了比較早。
Front End Manager	That's good because it's going to be a busy day. We have three large parties and one is a bridesmaid party.	這是一件好事，因為今天會是忙碌的一天。我們有三個大的派對，其中一個是伴娘派對。
Bartender	Thanks for the <u>warning</u>! I need <u>to cut up more lemons, limes and oranges.</u> I also need to check if I have enough oranges and orange juice. The **bridesmaid** party specially requested a variety of Sangria.	謝謝你的提醒！我需要削更多的檸檬、萊姆和柳橙。我還需要檢查是否我有足夠的柳橙和柳橙汁。伴娘派對有要求我們提供不同的桑格利亞雞尾酒。

Front End Manager	Are we <u>running low</u> on anything?	我們有什麼材料儲量比較少的嗎？
Bartender	Let me see. I might need more Brandy and **chilled** dry red wine. I also need to check if we have the special ordered pink grapefruit vodka. Can you ask the kitchen to bring me more ice?	我來查查看。我可能需要更多的白蘭地和冷凍的乾紅葡萄酒。我還需要檢查看看我們是否已經有特別訂製的粉紅葡萄柚伏特加。你是否可以請廚房給我拿來更多的冰塊？
Front End Manager	Do you need someone <u>to help you with</u> cutting up fruits?	你需要有人幫你切水果嗎？
Bartender	Yes. I probably need extra hands to help cut the strawberries. The bridesmaid party specially requested us to make Strawberry-Pink Grapefruit Rose Sangria.	是的。我可能需要額外的助手來幫我切草莓。伴娘派對特別要求我們做出草莓和粉紅葡萄柚的玫瑰桑格利亞酒。

Words
單　字

* stool /stul/　*n.* 凳子
* stock /stɑk/　*v.* 存貨
* warning /ˈwɔrnɪŋ/　*n.* 警告；告誡
* bridesmaid /ˈbraɪdzˌmed/　*n.* 伴娘
* chilled /ˈtʃɪld/　*adj.* 已冷的；冷凍的

Grammar
文法片語

1. Thanks for the warning! 謝謝你的提醒！

★小提點：〈Thanks〉就是〈Thank you〉，介係詞加〈for〉後面要接名詞或動名詞。〈Thanks for the help.〉謝謝你的幫忙。〈Thanks for the email.〉謝謝你的電子郵件。〈Thank you for helping me yesterday.〉謝謝你昨天幫我。

★小提點：如果要加強語氣，可以説〈Thanks again for ...〉或〈Thank you again for... 〉。

例三：Thank you again for the feedback. 再次謝謝你回饋的意見。

2. I need to cut up more lemons, limes and oranges.
我需要切更多的檸檬、萊姆和柳橙。

★小提點：動詞片語〈cut up〉把東西切的一塊一塊的。

At this stage, your child will need someone to cut up her food for her.
在這個階段，你的孩子會需要你把她的食物切好給她吃。

3. running low 快要沒有了

★小提點：〈running〉的原形動詞是〈run〉「跑」，〈low〉「低；少」，這個片語是表達東西快要沒有了。

例一：My phone battery is running low. 我的電話電池快要沒有電了。

★小提點：〈running low〉後面若想要解釋什麼東西，則可以用介係詞〈on〉。

例二：We are running low on sugar. We need to buy more. 我們快要沒有糖了，我們需要買多一點的糖。

4. to help you with 幫助你做……

★小提點：〈help〉幫助，在一起的介係詞是〈with〉「和」，通常是有具體性的幫忙做什麼事。

例一：Can I help you with something? 我可以幫你嗎？

例二：Please allow me to help you with the bag. 請讓我幫你提這個袋子？

Short Sentences
不尷尬短句

❶ We have liquor, beer, wines, cocktails, and some special local wines are available.
我們有烈酒、啤酒、葡萄酒、雞尾酒，還有一些特別當地出產的東西。

❷ Are the bar mats and menu holders ready for the customer yet?
吧墊和菜單架準備好可以讓客人使用了嗎？

❸ After you cap the liquor bottles tonight, please take inventory so we know what needs to be ordered in the morning.
當你今天晚上蓋上酒瓶時，請寫下庫存，這樣我們可以知道哪些需要在早上進行訂貨。

❹ If the restaurant gets busy, we will be seating people in the bar area tonight so you will have to multi-task.
如果餐廳太忙的時候，我們今晚會請一些人坐到酒吧區，這樣你會不得不有很多工作同時進行。

❺ Do you want to try the new shot recipe I just learned?
你想試試我剛剛學做的調酒嗎？

❻ We charge $2.00 extra for a double.
我們雙份酒有多兩塊美元的價格。

❼ We can make standard drinks.
我們可以做一般的飲料。

❽ Every bar is different and my goal is have the customer leave feeling good.
每個吧台都不一樣，我的目標是讓顧客離開時心情很好。

❾ On the rocks means adding ice.
所謂的 "On the rocks" 就是加冰塊。

Part II 餐廳英語

Speak Up!
說出來！   MP3 044

Dialogue 01 對話

Bartender: What are today's specials? Is there anything I need to know from the kitchen?

調酒師：今天有什麼樣的特色菜？有什麼廚房的事我需要知道的呢？

Waiter: Let me check with the kitchen. I've not talked to them yet about the specials.

服務員：讓我和廚房查看一下。我還沒有跟他們講到特別菜的事。

Bartender: Thanks a lot. Please let me know as soon as possible.

調酒師：非常感謝。請趕快讓我知道。

Dialogue 02 對話

Bartender: I think I need to cut that customer off before he gets too drunk.

調酒師：我想在這個客人喝的太醉之前不要再給他酒了。

Manager: I will back you up on that decision. Don't forget to call a cab for him.

經理：我會支持你的這個決定。不要忘了要幫他叫輛計程車。

Bartender: Of course. That's best for his safety.

調酒師：當然，這對他來說是最安全的。

Dialogue 03 對話

Guest: I wish to buy this lady a drink. She likes fruity drinks.

客人：我希望請這位女士一杯，她喜歡有水果味的酒。

Bartender: Yes, of course. How about White Peach Sangria? It has lots of fruit in it.

調酒師：是的，當然。要不要試試看白桃桑格利亞？這種酒有加大量的水果。

The key to being a good bartender is to keep learning new shot and cocktail recipes and to multitask well. The more drink recipes you know, the faster you will be able to serve the customers. Multitasking is a requirement behind the bar. You will be taking orders, delivering drinks, collecting the payments and a lot of other things all at the same time. By prepping as much as possible before your shift begins, you can be better at multitasking. If the glassware, food stuff, and drinks are ready for a busy night and within easy reach, you can focus on the customer and their needs. Make sure you know your companies policies for dealing with drunk or disruptive customers and let your manager know before trouble starts that there might be some brewing. A good manager will back you when you decide to cut off a customer.

當一名優秀的調酒師的關鍵是要不斷學習新的配方,也要能同時做多種任務。你如果知道的更多調酒的配方,你就能夠為客戶提供更快的服務。多重任務是在吧檯工作的要求條件。你要接訂單,提供飲料,收集付款,和很多其他的事情都在同一時間進行。盡可能在你的工作時間之前就把工作準備好,這樣你就可以同時進行多重任務。如果玻璃器皿,食物,和飲料都在繁忙的夜晚開業之前就準備好了,也都在可以拿取的範圍內,這樣你就可以專注於客戶和他們的需求。你要確保你知道你的公司對處理酒醉或有破壞性的客戶的政策,在有人要製造麻煩之前,你就應該讓你的上司知道問題可能在醞釀中。如果你覺得某一個客人不能再喝了,一個好的經理會支持你不要再提供酒給這個客人的決定。

Conversations
不停住對話 MP3 045

The Waiter has a customer who wants a special dish but has food allergies and checks with the kitchen to see what substitutions they can make.
服務員有一個客人想要點一道特殊的菜，但他對食物過敏，所以服務員在與廚房查查看他們能做出什麼替代的材料。

Waiter	I have a customer who has several food allergies and was wondering if you could change some of the ingredients.	我有一個客人對多種食物過敏，所以他在想你是否可以改變某些材料。
Kitchen Manager	It depends on the dish.	這要看是什麼菜。
Waiter	They want the fried flounder encrusted in walnuts but they are allergic to eggs and nuts.	他們想點炸比目魚鑲核桃，但他們對雞蛋和堅果過敏。
Kitchen Manager	We can leave off the walnuts, but there are eggs in the batter we fry the fish in so I'd suggest they try a different dish.	我們可以不用核桃，但是我們炒魚的麵糊裡有雞蛋，所以我建議他們嘗試不一樣的菜。

Waiter	Like the mahi-mahi?	像鬼頭刀？
Kitchen Manager	That's a good <u>solution</u>. The mango salsa that comes with the mahi-mahi is exceptional and it's grilled with fresh pineapple and **papaya**.	這是一個很好的解決方案。鬼頭刀這道菜有附非常特別的芒果莎莎，這道魚是用新鮮的鳳梨和木瓜一起烤的。
Waiter	I will suggest that. Do you have a backup idea in case that fails?	我會向他們這樣建議。你有沒有另一個備份的意見以防這個意見沒有成功？
Chef	I have a brand new fish recipe I could try with the flounder. It's baked so there aren't any eggs in it and <u>I can top it with</u> a beautiful fresh ginger sauce.	我有一個全新魚的食譜，我可以嘗試用比目魚做。這是用烤的，所以沒有任何的雞蛋在裡面，我可以在上面加鮮薑汁。

Part II 餐廳英語

Words 單字

* substitution /ˌsʌbstɪˈtuʃən/ *n.* 替換
* flounder /ˈflaʊndɚ/ *n.* 比目魚
* walnut /ˈwɔlnʌt/ *n.* 胡桃
* solution /səˈluʃən/ *n.* 解決方法
* papaya /pəˈpaɪə/ *n.* 木瓜

Grammar
文法片語

1. It depends on the... 要看……來決定

★小提點：〈depend〉依靠，〈depend on〉依靠某件事或某人，句型是〈A depends on B〉。

例一：It will depend on the weather. 這要看天氣而定。

例二：It all depends on the traffic. 要看交通的情形來決定。

★小提點：相似詞〈rely on〉。

例三：We have to rely on the manger to get us a room tonight. 我們必須依賴經理今天晚上給我們一個房間。

2. leave off 不做了，停止

★小提點：〈leave〉「離開」，副詞〈off〉有「關掉；結束」的意思，〈leave off〉和〈stop〉有同樣的意思。

例一：Let's leave off now and have some coffee. 我們現在不要做了，喝咖啡吧。

例二：Where did we leave off yesterday? 我們昨天講到哪裡了？

3. That's a good solution. 是一個好辦法

★小提點：〈solution〉是名詞「解答；答案」，〈a good solution〉就是「好辦法；好主意」，因為〈solution〉是可數名詞，所以要加〈a〉。

例一：The manager came up with a good solution to the problem. 那個經理想了一個解決的好方法。

例二：Don't worry. We will eventually find a good solution. 不要擔心，我們最終會找出一個好方法。

4. I can top it with... 我可以在上面加……

★小提點：在這裡的〈top〉是動詞「放在上面」。

例二：Please ask the chef not to top it with any garlic. 請叫廚師不要把蒜頭加在上面。

★小提點：〈to top it all(off)〉除此之外。

例三：I lost my wallet in Taichung and to top it off I lost my cell phone too. 我在台中丟了我的皮夾，除此之外，我還丟了手機。

Short Sentences

不尷尬短句

❶ My customer can't eat onions so leave them off the salad for him, please.
我的客人不能吃洋蔥，所以請在沙拉裡不要加洋蔥。

❷ Can you make some macaroni and cheese for the child in the party?
你可以做一些通心粉和起司給參加派對的孩子吃嗎？

❸ Make sure you put the salad dressing on the side for this entire party.
請確保你把沙拉醬放在旁邊讓所有派對的人可以自己加。

❹ The customer wants his meat very rare.
客人希望他的肉要非常的生。

❺ The customer said the soup was cold when it arrived to the table.
那位客人說湯送到桌上的時候已經是冷的。

❻ When you make the fish for my table, can you cut off the heads first?
當你把魚送到我的桌上，可否先把魚頭切掉？

❼ Leave the peas off the plate and you don't have to substitute another vegetable for it.
請不要加豌豆，你也不需要替換其他蔬菜。

❽ Don't forget to make one of the hamburgers well done with cheese, but no egg with a side of fries.
不要忘了把其中一個漢堡煮全熟，也要加起司，不要有蛋，但要在旁邊放一些薯條。

❾ We are out of the fish special so don't take any more orders for it.
我們已經沒有魚的特別餐了，請不要再接受更多的訂單。

❿ We have lots of strawberry cake so see if you can convince customers to try it.
我們還有很多的草莓蛋糕，請你說服客戶來點這個吧。

Speak Up!

說出來！ MP3 046

Dialogue 01 對話

Waiter: I have a customer who can't have gluten. Is there any wheat in the batter?

服務員：我有一個客人不能吃麩質。在這個麵糊裡有沒有任何的麥？

Chef: There is, but why not suggest that they have grilled fish. It's gluten free and I will cook it on a grill that's clean and wheat free so there is no contamination.

廚師：是有麥的，建議他們吃烤魚好了。這是沒有麩質的材料，我會在燒烤架上烤魚，這個燒烤架是乾淨也沒有麥，所以沒有污染。

Waiter: That's a good idea. I will suggest that to the customer. What about the seasonings on the fish?

服務員：這是一個好主意。我會建議給顧客。魚的調味料是什麼呢？

Chef: I will just season it with salt and pepper.

廚師：我會用鹽和胡椒調味。

Dialogue 02 對話

Waiter: The customer said that there is too much salt on this dish.

服務員：客人說這道菜有太多的鹽。

Chef: Throw it out. I will make him a new one.

廚師：把它倒掉。我會重新做一份新的。

Dialogue 03 對話

Waiter: This order can't have any soy in it. The customer said soy gives her a skin rash.

服務員：這道點菜不能有任何的大豆。客人說大豆會讓她皮膚發疹。

Chef: Sure, no soy. We will fry the fish with olive oil instead of oil made with soy.

廚師：知道了，不能有大豆。我們會用橄欖油代替大豆製成的油來煎這個魚。

Your customers will occasionally not want the dish the way the chef created it for a variety of reasons and sometimes the dish can't be made with substitutions. If you are unsure about the ingredients or the substitutes, check with the kitchen before you take the order and then offer the guest a choice of options. If someone is allergic to gluten, cross contamination is a serious issue so check with your kitchen to see if what they're ordering can be made in a clean environment. Allergies to nuts can include allergies to peanut oil and other nut oils so you can prevent an emergency if you know that ahead of time. Being careful with your communication with the kitchen will make for a smooth dining experience for your guests. Even if things are chaotic behind the scenes, in the dining room, everything should be calm and restful.

因為各種原因，你的客人可能很少完全滿意廚師所做的菜，但是有時菜就是不能用替換材料的方式來做。如果你不確定的成分或代替材料，在拿訂單前要與廚房討論一下，然後為客人提供有選項的選擇。如果有人是對麩質過敏，交叉污染是一個嚴重的問題，所以你要和廚房查一下，看看是否他們所點的菜可以在一個乾淨的環境中來煮。堅果過敏可能包括對花生油和其他堅果油過敏，所以你如果在事前知道這些資訊，你就可以防止有緊急情況的發生。和廚房小心地溝通會為你的客人提供順利的用餐體驗。即使幕後是很混亂的，在用餐的地方一切都應該是平靜和寧靜的。

餐廳英語　Part II

2.2.5 Meals and Wine List 餐點與酒的搭配介紹

Conversations

不停住對話 MP3 047

Training conversation between Waiter and Wine Buyer
服務員和採購之間的訓練的對話

Buyer	This is full-bodied white Bordeaux. It **pairs** beautifully with pork and rich seafood.	這是一個口感濃郁的波爾多白酒。這和豬肉和豐富的海鮮可以配得很好。
Waiter	What doesn't it work with?	這和什麼不配呢？
Buyer	It does not work with spicy food. If you have a customer ordering a spicy dish, you might suggest one of the Blush wines from the wine list. Suggest a drier Riesling with a light seafood or chicken dish.	這和辛辣食物不配。如果你有一個客人點了辣的菜，你可能從酒單建議其中的玫瑰紅葡萄酒。你要推薦比較清爽的雷司令酒來配清淡的海鮮或雞肉。
Waiter	What about our new duck dish?	什麼和我們這道新的鴨肉菜色比較配？

Buyer	Recommend a Pinot Noir for the duck and saltier dishes. If it's **lamb**, beef, game, or pizza, the best wine is a robust red Burgundy.	鴨肉和比較鹹的菜可以配一款黑比諾酒。如果是羊肉、牛肉、野味或披薩，最好的搭配是烈的勃艮第紅酒。
Waiter	Is there anything you'd <u>avoid pairing</u> a Burgundy with?	有什麼你會建議避免和勃艮第酒一起配的呢？
Buyer	Nothing too **spicy**, **salty**, or pork, but if you have a full-flavored cheese, it will <u>wake up</u> the fruitiness of a good Burgundy.	不是太辣、過鹹、或豬肉，但如果你有一個風味濃郁的起司，這樣的搭配會喚醒勃艮第酒裡很好的果香味。
Waiter	What about a dessert wine?	那搭配甜點的酒呢？
Buyer	If you have an **intense** chocolate dessert <u>on the menu</u>, pair it with the intensity of a vintage Port.	如果你在菜單上有濃濃的巧克力甜點的話，用強烈的年份較久的波特酒來配是很適合的。

Part II 餐廳英語

Words

單　字

* pair /pɛr/　　*v.* 搭配
* lamb /læm/　　*n.* 羊肉
* spicy /ˈspaɪsi/　　*adj.* 辛辣的
* salty /ˈsɔlti/　　*adj.* 鹹的
* intense /ɪnˈtɛns/　　*adj.* 強烈的；緊張的

Grammar
文法片語

1. It does not work with... 這跟……不搭配

   ★小提點：〈work〉是動詞「工作」，〈with〉是介係詞「和……一起」，這句可以解釋為「不適合或不搭」。

   例一：It does not work with me. 對我來說不適合

   ★小提點：〈work with〉一起工作，這後面可以加某人或某件事

   例二：It is my pleasure to work with you. 我很榮幸可以和你一起工作。

   例三：Do you know how to work with the bread dough? 你知道怎麼弄麵團嗎？

2. avoid doing something 避免做某件事

   ★小提點：動詞〈avoid〉避免，後面需加動名詞或是名詞。

   例一：You need to avoid going out on a typhoon night. 你要避免在颱風夜外出。

   例二：How do I avoid the heavy traffic? 我要如何避免忙碌的交通？

   ★小提點：〈stay away from〉有「遠離或避免」的意思。

   例三：We should stay away from fried food. 我們應該不要吃炸的食物。

3. wake up 醒來

   ★小提點：除了睡醒的意思，還有將…人喚醒的意思。

   例一：A cup of coffee can wake me up. 一杯咖啡可以喚醒我。

   ★小提點：〈wake up〉也可以用在使某人要有警覺性

   例二：It is time for you to wake up and pay attention to the details. 你要有所醒悟，該要注意細節了。

4. on the menu 在菜單上

   例一：What's on the menu today? 菜單上有什麼？

   例二：Everything on the menu sounds really good. 所有菜單上的聽起來都不錯。

Short Sentences
不尷尬短句

❶ I would suggest a dry Riesling from our wine list to accompany your selection of grilled shrimp.
我建議點我們的酒單上的清爽的雷司令酒來配你選的烤蝦。

❷ Do you wish to order wine from our wine list?
你想從我們的酒單上點酒嗎？

❸ Do you want me to recommend the wine for the table based on our food selections?
你要我根據我們的菜單來幫你推薦酒嗎？

❹ We have several local beers and wines on our wine list that you might enjoy with your meal.
我們的酒單上有幾個當地的啤酒和葡萄酒，你可能會喜歡點這些來搭配你的餐點。

❺ If you can't decide what wine you want to order, I can help you.
如果你不能確定你想要點什麼酒，我可以幫你。

❻ A good wine compliments and contrasts with the food all at the same time.
一個好的葡萄酒在同一個時間可以把食物的好的味道和對比味道提出來。

❼ We have a complete wine list with a nice selection of white, red, and rose wines.
我們有一個完整的酒單，有很不錯的白酒，紅酒和玫瑰葡萄酒的選擇。

❽ I can get the wine steward for you if you like.
如果你要的話，我可以幫你請來侍酒師。

❾ Would you like to see our wine list tonight?
你今天晚上想要看看我們的酒單嗎？

Dialogue 01 對話

Customer: I'm having the duck. What wine would you recommend?

顧客：我點的是鴨肉。你會推薦什麼酒？

Waitress: I'd suggest one of our Pinot Noirs or Zinfandels. We have several good choices on our wine menu.

服務員：我建議我們的黑比諾酒或金芬黛葡萄酒。我們在我們的酒單上有幾個不錯的選擇。

Dialogue 02 對話

Customer: Is there a good dessert wine to go with the apricot cake?

顧客：有沒有好的點心酒可以配那個杏桃蛋糕？

Waiter: What about a Muscat? There are several delicious dessert wines that match the tartness of the apricots with the fruitiness of the wine.

服務員：要不要試試蜜思嘉酒？我們有幾個不錯的點心酒的水果味可以搭配杏桃的酸味。

Customer: That sounds delicious! We'll order it.

顧客：那聽起來不錯，我們就點這個。

Waiter: Okay. I will be right back with the order.

服務員：好的，我馬上把你點的帶過來。

Dialogue 03 對話

Waiter: Would you like to see the wine list?

服務員：您要看看酒單嗎？

Customer: No, thank you. I can't drink since I am driving tonight.

顧客：不，謝謝。我不能喝酒因為我今晚需要開車。

Waiter: Sure. Would you like something else?

服務員：當然。你需要別的東西嗎？

Learning what wines go with which dish can be tricky. Sometimes your restaurant will have training sessions so make sure you don't miss them. It's the fastest way to learn which wines enhance the meals the Chef makes. Take time to learn how to open a wine bottle, how to pour it, and how to check to see if the customer likes it. It will help you give better service and will encourage your guests to be more adventurous in their personal choices if they have confidence in your knowledge. There is a lot to know, but take the time to figure out the difference between the different kinds of wines and beer. Beer is currently a trendy drink, especially if it is made locally by small breweries in tiny batches. It gives an upscale feeling to the drinkers and encourages small businesses.

學習什麼菜配什麼酒不是一件簡單的事。有時候，你的餐廳會有培訓課程以便確保你不會錯過這些資訊。這是最快方法來學習什麼樣的酒可以提高廚師所做的菜的味道。你要慢慢學習如何打開一瓶酒，怎麼倒酒，以及如何查看顧客是否喜歡這個酒。這會幫助你提供更好的服務，如果客人對你的知識有信心，這樣也會鼓勵你的客人用比較開放的態度來做出個人的選擇。有很多要學習的，所以需要花時間去找出不同種類的葡萄酒和啤酒之間的差異。啤酒是目前流行的飲料，尤其如果是當地小型啤酒廠所做微量製造的。這樣會讓飲酒者有高檔的感覺，並可以鼓勵小企業的成長。

Part II 餐廳英語

Conversations
不停住對話 MP3 049

Server is introducing special appetizers and soup to two guests.
服務員在向兩位顧客介紹特別的開胃菜和湯。

Server	Would you like to start with an appetizer tonight? Our chef has created a baked lobster dip with crostini.	你今晚想一開始就吃開胃菜嗎？我們的廚師有自創了烤龍蝦沾醬和義大利小圓餅一起吃。
Guest 1	What else is in it?	裡面還有什麼呢？
Server	It has artichoke hearts, garlic, cheese and is served hot from the oven.	這裡面還有朝鮮薊心、大蒜、起司，是從烤箱烤熱後趁熱吃的。
Guest 2	It sounds wonderful but I am allergic to seafood.	這聽起來很棒，但我對海鮮過敏。
Server	A better choice for you might be the tomato basil bruschetta served on toasted Italian bread that is brushed with olive oil and garlic.	對你來說更好的選擇可能是番茄羅勒麵包片，這是烤過的義大利麵包刷上橄欖油和大蒜一起烤的。

157 ◀ Unit 2   Dining Services   用餐服務

Guest 1	Let's order that since we can **share** it and not worry about allergies. <u>Plus it's</u> vegetarian.	讓我們就點這個吧，因為我們可以一起吃也不用擔心過敏。再加上這是素食的。
Server	If you are vegetarian, we have a coconut tofu soup you might want to try. It has tofu, garlic, kaffir lime leaves and Thai ginger.	如果你是素食者，我們有你可能會想嘗試的椰子豆腐湯。這裡有豆腐、大蒜、檸檬葉和泰國生薑。
Guest 2	Let's try it!	讓我們試試吧！
Server	I can bring you a small **sample** if you like to help you decide.	如果可以幫助你決定的話，我可以為你提供小量讓你試試。
Guest 1	<u>Why don't we</u> order the bruschetta and a small cup of the coconut tofu soup?	我們為什麼不點那個義大利麵包片和小杯的椰子豆腐湯呢。
Server	Would you like an aperitif with your appetizers? We have a classic Martini that will **complement** your choices.	你想點開胃酒和你的開胃菜嗎？我們有經典的馬丁尼，這個和你所選擇的開胃菜很配。
Guest 2	None for me, but I'm sure my friend would like one.	我是不需要，但我敢肯定我的朋友會想來一杯。

Part II 餐廳英語

Words
單　字

* lobster /ˈlɑbstɚ/　*n.* 龍蝦
* dip /dɪp/　*v.* 沾（醬）
* share /ʃɛr/　*v.* 分享
* sample /ˈsæmpəl/　*n.* 樣品
* complement /ˈkɑmpləmənt/　*v.* 互補

Grammar
文法片語

1. What else　還有什麼

　★小提點：副詞〈else〉「不同；代替」，這是口語用法，後面可以加動詞或助動詞。

　　例一：What else did he say? 他還説了些什麼？

　　例二：What else do you want me to do? 你還要我做什麼事呢？

2. brushed with ...　擦上……

　★小提點：動詞〈brush〉「擦；梳；刷」，生活中常用還有〈brush your hair〉梳頭髮，〈brush your teeth〉刷牙，食物上面刷上一層醬的動作也是用〈brush〉。

　　例一：Please brush the top of the pie with a little milk. 請在派的上面刷上一層牛奶。

　★小提點：〈a brush with〉這個片語的〈brush〉是名詞「摩擦」，〈a brush with〉是與人有摩擦。

　　例二：He had a brush with the manager. 他和那個經理發生摩擦。

3. Plus it's...　還有，這是……

　★小提點：連接詞〈plus〉「還有；加上」，用來連接兩個句子。

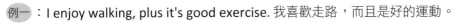

例一：I enjoy walking, plus it's good exercise. 我喜歡走路，而且是好的運動。

★小提點：這個片語〈pluses and minuses〉中文的直譯是「加和減」也就是「優缺點」。

4. Why don't we...? 為什麼不做……?

　★小提點：〈Why don't we + 原形動詞〉，這是有點建議性但是不是很直接的說法，讓對方有考慮的餘地。

　　例一：Why don't we try the Stew in a Coffin? 我們為什麼不試試棺材板呢？

　　例二：Why don't you say what you mean? 為什麼不直接講出你內心的話呢？

Short Sentences

不尷尬短句

❶ Can I bring you an appetizer while you wait?
你在等的時候我可以幫你送上一道開胃菜嗎？

❷ The Five Spices Beef Shank is a cold appetizer.
五香滷牛腱是一道冷盤。

❸ The avocado salad is very good for a light appetizer dish.
酪梨沙拉很適合當清爽的前菜。

❹ We have four choices for salad dressing: Caesar, oil and vinegar, Thousand Island and yogurt dressing.
我們有四種沙拉醬可以選擇，凱薩醬、油醋醬、千島醬、優格醬。

❺ Do you want to order salad or soup?
要不要點個沙拉或湯？

❻ Some salads go perfectly with some of our special dishes.
有一些沙拉和我們的一些特色菜可以配得很完美。

❼ I would like to recommend you our chicken salad, with baked thighs that have been sprinkled with basil or rosemary.
我想要推薦我們的雞肉沙拉給您，有烤過的雞腿肉上肉撒上羅勒和迷迭香。

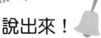

Dialogue 01 對話

Guest: Do you serve any local appetizers?

顧客：你們有提供當地口味的開胃菜嗎？

Server: Yes. You can try something called stewed mixed Taiwanese cold dish. It's a cold dish with long cooked eggs, thin slices of beef and slices of tofu and top with finely chopped green onion, soy sauce and sesame oil.

服務員：有的。你可以試試台式滷味冷盤，滷味裡的雞蛋是煮了很久的，然後有牛肉切片和豆腐，上面會加蔥花、醬油和芝麻油。

Guest: I would like to try that.

顧客：我會想試試。

Dialogue 02 對話

Guest: I can't decide between an appetizer and soup. I don't want too much food because I am not that hungry.

顧客：我無法決定是要點開胃菜或湯，我不需要吃太多，因為我不太餓。

Waiter: That can be a difficult choice, but remember the purpose of an appetizer is to stimulate your appetite and our appetizers are small tasty bites of food for that specific purpose.

服務員：這是很難的選擇，但你要知道開胃菜的目的是為了刺激你的食慾，我們的開胃菜的特別目就是好吃少量但可以刺激你的食慾。

Dialogue 03 對話

Guest: Which salad do you recommend?

顧客：你會推薦哪一道沙拉呢？

Waitress: My favorite is the Cobb Salad, but many of my customers love the Harvest Salad. The combination of apples, cranberries, and sugared pecans is distinctive.

服務員： 我最喜歡的是科布沙拉，但我有很多的顧客喜歡的豐收沙拉，這道沙拉有蘋果，蔓越莓，以及加糖山核桃的組合是很獨特的。

A classic sales technique is called up-selling and a good server will offer his/her customers the opportunity to add something extra to their meal. You begin by offering them the latest or newest appetizers on the menu or suggesting an old classic that is a favorite at your restaurant. This only works if you can explain why a dish is unique or special as well as what modifications the chef is willing to make to his dishes. If a guest says that they have special concern (like allergy or diet preference), make sure you suggest food that fits their guidelines. Work on your descriptions of the food choices so that they are appealing, mouth-watering, and difficult to refuse. Your customers may not have known how much they wanted to try something until you described it to them. That is good up-selling: classy and helpful!

有一種典型的銷售技巧叫做向上銷售，一個好的服務員知道如何找機會提供給他／她的客戶讓他們點額外的餐點，你一開始是為他們提供的菜單上最流行的或最新的開胃菜，或建議餐廳的經典受歡迎的菜。這樣的技巧能行得通的狀況是，如果你能解釋為什麼這個菜是獨特的或特殊的，以及說明些廚師是願意為他的菜變換不同的做法，如果客人說，他們有特殊的關注（如過敏或飲食的偏好），你要確保你所建議的食物有適合他們的標準。你要在食物的選擇的說明上做功課，這樣你的形容會讓你所要推薦的食物能有吸引力，令人垂涎欲滴而且難以拒絕。在你形容所要推薦的食物給他們之前，你的客戶可能不知道他們會想嘗試。這是很好的向上銷售的技巧，也是很經典和有幫助的方式！

Conversations
不停住對話   MP3 051

Waiter is recommending one main course.
服務生在介紹一道主菜。

Waiter	May I <u>recommend</u> the Pumpkin Curry soup and the Chef created a special fish dish for tonight.	我可以推薦南瓜咖哩湯還有廚師今晚做的特別的一道魚嗎？
Customer	Do you use coconut milk in the curry?	咖哩裡有加椰奶嗎？
Waiter	The **ingredients** in the pumpkin curry are fresh **organic** pumpkin that we roast and puree with fresh coconut and some red chilies for heat. It is the perfect blend of sweet and warm spiciness.	南瓜咖哩的配料是我們用烤過的新鮮有機南瓜，然後與新鮮椰子打成漿加上一些紅辣椒提味。這道菜完美融合了香料的甜度和溫度。
Customer	<u>What kind of fish</u> did the Chef use in the special?	廚師在那道特別的菜用什麼樣的魚？

Waiter	Because Taiwan is an island, all our fish is <u>locally caught and very fresh.</u> Today the Chef stir-fried catfish filets with fresh ginger and green onions in his special sauce.	因為台灣是一個小島，我們所有的魚都是本地捕獲的，非常新鮮。今天，廚師炒鯰魚魚片加上他用新鮮生薑和蔥所調的特製醬汁。
Customer	What is in the shrimp dish?	那道蝦裡有什麼呢？
Waiter	That dish is very **spicy**. If you don't like things so hot but want seafood, try the steamed clams. They were caught this morning and steamed with fresh basil and garlic <u>in a white wine sauce.</u>	那道菜是非常的辣。如果你不喜歡吃這麼辣的菜，但想吃海鮮，你可以試試蒸蛤蜊。這是今天早抓的，這道菜是用新鮮九層塔和大蒜用白酒醬所蒸的。

Part II 餐廳英語

Words 單 字

* recommend /rɛkə`mɛnd/   *v.* 推薦；介紹

* ingredient /ɪn`gridɪənt/   *n.* 成分；因素

* organic /ɔr`gænɪk/   *adj.* 有機的

* locally /`lokəli/   *adv.* 當地地

* spicy /`spaɪsi/   *adj.* 多香料的；辛辣的

Grammar

文法片語

1. May I recommend...? 可否讓我推薦……？

★小提點：:〈May I...〉是一種禮貌的問句，可以直接加動詞，雖然服務人員有心要幫忙，但是也不能講的太強求，所以用〈May I〉來謙虛地表達服務人員的誠意！

例一：May I recommend the milk bubble tea? 可以讓我建議你試試看波霸奶茶嗎？

2. What kind of ...? 哪一種……？

★小提點：:〈What kind〉可以解釋為「什麼類型」，〈of〉介係詞可以想成中文「的」，〈What kind of ＋ N〉後面直接加名詞即可。

例一：What kind of food do you like? 你喜歡什麼樣的食物呢？

例二：What kind of room do you want, single or double? 你想要什麼樣的房間，單人房或雙人房？

2. locally caught and very fresh 本地捕獲的，非常新鮮

★小提點：如要表達「當地生產」可以説〈locally grown〉。〈grown〉是p.p.，因為東西是被種植所以要用過去分詞形容，〈locally〉是副詞「當地」形容分詞。

例一：This is all locally grown produce in Tainan. 這全部是台南當地出產的農產品。

例二：This is freshly baked bread. 這是剛烤好的麵包。

3. in a white wine sauce 加在白酒醬裡

★小提點：:美國人很習慣吃東西時加醬料，不然他們會覺得沒味道，〈in the sauce〉會是很好用的片語，通常加在句子的最後面。

例一：The fish is cooked in the chef's special sauce. 那道魚是用廚師的特別醬料所煮出來的。

例二：I put a lot of garlic in the sauce. 我在醬裡放很多的蒜頭。

Short Sentences

不尷尬短句

❶ What would you like for the main course?
你主餐想要吃什麼？

❷ Sorry, it's sold out already. Would you like to change it for something else?
對不起，已經賣完了。您需不需要換別的菜？

❸ If you are allergic to seafood, you should not try oyster vermicelli.
如果你對海鮮過敏的話，你不應該吃蚵仔麵線。

❹ Can you please recommend something good and inexpensive?
你能不能推薦好吃有不太貴的菜？

❺ Do you have any questions about the menu or today's special dishes?
你對今天的菜單或特別菜有任何問題嗎？

❻ Are you in the mood for something fried or would you like a lighter dish?
你想吃油炸的東西或你想一吃比較清淡的菜？

❼ The chef's special pasta dish is exceptional if you're in the mood for pasta.
如果你想吃義大利麵的話，這個廚師的特製義大利麵是非常好吃的。

❽ I would recommend the shrimp dish for someone who is visiting Taiwan for the first time.
我會建議第一次來台灣的客人點這道蝦。

❾ You can't go wrong if you order the pork.
如果你點豬肉是不會有錯的。

❿ If I were you, I'd try the prawns. They are in seasons at the moment.
如果我是您，我會選大明蝦。現在正值盛產。

⓫ If you don't like spicy food, this dish might not be a good choice for you.
如果你不喜歡吃辣，這個菜對你來說可能不是一個好的選擇。

Part II 餐廳英語

Speak Up!
說出來！　　　　MP3 052

Dialogue 01 對話

Waiter: Would you like to try Taiwanese chicken legs simmered with basil, garlic, and chili in a wine sauce? In Taiwan, many people prefer the dark meat.

服務員：您會想要試試用慢火在九層塔，大蒜和辣椒加酒所煮的台式雞腿？在台灣，很多人比較喜歡黑色肉質的雞肉。

Guest: That's funny. In the United States, white meat is the favorite of most people.

顧客：那很有趣。在美國大多數人的最愛的是白色雞肉。

Dialogue 02 對話

Guest: Can you recommend a local dessert?

顧客：你可以推薦一道當地的甜點嗎？

Waiter: The most classic one is shaved ice with brown sugar syrup on top. Would you like to try it?

服務員：最經典的是刨冰加糖漿在上面。你想嚐嚐嗎？

Dialogue 03 對話

Guest: I am very reluctant to try the Stinky Tofu.

顧客：我很不想嘗試臭豆腐。

Waiter: Well, the smell indeed is very offensive, but many people still like to eat it. If you don't want to try it, you can try our Fried Tofu. The tofu for this dish is not fermented so is not stinky. You might like it.

服務員：喔，那個味道確實會讓人反感，但很多人還是喜歡吃。如果您不想試試，你可以試試我們的炸豆腐。這道菜的豆腐是沒有發酵所以不會臭。你可能會喜歡吃。

Job Wisdom
職業補給站

Many typical Taiwanese foods and spices are different for the foreign traveler and those that are similar use different names in English. Knowing the English names of spices and foods will help the guest decide if they are willing to try a new dish and stray from their ordinary food choices. When recommending dish, try to stress how fresh it is, or if it's organic, or local. Those are all things that Westerners value and will encourage them to be more adventurous in their eating. Cooking techniques are similar, but let them know that your kitchen uses local wines and ingredients if possible. If a dish is spicy (hot), make sure you let them know on a scale of one-to-ten how spicy it is so that they can decide if it's too spicy for them. Giving them the health information about the food they are consuming isn't typical but will help them make better choices. Most people are health conscious and tend to shy away from fried foods or foods in heavy sauces so select healthy choices to recommend to them when they are available.

對外國遊客來說，許多典型的台灣食品和調料是很不一樣的，還有一些類似的東西但英語用的是不同的名字。知道一些香料和食品的英文名稱可以幫助顧客決定他們是否願意嘗試和他們的日常食物很不一樣的新菜。當你在推薦菜的時候，可以盡量強調這個菜是多麼的新鮮，或者是它是有機的，還是本地的。這些都是西方人對吃很重視的條件並可以同時鼓勵他們可以冒險嘗試新的食物。烹飪技術是相似的，但如果可能的話，可以讓他們知道你的廚房使用的是米酒和成分。如果這道菜是辣的，你要確定提供資訊讓他們知道就以辛辣的程度 1 到 10 來說，是哪一個程度，使他們能夠決定是否對他們來說他們會太辣。一般人不會對他們所吃的東西的營養成分有多大的興趣，但如果你能提供營養成分的資料還是可以幫助於他們做出更好的選擇。大多數的人是注重健康，而且往往比較不吃油炸食或太多醬汁的食物，所以在所以推薦給他們時食物時，如果有健康的選擇的話，可以主動告訴他們。

Part II 餐廳英語

Conversations
不停住對話   MP3 053

An elder western guest is asking the waiter about the use of chopsticks.
一位年長西方客人在問服務員有關於筷子的使用。

Guest	I was told that your restaurant offers very **exceptional** Chinese food.	有人告訴我，你的餐廳提供非常出色的中國菜。
Waiter	Well, thank you.	是的，謝謝你。
Guest	This is my first time to dine at a real formal Chinese restaurant.	這是我第一次在真正的正式的中國餐廳用餐。
Waiter	Our restaurant tries to create a **traditional** dining experience for our guests.	我們的餐廳試圖為我們的客人提供傳統的用餐經驗。
Guest	I am <u>not very good at</u> using chopsticks.	我不是很擅長使用筷子。

Waiter	That's no problem. Although the custom is to use chopsticks for Chinese food, we also offer fork, spoon and knife. It is always helpful to use spoon and chopsticks together. <u>It is fun to</u> try, but you don't have to use chopsticks really. Would you like some hot tea first?	這是沒有問題的。雖然一般的習慣是吃中國菜時用筷子，我們還是有提供叉子、湯匙和刀子。湯匙和筷子在一起是很好用的。這是有趣的組合你可以試試看，但其實你不一定要使用筷子。你想先喝些熱茶嗎？
Guest	Yes please. Also, do you have the menu in English?	是的，請給我。另外，你有英語的菜單嗎？
Waiter	Yes, of course. All our menu are in Chinese, English and Japanese. We have many foreign guests. I hope you find the menu easy to read in English.	是的，當然。我們所有的菜單都有中文，英文和日文。我們有很多外國客人。我希望你會覺得英文的菜單容易看得懂。
Guest	Can you recommend some dishes? <u>I have no idea</u> what to **expect**.	你能推薦一些菜嗎？我不知道點的會是什麼樣的菜。
Waiter	You can start with some Cantonese Dim Sum and Taiwanese style **snacks**. Each dish comes as a small quantity and it can be a good sample. Our most famous one is BBQ eel.	你可以先點一些粵式點心和台灣小吃。每道菜都是少量的，所以可以是一個很好的試菜方式。我們最有名的是烤鰻魚。

Words
單 字

* chopstick /ˈtʃɑp͵stɪk/　*n.* 筷子（常複數）
* exceptional /ɪkˈsɛpʃənəl/　*adj.* 例外的；異常的
* traditional /trəˈdɪʃənəl/　*adj.* 傳統的；慣例的
* expect /ɪkˈspɛkt/　*v.* 預期；期待
* snack /snæk/　*n.* 零食

Grammar
文法片語

1. not very good at... 對……不在行
   ★小提點：片語〈be good at〉「擅長」，後面可以直接加名詞或動名詞。
   例一：Our manager is very good at management. 我們的經理對管理很在行。
   例二：The chef is very good at making seafood dishes. 廚師對煮海鮮類的菜很在行。

2. It is fun to... 做……是很有趣的
   ★小提點：形容詞〈fun〉有樂趣的，別人問你好不好玩，你可以直接回答〈It is fun.〉「好玩」，如果要繼續解釋好玩的動作，就用〈It is fun to + 原形動詞〉。
   例一：It is fun to take the train. 坐火車很好玩。
   例二：We had so much fun visiting Japan. 我們去日本玩的好開心。

3. I have no idea. 我想不出什麼辦法
   ★小提點：名詞〈idea〉「意見，想法」，最常用到的是〈It is a good idea.〉真是一個好辦法，因為〈idea〉是可數名詞，所以要記得加〈a〉。
   例一：What a good idea! 真是好意見！
   例二：It is a good idea to make a reservation. 做預約會是一個好想法。

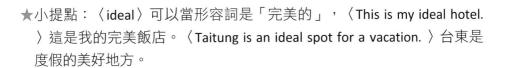

★小提點：〈ideal〉可以當形容詞是「完美的」，〈This is my ideal hotel.
〉這是我的完美飯店。〈Taitung is an ideal spot for a vacation.〉台東是
度假的美好地方。

Short Sentences
不尷尬短句

❶ Our most ordered dish is grilled squid.
我們客人最喜歡點的是烤魷魚。

❷ Do you like spicy food or non-spicy food?
你比較喜歡辣的菜還是不辣的菜？

❸ Have you tried steamed fish?
你有吃過蒸魚嗎？

❹ Would you like plain rice or fried rice?
你要點白飯還是炒飯？

❺ The radish cake tastes better with thick soy sauce.
蘿蔔糕沾點醬油膏會更好吃。

❻ Do you want to try marinated jellyfish salad?
你們要不要試試看涼拌海蜇皮？

❼ Our fried noodles are the most loved.
我們最受歡迎的是炒麵。

❽ I can divide your soup into six small bowls for your soup.
我可以把你們的湯分成六小碗。

❾ I strongly recommend the Stir Fry Cabbage.
我很強烈的推薦炒高麗菜。

❿ How about blanched kale with oyster sauce?
要不要試試蠔油芥藍？

Speak Up! 說出來！

MP3 054

Dialogue 01 對話

Guest: It is not easy to eat with chopsticks, but it is fun.

顧客：用筷子吃飯是不容易的，但是很有趣。

Waiter: The more you practice the better you will get. If you want, I can bring you the practice style chopsticks.

服務員：你練習得越多就越容易上手。如果你願意，我可以拿給你練習用的筷子。

Dialogue 02 對話

Guest: Can you recommend any interesting local dish?

顧客：你能推薦什麼有趣的地方菜嗎？

Waiter: How about deep fried squid ball?

服務員：要不要試試炸花枝丸？

Guest: Squid ball? That's definitely interesting. Sure, please give us that order.

顧客：花枝丸？那聽起來真的很有趣，好的，請就給我們這道菜。

Dialogue 03 對話

Waiter: All the orders are here. I will bring you the red vinegar.

服務員：餐點都到齊了，待會會上紅醋給您。

Guest: What's the red vinegar for?

顧客：紅醋是做什麼用的？

Waiter: If you add it in the soup, it will bring out the taste of the soup.

服務員：加一點在湯裡會使湯更鮮美好喝。

It is very possible that your foreign customers will ask you this question "What is difference between Chinese food and Taiwanese food?" You may have never thought about this before. Chinese food has a huge variety: such as Szechuan, Pekinese and Cantonese. However, when we think of Taiwanese food in Taiwan, it is more of a local taste with lots of pork and seafood. The classic Taiwanese dishes are oyster omelet, salty and crispy chicken, stew in coffin, meat sphere, and braised ground pork. Taiwanese style sausage made with pork has a very unique taste. It is sweeter than most sausage in general. Beef, however, was not used in local Taiwanese dishes in the past. Cows were very sacred to farmers in Taiwan. Although beef is now popular, there are many older people who do not eat beef and even dislike the idea of their family members eating beef. Traditionally, rice is the main diet in Taiwan. After WWII, Taiwanese food had a lot of influence from China. People from China migrated to Taiwan and brought flour-based food such as steamed bun, steamed bun with meats, green onion flat bread, and beef noodles. All these became regular food choices.

你所服務的國外顧客是非常有可能問你這個問題："中國菜和台灣菜之間的區別是什麼？"你可能從來沒有想過這個問題。中國菜包含很廣的範圍，如四川菜、北京菜和廣東菜。然而，當我們想到的台灣菜是有很多豬肉和海鮮材料的當地的口味。經典的台灣菜有蚵仔煎、鹹酥雞、棺材板、肉圓和紅燒豬肉。用豬肉製成的台灣風味的香腸具有非常獨特的味道。這種香腸比一般的香腸還要甜。然而，牛肉在以前不太算是台灣本地菜。對台灣農民來說牛是非常神聖的。雖然牛肉現在是流行的，還有很多年長者是不吃牛肉，甚至不喜歡自己的家人吃牛肉。傳統上，在台灣稻米是主要的飲食。在二戰結束後，台灣食品受到很多來自中國的影響。中國人移民到台灣帶來麵粉類的食物，如饅頭、包子、蔥油餅和牛肉麵。所有這些都已經成為一般食物的選擇。

2.2.9　Introducing Desserts and Drinks After the Meal 介紹甜點和餐後飲料

Conversations
不停住對話 　MP3 055

Waiter is trying to convince guests to try a dessert dish.
服務員正在說服顧客試試一道甜點。

Waiter	Let me take these dishes away. Was everything delicious?	讓我把這些盤子先拿走。一切都好吃嗎？
Guest 2	It was. I think we'd like coffee now.	是的。我想我們現在想要咖啡。
Waiter	Would you like to try a slice of our **homemade** chocolate cake with your coffee? It has a layer of fresh raspberry filling and the frosting is our Chef's grandmother's **fudge** topping. It is served warm with a side of homemade ice cream.	你想試試我們的自製的巧克力蛋糕配上你的咖啡嗎？這個蛋糕裡有一層新鮮的覆盆子的夾心，糖霜醬則是我們廚師的祖母的巧克力糖霜醬。這個甜點要趁熱吃，在吃的時候是會在甜點旁邊加一些自製冰淇淋。
Guest 1	I'm not sure. I've already eaten so much.	我不確定。我已經吃了好多。

Guest 2	But it sounds very good.	但是聽起來很不錯。
Waiter	You can share one if you like. I'll bring two **spoons** and it will make you both very happy that you decided to try it.	如果你要的話，你們可以一起吃一個。我會給你們兩個湯匙，這道甜點會讓你們覺得很高興你們有決定試一試。
Guest 1	But I skipped the gym today.	但是我今天沒有去健身房。
Waiter	It is the perfect night <u>for a walk</u> along the Love River and you can **continue** your conversation in the moon light. It's the perfect excuse.	這是一個完美的夜晚可以沿愛河岸邊散步，你可以在月光下繼續你們的談話。這個甜點會是很完美的藉口。
Guest 1	<u>You convinced me</u>. One chocolate cake and two spoons.	你說服我了。那就來一個巧克力蛋糕和兩個湯匙。
Guest 2	And coffee- black with **cream** on the side.	還有咖啡，黑咖啡，請把奶精放在旁邊。

Part II　餐廳英語

Words
單　字

* homemade /ˈhomˈmed/　　*adj.* 自製的
* fudge /fʌdʒ/　　*n.* 糖醬
* spoon /spun/　　*n.* 湯匙
* continue /kənˈtɪnju/　　*v.* 繼續
* cream /krim/　　*n.* 奶精

Grammar
文法片語

1. a slice of 一片

★小提點：名詞〈slice〉一片，〈a slice of〉後面可以加水果或麵包類，〈a slice of bread〉一片麵包，〈a slice of apple〉一片蘋果，〈a slice of cake〉一小塊蛋糕。

例一：Would you like a slice of bread with butter? 你想要有一片麵包加奶油嗎？

例二：May I have a slice of cheesecake? 我可以要一片的起司蛋糕嗎？

★小提點：〈slice〉也可以當動詞，就是「切」的動作，和動詞〈cut〉「切」很類似但有點不一樣，〈slice〉是指可以「切片」的動作，〈cut〉的「切」的範圍比較廣，沒有一定的形狀。

例三：Can you slice the bread? 你可以切麵包嗎？

2. It is served with... 和……一起配

★小提點：過去分詞〈served〉「被端上」，原形動詞是〈serve〉。

例一：The chicken is served with salad. 雞肉上菜的時候是和沙拉配在一起的。

例二：Chinese food is often served with rice. 中餐通常是和飯配在一起吃的。

3. for a walk 散步

★小提點：這個片語之前的動詞可以用〈go for a walk〉或〈take a walk〉中文是「去散步」。

例一：Let's take a walk. 我們去散步吧！

例二：We went for a walk by the beach yesterday. 我們昨天去海邊散步。

4. You convinced me. 你說服了我

★小提點：動詞〈convince〉說服，後面直接加受詞。〈convinced her〉說服她，〈convinced them〉說服他們，〈convinced us〉說服我們。

例一：Are you convinced? 你有被說服了嗎？

例二：Please don't try to convince me. 請不要試著說服我。

Short Sentences
不尷尬短句

❶ We have both cold and hot desserts.
我們有冷的與熱的甜點。

❷ Our dessert comes with the meal.
我們的甜點是隨餐贈送的。

❸ The cheesecake goes really good with coffee.
乳酪蛋糕和咖啡很配。

❹ You may choose a dessert that is low calorie.
你可以選擇低熱量的甜點。

❺ Do you want to add honey on your strawberry waffle?
你的草莓鬆餅需要加點蜂蜜嗎？

❻ Just a reminder that this dessert has cinnamon in it.
跟你說一下，這個甜點有加肉桂粉。

❼ We have several different kinds of ice cream.
我們有幾種口味的冰淇淋。

❽ Would you like to try Bubble Tea?
你要不要試試波霸奶茶？

❾ The star fruit juice is made with fermented start fruit.
楊桃汁是用發酵過的楊桃所做的。

❿ Have you ever had mochi ice cream?
你有吃過麻糬冰淇淋嗎？

Speak Up!
說出來！ MP3 056

Dialogue 01 對話

Customer: Can you recommend a local dessert?

顧客：你能推薦一個當地的甜點嗎？

Waiter: In the winter, we like Sweet Bean Soup because it's beneficial to your circulatory system and helps your kidneys and in the summer it's perfect over shaved ice. Would you like to taste it?

服務員：在冬季，我們喜歡紅豆湯，因為這個有益於你的血液循環系統及腎臟，在夏天紅豆和刨冰是完美的組合。你想嚐嚐嗎？

Dialogue 02 對話

Guest: I heard you are famous for some kind of shaved ice dessert. Can you tell me what's in it?

顧客：我聽說你們某些種類的刨冰甜品很有名。你能告訴我裡面有什麼嗎？

Waitress: Certainly. Our special is called 8 Treasures Ice and it has 8 special ingredients like taro, azuki beans, peanuts, mung beans, and fruit over shaved ice and then condensed milk is pour over it. It's a favorite in the summer, but you can get any kind of fruit on yours.

女服務員：當然可以。我們有名的是八寶冰，這裡面有 8 個特殊食材，如芋頭、紅豆、花生、綠豆和水果，這些材料是放在刨冰上面，然後再把煉乳淋在上面。這是夏天大家最愛吃的，但你可以選任何一種水果放在上面。

People love dessert. They love dessert more than salad and steak, and yet, often they feel guilty ordering it and will deny themselves the pleasure. Ordering dessert is an emotional decision- not a logical one- and you have to appeal to their senses and convince them that the pleasure of the dessert will outweigh the guilt of eating it. You can suggest the table order a couple of desserts to share with their after meal coffee or drinks so that they can vote on their favorite, or you can remind them that it's a beautiful night for a walk after their meal and that they can walk off the dessert. By describing the dessert with words that tempt and allure the guests into continuing their dining experience with you, they will leave feeling satisfied and content.

一般人都是很喜歡甜點的。他們喜歡甜食多於沙拉和牛排，然而，他們對點甜點往往感到內疚，所以會拒絕自己有這樣的享樂。點甜點是一種情緒上的決定而不是一個邏輯的決定，並且你要讓甜點看起來很好吃，也要說服他們吃甜點的樂趣會超過對吃甜點的內疚。你可以建議客人點一些甜點來配他們餐後喝的咖啡或飲料，這樣可以幫助他們決定自己喜歡的甜點，或者你可以提醒他們，這是一個美麗的夜晚，他們可以在用餐後散步，這樣可以幫助他們消耗吃甜點的熱量。透過用字來描述甜點來誘惑客人以讓客人繼續因為你而有好的用餐體驗，他們在用完餐離開後會感到滿意和滿足。

2.3.1 Problems While Serving 服務時的問題 (1)

Conversations
不停住對話 MP3 057

A waiter notices that a guest isn't eating her meal.
服務員注意到客人沒有在吃她點的菜。

Waiter	How's your fish? Is it cooked to your liking?	你的魚好吃嗎？是否合你的口味？
Guest 1	It smells off to me. I'm not sure it's fresh.	對我來說聞起來有味道。我不確定是否是新鮮的。
Waiter	I'm sorry, Ma'am. Let me take it to the kitchen and **replace** it with another one. I'll take it off your bill immediately.	對不起，夫人。讓我把這道菜拿到廚房，並替換另一道菜。我馬上把這道菜從你的帳單上劃掉。
Guest 1	I'm not sure I want another one. It's kind of ruined the idea of fish for me tonight.	我不知道我是否想要再點一道魚。我今晚想吃魚的想法已經毀滅了。
Waiter	I would be glad to substitute another dish for it. Would you like to try something different? Perhaps the pork special or a pasta?	我會很樂意替換另一道菜。你想嘗試不同的東西？或許是豬肉特餐或義大利麵？

| Guest 1 | May I see a menu? I can't remember what was on it. | 我可以看菜單嗎？我不記得菜單上有什麼。 |

| Waiter | Certainly. Let me take this away and get you the menu. | 當然可以。讓我把這個拿開，然後給你菜單。 |

| Guest 2 | Ewww! There's a hair in my pasta! | 唉呦！有一根頭髮在我的義大利麵裡！ |

| Waiter | Oh no! I'll will tell the kitchen **instantly** when I return both dishes. Would you like me to reorder the dish or would you like the menu? | 哦，糟了！當我把這道菜送回時，我會馬上告訴廚房。你要我再重新幫你點一樣的嗎？還是你想看一下菜單？ |

| Guest 2 | I'm not hungry anymore! This place is terrible. Her fish wasn't fresh and there was a hair in my pasta. That's just **gross**! | 我已經不餓了！這個地方是很糟糕。她的魚不新鮮，我的麵裡有頭髮。真是噁心！ |

| Waiter | I'm sorry, Ma'am. I am sure the Chef will be upset as well. He prides himself on the quality of food that he sends out. Let me get you a menu and you can try something different, **on the house**. | 對不起，小姐。我相信廚師也會覺得很生氣。他自己對食物的品質是很自豪。讓我給你菜單，你可以試試不同的菜，這次我們買單。 |

Part II 餐廳英語

Words

單　字

* notice /ˈnotɪs/　*v.* 注意

* replace /rɪˈples/　*v.* 替換

＊ instantly /ˈɪnstəntli/　*adv.* 立即地

＊ gross /gros/　*adj.* 噁心的

＊ on the house　*ph.* 免費

Grammar
文法片語

1. A waiter notices that a guest isn't eating her meal.　服務員注意到客人沒有在吃她點的菜。

　★小提點：〈notice〉察覺，動詞。後面可接一個名詞子句。

　　例一：I noticed that the door was open.　我發現這個門開了。

　　例二：She didn't notice that something was missing.　她沒有發覺有東西不見了。

2. take it off　把……拿掉

　★小提點：在代名詞 it 的地方可以用其他名詞代替。

　　例一：〈Please take your jacket off.〉和〈Please take off your jacket.〉「請把你的夾克脫掉」，這兩句意思完全一樣。是可以分離的動詞片語。

　★小提點：〈take off〉也可以用在飛機起飛時的動作。

　　例二：The plane will take off soon.　飛機即將起飛。

3. to substitute it for...　用……來代替

　★小提點：動詞〈substitute〉替換。用介係詞〈for〉。to substitute A for B (or A be substituted for B) 意為「用 A 來替換 B」，亦即「B 被 A 所取代」。

　　例一：If you don't like noodles, we can substitute rice for it.　如果你不喜歡麵，我們可以換成飯。

　　例二：Can you substitute olive oil for butter? 你可以把奶油換成橄欖油嗎？

　★小提點：〈substitute〉也可以當名詞，最常見的是〈a substitute teacher〉代課老師，〈a substitute ingredient〉代替的材料。

不尷尬短句

❶ Is there something wrong with the rice?
飯是不是有什麼不對嗎？

❷ I can send back food if you just don't like the order.
如果你不喜歡你所點的，我可以把食物送回廚房。

❸ Would you like a different order?
你想要點不一樣的嗎？

❹ Someone just complained about a dish.
有人剛剛抱怨了一道菜。

❺ We are sorry that you are not pleased with this dish.
我們感到很抱歉，你對這道菜不是很喜歡。

❻ We will resolve the problem right away.
我們馬上解決這個問題。

❼ I am so sorry that we gave you the wrong order.
我很抱歉，我們給你錯誤的菜。

❽ I can send back the dish and ask the chef to make a different one.
我可以把菜送回廚房，並要求廚師做一道不同的菜。

❾ The chef apologized for the mistake and he wants to assure you that it was just a one time only mistake.
那個廚師對所造成的錯誤道歉，他想向你保證，這只是僅僅一次的失誤。

❿ Would you like the chef to rework the dish?
你希望廚師重新做這道菜嗎？

Speak Up!

說出來！

MP3 058

Dialogue 01 對話

Guest: Waiter! I ordered a salad with beef and this salad has shrimp on it!

顧客：服務員！我點的是牛肉沙拉但是這個沙拉裡有蝦！

Waiter: I'm sorry sir! I must have mixed up the salads. Let me get you a new one.

服務員：對不起，先生！我一定是把沙拉混淆了。讓我再給你一個新的。

Guest: Please do. I'm allergic to shrimp.

顧客：請務必這樣做。我對蝦是過敏的。

Dialogue 02 對話

Guest: We have been waiting for forty minutes and our meals still aren't here. We are getting very hungry.

顧客：我們已經等了四十分鐘，我們的菜還沒有來。我們越來越餓了。

Waitress: I'm sorry, Ma'am. I'll go check with the kitchen and see what happened to them. Would you like another appetizer while you wait- free of charge?

服務員：對不起，女士。我會去廚房看看是有什麼問題。在你等待時你還想再來一道開胃菜嗎？這是免費的。

Dialogue 03 對話

Guest: I'm the only one not served at my table. It's been a long wait.

顧客：我的桌子是唯一還沒有上菜的。真是一個漫長的等待。

Waiter: I'm sorry sir, but I checked on your meal in the kitchen and they lost your order. They are cooking it right now so it won't be much longer.

服務員：先生，真的很對不起，我已經和廚房查了你的菜，他們把點菜單弄丟了。他們現在正在煮，所以不會太久的。

Job Wisdom
職業補給站

Mistakes happen in any job, but they are upsetting when it happens to your guests that you are serving. You have gone above and beyond with your service and yet something distasteful occurred. Stay calm and remember it's not personal. Deal with the problem immediately and let the guest know your results. If the dish needs to be returned to the kitchen, offer to order them a new one immediately and put a rush on it in the kitchen so they don't have to sit there while others in their party eat. If a strange item is found in the dish or the food isn't fresh, offer to take it off the bill immediately and suggest that you have the dish remade for free. You can also offer to fetch them something different for free as well. Listen to the problem carefully and make sure your body language is respectful at all time. Even if you're exasperated, be careful not to roll your eyes or cross your arms. Instead, nod and smile as you solve their problem. Be sincere and try to accommodate any reasonable request.

　　雖然在任何工作裡，錯誤是會發生的，但是對你服務的客人來說，他們還是會感到生氣。你已經做到超越了你的服務能力，但是顧客抱怨難吃的事還是會發生。你要保持冷靜，也要記住這不是針對個人而來的。你要馬上處理這個問題，讓客人知道你所處理的結果。如果點的菜需要被送回廚房，馬上提供給客人他們可以點的另一道新菜，讓廚房的人知道這道菜是要馬上做的，這樣客人不必坐在桌子上看著他們同夥的人在吃東西。如果一道菜裡被發現有奇怪的東西或食物不新鮮，要馬上在賬單上取消這道菜的收費。你也可以建議他們可以有另一道免費的菜。你對他們的問題要聽清楚，也要隨時隨地確定你的肢體語言表現出來是尊重的。即使你感到被激怒，你也要小心不要翻白眼或交叉雙臂。相反的，在解決他們的問題的同時你要點頭和微笑。你要表現出你是真誠的，並盡量滿足所有合理的要求。

Part II 餐廳英語

2.3.2 Problems While Serving 服務時的問題 (2)

Conversations

不停住對話 MP3 059

A bus boy dropped a loaded tray of dirty dishes and leftover food sprayed all over a guest's pants leg.
推餐員把放置吃剩食物的托盤不小心打翻到客人的褲管上。

Guest 1	He got stuff on my pants!	他把髒的東西濺在我的褲子上！
Waiter	(Offering a **damp** clean towel) Oh no! I'm so sorry! Let me help you with that! Here's a clean towel to use on your pants.	（同時提供一個乾淨的濕毛巾）哦，不好了！我很抱歉！讓我來幫你！這裡有一個乾淨的毛巾可以用在你的褲子上。
Guest 1	Let me try to get it off with your towel. What are you going to do about this? I just had these pants cleaned.	讓我用你的毛巾把它清掉。你打算怎麼辦呢？我這條褲子才剛剛清洗。
Waiter	We will pay for your cleaning bill, of course. It's our fault they got **dirty**.	我們當然 可以支付你的清潔費用。弄髒你的褲子是我們的錯。

Guest 2	It was an accident. <u>Don't worry about it.</u>	這是一個意外。不用擔心啦。
Guest 1	What do you mean don't worry about it? I have an important meeting after this and I can't go like this.	你說不擔心是什麼意思？我在用餐後有一個重要會議，我不能穿這樣去。
Waiter	There is a men's store next door if you want to step over and see if they have anything you can wear to the meeting. I will show you where it is, if you like.	隔壁有一個男裝店，如果你想進去看看他們是否有什麼你可以穿到會議的。如果你要的話，我會告訴你這個店在哪裡。
Guest 1	I'm never eating here again.	我以後都不會來這裡吃飯了。
Waiter	I'm sorry that you feel that way, sir. May I give you a **voucher** for a free meal some other time to make up for your **inconvenience**?	先生，對不起讓你有這樣的感覺。我可以給你一個優惠券，下次有空再來時你可以有免費的一餐，這樣希望可以彌補你的不便？

Part II 餐廳英語

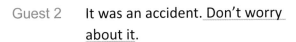

Words
單 字

* leftover /ˈlɛftˌovɚ/　*n.* 剩菜
* damp /dæmp/　*adj.* 潮濕的
* dirty /ˈdɚti/　*adj.* 骯髒的
* voucher /ˈvɑʊtʃɚ/　*n.* 餐券
* inconvenience /ˌɪnkənˈvinjəns/　*n.* 不方便

Grammar
文法片語

1. all over 到處都是

★小提點：形容詞〈all〉全部，副詞〈over〉越過，〈all over〉「到處都是」是非正式口語用法。

例一：It is raining all over Tainan. 台南到處都在下雨。

★小提點：〈all over〉再一次，〈Do it all over!〉和〈Do it again!〉完全一樣，都是從新做一次。

例二：You need to do it all over because it was not good enough. 因為做的不好所以你需要重新再做一次。

★小提點：〈all over〉也可以解釋為「結束了」，和〈finish〉、〈end〉的意思一樣。

例三：It is all over between us. 我們之間已經完了。

2. pay for 為……付款

★小提點：動詞〈pay〉付款，〈pay for〉後面直接接名詞。

例一：How much did you pay for the drink? 這個飲料你付了多少錢？

例二：Who will pay for the train tickets? 誰會付火車票？

★小提點：〈pay for〉也可以用來做「賠償」或「付出代價」。

例三：Let us pay for the missing towels. 讓我們來賠償遺失的毛巾。

3. Don't worry about it. 不要擔心

★小提點：這裡的代名詞〈it〉指的是說話者在講的事情，因為說話者和聽話者知道對話的內容所指的事情，所以直接用〈it〉，〈it〉也可以用其他字代換，如〈Don't worry about what happened.〉不用擔心發生了什麼事。〈Don't worry about the money.〉不用擔心錢的事。

例一：Please don't worry too much about us. 請不用替我們太擔心。

例二：Bobo worried that he didn't do it right. Bobo 擔心他沒有把事情做對。

不尷尬短句

❶ The coupon can be used once only.
此優惠券只能使用一次。

❷ The manager said he can give you a small discount.
這個經理說他可以給你一個小小的折扣。

❸ There is a 10 % discount for cash payment.
如果是現金支付則有 10%的折扣。

❹ You can find some coupons from our website.
你可以在我們的網站上找到一些優惠券。

❺ We do not take American Express.
我們不接受美國運通卡。

❻ You can pay by cash or credit card.
你可以用現金或信用卡支付。

❼ Do you need your receipt?
你需要你的收據嗎？

❽ The coupon is still valid.
這個優惠券仍然有效。

❾ Do you need the uniform invoice for your company?
你需要有統一發票嗎？

❿ We always have 20% discount every Monday.
我們每星期一都有 20%的折扣。

說出來！ MP3 060

Dialogue 01 對話

Guest: I'd like to use this coupon today?
顧客：我想今天使用這個優惠券？

Server: I'm sorry, but that coupon is no longer valid. It expired six months ago.
服務員：對不起，但這個優惠券已經無效。已經過期半年了。

Guest: But I planned on using it today. What am I to do?
顧客：但是我計劃今天要用這個優惠券。我該怎麼做？

Server: Why don't I give you my discount today?
服務員：要不然就讓我給你點折扣吧！

Dialogue 02 對話

Waiter: I'm sorry, Miss, but this credit card has been declined. Do you have another one?
服務員：對不起，小姐，但這張信用卡已經被拒絕。你有另一張卡嗎？

Guest: Can you run it again? I'm sure it works.
顧客：你能再試一次嗎？我很確定這是可以用的卡。

Waiter: We tried it twice. You may need to contact your bank. Do you want to try another card?
服務員：我們已經試了兩次。你可能需要與銀行聯繫。你要試試另一張卡嗎？

Dialogue 03 對話

Guest: We asked for separate checks and yet everything is on one bill.
顧客：我們要求分開付賬，但全部都寫在一個賬單。

Waitress: I'm sorry, Ma'am. Let me re-run the bill and put it on separate bills.
服務員：對不起，女士。讓我重新印各自的賬單。

You have done everything right. You went above and beyond with your service and did it with a pleasant attitude and smile. You've done everything right- except you were walking too fast and tripped, spilling a pitcher of water all over a customer and ruining her outfit! Things happen. It was an accident, but you have an upset guest. Apologize immediately and offer to pay for the cleaning of her outfit. Assure her that her meal will be free and that you didn't mean to drench her in water. She probably won't be happy about the experience, no matter how much you apologize. If you need help, ask your front end manager to come talk to her to smooth things over. Some people will accept your apology and act like it's not a big deal. Make sure you still treat them like VIP guests and offer them a voucher for a free meal next time they come in.

你所做的一切都是對的。你已經超越了你的服務能力，也用愉快的姿態和笑容做到這樣的服務。你所做的一切都是對的，但是你走得太快而絆倒了，也把溢出的水濺在客人的身上並破壞了她的衣服！不幸的事情是會發生的。 這是一個意外，但你有一個在生氣的客人，你要立即道歉並提供支付她的衣服的清洗費用。也要向她保證，她的用餐是免費的，你不是故意用水淋到她的。無論你多麼深的表歉意 ，她對這樣的經驗大概也不會感到太開心。如果有需要幫助，請向你的外場經理來跟她說話打圓場。有些人會接受你的道歉，也會覺得這不是什麼大不了的事。但是你要確保你仍然像對待他們像貴賓一樣，為他們提供一個優惠券和下次他們來時的免費用餐券。

Part II 餐廳英語

Part III

Hotel English
旅館英語

Unit 01 Front Desk 櫃台

3.1.1 Reservation Department 訂房服務

不停住對話 MP3 061

Reservationist is talking on the phone with a possible guest about booking a room.
接待員在電話中和有可能預訂一個房間的客人交談。

Receptionist	Thank you for calling The West Inn Luxury Hotel. <u>This is</u> Anna speaking. How may I help you?	謝謝您打電話到西方酒店豪華飯店。我是安娜。我可以如何幫助你呢？
Guest	I was wondering if you had any rooms <u>available for</u> next weekend. We'd like to arrive late Friday night and stay through Sunday.	我是想知道，你下個週末是否有空房。我們預計週五晚上到，然後一直留到週日。
Receptionist	One moment please and I'll check. While I'm checking, are there any questions you have about our hotel or the area around the hotel?	請稍等，我查一下。當我在查資料時，你對我們的飯店或飯店附近的區域有任何問題嗎？
Guest	<u>What kind of</u> breakfast do you offer and is it free?	你有提供什麼樣的早餐，是免費的嗎？

Receptionist	We serve a free **continental** breakfast from 6 am to 9 am, but you can have a sit down breakfast in one of our restaurants any time. We have a few vacancies still available, but not many. Would you like a suite or a room with two double beds?	我們是有免費的歐陸式早餐，時間是早上 6 時至 9 時，但你任何時候都可以到我們餐廳吃正式早餐。我們是有一些空缺，但不是很多。你想要套房或一間有兩張雙人床的房間？
Guest	A room with two double beds. How much will that cost?	一個有兩張雙人床的房間。這需要多少的費用？
Receptionist	The **usual** rate for our standard double room is $150 a night, but I can **extend** a special rate for the **entire** weekend for $350 plus tax. It would usually cost you $450 for the weekend so you'd save $100.	我們的標準大床房間的一般價格為一晚 $150 美元，但我可以延長特價時間給你，整個週末就 $350 美元加稅，這通常費用會是 $450 美元，所以你可以省 $100 美元。
Guest	We'll take the **suite** then since it's not that much more.	我們就訂套房，因為價格沒有多很多。

Part Ⅲ　旅館英語

Words

單　字

* continental /ˌkɑntəˈnɛntəl/　*adj.* 大陸的；洲的
* usual /ˈjuʒuəl/　*adj.* 平常的
* extend /ɪkˈstɛnd/　*v.* 延長
* entire /ɪnˈtaɪɚ/　*adj.* 全部的
* suite /swit/　*n.* 套房

Grammar
文法片語

1. This is … 這是……
   ★小提點：〈This is...〉是基礎英文的句子，看似簡單但是用法很廣泛。介紹朋友給另一個人時可以用〈This is Mary.〉這是瑪麗，打電話給別人時要表達自己是誰時可以說〈This is Amy.〉我是艾米，在端給客人所點的菜時可以說〈This is your order.〉這是你所點的菜。在拿給客人菜單時可以說〈This is the menu.〉這是菜單，導遊在介紹景點給遊客時可以說〈This is the Confucius Temple〉這是孔子廟。

2. available for 有空位
   ★小提點：形容詞〈available〉可用的，介係詞〈for〉用於，〈available for〉後面加名詞或時間。
   例一：We have one room available for tomorrow. 我們明天有一個空房。
   ★小提點：形容詞〈available〉也可以單獨使用後面不用加詞，意思是「有空」，同樣的意思也可以用〈free〉「有空」。要注意〈available〉還有「單身」的意思，要小心用。
   例二：〈I am available now.〉我現在有空（我單身）。〈I am free now.〉我現在有空。〈I am not free now.〉我現在沒有空。

3. It would usually cost you $450. 這會花你 450 元
   ★小提點：〈cost〉花費，三態變化 cost 同型。
   例一：How much would it cost us to replace? 我們要花多少錢去代換？
   ★小提點：〈cost〉也可以當作名詞用，常出現的句型〈The cost of…〉「某東西的花費…」。
   例二：The cost of rebuilding the theater will be 5 million. 重建劇院的花費應該會要 500 萬。

Short Sentences
不尷尬短句

❶ There will be two adults and one infant so we will need a crib in the room.
我們有兩個大人和一個嬰兒，所以我們需要在房間裡有一個嬰兒床。

❷ There is no charge for the crib and I will make sure it is in your room before you check in.
嬰兒床是不收費的，我會在你入住之前確定放嬰兒床在你的房間。

❸ Is it necessary to book the room ahead of time?
是否一定要提前預訂房間呢？

❹ It's currently peak tourist season so you need to reserve your room ahead of time to guarantee that one will be available for you.
這是目前旅遊旺季，所以你需要提前預訂你的房間，才能確保你會訂到房間。

❺ I need to book my cheerleading group so do you do group bookings?
我需要替我的啦啦隊預訂房間，你們有做團體預訂嗎？

❻ Is there a discount if we reserve a block of rooms?
如果我們預訂整區的房間是否有折扣呢？

❼ How long will you be staying?
你會住多久呢？

❽ How many adults are in your party?
你們這團有多少成年人？

❾ There is a $10 charge for extra guests in your room and you need to put their names on the registration when you check in.
如果你的房間有額外的客人，這樣會有 10 美元的費用，你辦理入住手續時，你需要把他們的名字寫在登記資料裡。

Speak Up!
說出來！ MP3 062

Dialogue 01 對話

Caller: I would like a room for four people, two adults and two children the week of September 10th.

來電者：我想要一個有四個人的房間，我們在 9 月 10 日那週有兩個大人和兩個小孩子。

Reservationist: I'm sorry. We are completely booked that week. There is a tennis tournament that week and many guests have already reserved rooms.

接待員：對不起。我們那週全部訂滿了。那週有一個網球比賽，有很多客人已經預訂房間了。

Dialogue 02 對話

Receptionist: How many people will be staying in the room?

接待員：有多少人會住在房間裡？

Caller: Two adults. Is there a fridge in the room? I need to keep my medicine cold.

來電者：有兩個成年人。在房間裡有沒有冰箱？我的藥需要冷藏。

Receptionist: I can reserve you our standard king size room with a refrigerator but a credit card is required for all reservations.

接待員：我可以幫你預約一個有標準大床的房間，這個房間配有冰箱，但所有的預約都需要信用卡。

If you get a kick out of working with people and have dazzling phone and communication skills, you will excel while working reservations at a hotel. Another requirement is to have strong IT skills- meaning you are comfortable working with computers and learn software programs quickly. You have to be confident in your negotiating and sales skills because you will be expected to promote more expensive rooms when you spot an opening. Also, you will have to know all the rate strategies and to be thorough in your recording of the bookings. If you get sloppy or aren't careful with the information you gather, not only will the guests be upset, but it will result in lost bookings in the future. Keeping the hotel rooms full is a critical aspect of the receptionist job. It's not about answering the phone, but about helping the hotel achieve a profit during the year. A good receptionist is priceless! So be friendly, yet professional in all you do.

　　如果你很喜歡和別人一起工作，並擁有高超的電話和溝通的技巧，你在飯店負責預約工作將會脫穎而出。另一個要求是要有電腦的技能，這意味著你對使用電腦要感到很自然，也要很快速的學習電腦軟體。你必須對你的談判和銷售技巧要有自信，如果你有看到有不同價位的空房，你會被寄望要推薦客人來訂比較昂貴的房間。此外，你必須知道所有的價格策略，並要做訂房記錄。如果你對你所拿到的資料很草率或不小心，不僅讓客人會很生氣，這樣也會導致失去的預訂機會。保持飯店客滿的訂房是接待員的一個重要工作。這不是接電話的問題，而是幫助這個飯店實現盈利的狀況。一個好的接待員是無價的！所以，你要表現出你可做到最友善也最專業的一面。

Unit 01 **Front Desk**
櫃台

3.1.2 Introducing Different Types of Rooms 房型介紹

不停住對話 MP3 063

The Front Desk is helping a guest decide on rooms for her and her parents.
櫃檯在幫助客人決定為她和她的父母訂什麼樣的客房。

Guest	I need two rooms for the week of June 1st. <u>Do you have any</u> vacancies then?	我需要兩個房間,時間是 6 月 1 日那個星期。你有任何的空房嗎?
Front Desk	We have a **variety** of rooms available for that week. Do you have preference for King Size beds or Suites?	我們那個星期是有各種客房的空缺。你想要訂的是超大床或套房?
Guest	My parents would like two **Queen Size beds** in their room, but I would like adjoining rooms, if possible. I only need a twin bed for me.	我的父母會想要他們的房間內有兩個大號床,如果可能的話,我想住在隔壁的房間。我自己只需要一張單人床。

Front Desk	I have two adjoining rooms available. One of them has two Kings and the other room has two **double** beds. Another choice is our **luxury** suite. It has two bedrooms and a living area.	我有兩個相鄰的房間。其中一人有兩個加大雙人床，另一個房間有兩張雙人床。另一種選擇是我們的豪華套房。這裡有兩間臥室和一個客廳。
Guest	What kind of beds are in the Suite?	套房裡有什麼樣的床？
Front Desk	There are two King beds in the first bedroom, and a double in the smaller bedroom. It also has a pull out sofa in the living room.	第一間臥室有兩個加大雙人床，比較小的臥室有一般雙人床。在客廳也有一個沙發床。
Guest	That might be the perfect solution. My brother may **join** us later in the week. He could sleep on the pull out bed.	這可能是最完美的解決方案。我哥哥那一星期可能會加入我們。他可以睡在沙發床。
Front Desk	Would you like to reserve it? It requires a credit card and a deposit.	你想預定嗎？我們需要信用卡和訂金。

Part III 旅館英語

Words 單字

* variety /vəˈraɪətɪ / 　*n.* 多種多樣
* Queen Size bed /kwin/ /saɪz/ /bɛd/ 　*ph.* 大號雙人床
* double /ˈdʌbəl/ 　*adj.* 兩倍的；雙重的
* luxury /ˈlʌgʒəi/ 　*n.* 奢侈；豪華
* join /dʒɔɪn/ 　*v.* 連接；參加；聯合

Grammar
文法片語

1. Do you have any …? 你有任何的……嗎？

★小提點：形容詞〈any〉任何，這個後面可以加名詞。

例一：Do you have any hot water? 你有熱水嗎？

例二：Do you have any Taiwanese money? 你有任何的台幣嗎？

例三：We don't have any clean towels. 我們都沒有乾淨的毛巾。

★小提點：否定句型是〈We don't have any food in the bag.〉「我們袋子裡沒有任何的食物」，〈She does not have any appointment.〉「她沒有任何的預約。」

2. Another choice 另一個選擇

★小提點：形容詞〈Another〉另一個，單數的限定詞所以後面要加單數。

例一：Do we have another choice? 我們有其他的選擇嗎？

例二：Another choice is to take the shuttle bus. 另一個選擇是搭接駁車。

★小提點：和〈Another〉類似的有〈one more〉「再一個」。

例三：〈I have one more question.〉和〈I have another question.〉意思相同都是「我有另一個問題。」

3. pull out 拉出來

★小提點：動詞〈pull〉拉，副詞〈out〉出來，所以這是一個動詞的片語，但是也可以當名詞片語如〈a pull out sofa〉拉出式沙發。

例一：The drawer in the hotel room does not pull out. 飯店房間內的抽屜拉不出來。

例二：The dog pulled out a bone from under the sofa. 那隻狗從沙發下拉出一根骨頭。

★小提點：〈pull out〉也可以被解釋為「退出；撤離」。

例三：He was forced to pull out of the game because of the injury. 因為受傷他被迫退出比賽。

Short Sentences
不尷尬短句

❶ If you need an extra bed, we can provide a roll-away cot for an additional $10 a night.
如果你需要加床，我們可以提供一晚額外 $10 美元可移動的折疊床。

❷ In the hostel, you won't have your own room, but will share it with strangers.
在青年旅館裡，你不會有自己的房間，而是會與陌生人共用房間。

❸ The family of four requested a room with two double beds.
那一家四口要求有一間兩張雙人床的房間。

❹ The rooms with king size beds cost more than rooms with doubles.
有特大號床的客房價格比雙人床的客房貴。

❺ They reserved a room with a queen size bed and a cot for the child.
他們預訂了一個有大號床和一張給小孩的嬰兒床的房間。

❻ The room contains a sofa bed so it can actually sleep five people and there is no charge for the extra person in the room.
那個房間裡有一張沙發床，所以實際上可以睡五個人，額外的人也不用加收費。

❼ Would you like to look at the Junior Suite before you decide and see if it's enough space for your family?
你想先看看普通套房，然後再決定是否這個房間對你的家人來說有足夠的空間？

❽ A room with two beds is perfect for a family of 4.
一個房間有兩張床對一家四口來說是完美的選擇。

❾ The Luxury Suite has a small kitchen and it is large enough for four adults to be comfortable in the space.
豪華套房內設有一間小廚房，這樣的空間是足夠讓四個成年人感到舒適。

❿ The Suite is very nice and may end up costing you less than two rooms.
這個套房是非常好的，最後還是比你訂兩個房間便宜。

Part Ⅲ 旅館英語

Speak Up!
說出來！
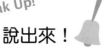
MP3 064

Dialogue 01 對話

Guest: I need a room that sleeps five but isn't too expensive.

顧客：我需要一個可以睡五個人的房間，但也不要太貴的。

Front Desk: I can give you a room with two double beds and we can put a cot in it for $10 a night, if you like.

櫃檯：我可以給你一個有兩張雙人床的房間，如果你要的話，我們可以加一張小床，但一晚要多加 $10 美元。

Dialogue 02 對話

Guest: I need to reserve a block of rooms for a wedding party

顧客：我需要預訂婚禮派對用的幾個房間。

Front Desk: Do you want the standard double rooms?

櫃檯：你想要標準雙人房嗎？

Dialogue 03 對話

Guest: I requested a room with a Queen size bed but there are two double beds in our room.

顧客：我要求一間有一張大號床的房間，但我們的房間有兩張雙人床。

Front Desk: I'm sorry, Sir. Let me check that. We have one left that has a King size bed in it. Since it's our mistake, I will give it to you for the cost of the Queen.

櫃檯：對不起，先生。讓我查查看。我們只剩下一間有一張特大號床的房間。因為這是我們的錯，我會提供給你這個房間但只收大號床房間的費用。

　　Your hotel has a variety of room layouts and matching your guest with the perfect layout for them takes good listening skills and some quick thinking at times. They may ask for two adjoining rooms, but the better fit might be a suite or a junior suite. If someone is bringing a group of people for a sporting event like a tennis or swimming match, standard twin rooms may fit their needs perfectly. A couple with a baby will need a room with floor space to put a crib and other baby paraphernalia. A room with a California King bed, a king size bed that is extra-long, may be difficult to find and should cost more than other rooms. The standard bed size used to be a double bed, meaning two people can sleep in it, but lately that has been replaced with the Queen size bed, which should have plenty of space for two people and a small child, if need be. The harder rooms to sell are the luxury rooms so you may want to offer specials on them when business is slow. Once people stay in the luxury room, it is harder for them to go back to a standard room the next time they visit.

　　你的酒店有多種房型的佈局，為你的客人做出適合他們的完美分配需要良好的傾聽技巧，有時也需要一些敏捷的思維，他們可能要求兩個相鄰的房間，但是更適合他們的可能是套房或小型套房。如果有人為了體育賽事如網球或游泳而帶來了一群人，標準雙人房對他們的需求可能會比較完美。一對有帶寶寶的夫婦可能需要一個較有空間的房間來放嬰兒床等嬰兒用具，一個配有加州特大床的客房（一張超長的特大號的床），都是可能較難找到，所以應該比其他房間貴。以前標準的床是一張雙人床，這意味著兩個人可以一起睡這樣的床，但最近這樣標準的床已被大號雙人床所替換，這樣如果需要的話。對兩個人和一個小孩子來說應該有足夠的空間，比較難推銷的房間都是豪華房間。所以在淡季的時候，你可能要提供這種房間的特別價。一旦客人住過豪華的房間，下一次他們再來時，他們就會不會想住標準房間。

3.1.3　Greeting Guests and Safekeeping 接待及保管物品

Conversations

不停住對話 　MP3 065

Greeting a Guest who wants a **different** room than what was reserved for them.
接待一個想要不同房間的顧客，這個顧客預訂一個房間但想要換不同的房間。

Desk Clerk	Welcome! What name is the reservation under?	歡迎光臨！請問是用什麼名字做預約的呢？
Guest	It should be under Charles. John Charles.	應該是查爾斯。約翰‧查爾斯。
Desk Clerk	I'm sorry I'm not finding it. Is there another name I can check?	對不起，我沒有找到這個名字。是否還有其他的名字我可以用來查查看呢？
Guest	My boss' **secretary** made them. Maybe she put all the rooms under his name. Try Thomas. Fred Thomas. I know she made a **deposit** for them on the company credit card.	是我老闆的秘書預約的。也許她用他的名字做所有房間的預約。試試看托馬斯。弗雷德‧托馬斯。我知道她有用公司的信用卡為這預約付了押金。

Desk Clerk	What's the name of the company? I'll **search** for that as well.	公司的名稱是什麼呢？我也可以用這個做搜尋。
Guest	IT Manufacturing.	IT 製造。
Desk Clerk	Here it is. All the rooms are under the company name. We have a standard double room for three nights, the 17th through the 19th with check out on the 20th waiting for you.	找到了。所有的房間的預約都在公司的名稱下。我們的資料顯示是標準雙人房三個晚上，從 17 日到 19 日，退房時間是在 20 日。
Guest	Is there any way you can **upgrade** that room to a slightly larger bed?	你是否有什麼辦法可以把那個房間升級到一個稍大的床？
Desk Clerk	I can do that for another $20 a night. Would you like a room with a single Queen or one with a double?	我是可以這樣做，但有另外一個晚上 20 美元的費用。你想要有一張加大雙人床的房間或有一般雙人床的房間？
Guest	The single Queen is fine.	那個有一張加大雙人床的房間好了。
Desk Clerk	That will be room #435. It's down the hall from the ice machine and the elevator. Does that work?	這個房間是 # 435 。從製冰機和電梯的走廊一直走到底就會到房間。這樣可以嗎？
Guest	It does.	可以的。

Part II 旅館英語

Words
單 字

* different /ˈdɪfəənt/　*adj.* 不同的
* secretary /ˈsɛkrəˌtɛri/　*n.* 秘書
* deposit /dəˈpɑzɪt/　*n.* 儲蓄；保証金
* search /sətʃ/　*v.* 搜尋
* upgrade /əpˈgred/　*v.* 升級

Grammar
文法片語

1. under his name 以他的名字
　★小提點：介係詞〈under〉「在……之下」。
　　例一：I did not open the account under my name. 我沒有用我的名字來開戶。
　★小提點：另一個常用的片語是〈under the name of〉。
　　例二：Please book the ticket under the name of Mr.Lin. 請用林先生這個名字來訂票。
　★小提點：換了介係詞意思就完全不一樣〈in the name of〉「為了某人在做一件榮譽的事」。
　　例三：They donated the money in the name of their father. 他們以他們父親的名義來捐款。

2. Here it is. 這是給你的
　★小提點：副詞〈here〉這裡，〈Here it is.〉是很口語化的用法，通常是要拿東西給對方時會說的話，視情況而定，這句話有「拿去吧！」、「就是這個」、「給你」、「這是你要的東西」，另外一個類似的句型是〈Here you are.〉「這是你要的東西。」，也是口語化的用法，只是有一點點的差別，〈Here it is.〉比較注重所給的東西，〈Here you are.〉比較注重的是對方。如果你買車票，服務員給你車票時會說〈Here it is.〉，也可能會說〈Here is your ticket.〉。

3. Does that work? 這樣可以嗎？

　★小提點：動詞〈work〉「工作；運作；操作」，看對話的情況而定，〈Does that work?〉有很多的意思，可以是禮貌地在問對方〈Does that work for you〉「你認為這樣好嗎？」，當在問事情的操作時，這句就變成〈Does the car work?〉「車子可以開嗎？」，〈Does the air conditioner work?〉「冷氣可以用嗎？」，〈Does the escalator work?〉「手扶梯可以用嗎？」。

Short Sentences
不尷尬短句

❶ If you need help with your luggage, we have baggage carts that you can use.
如果你需要行李上的幫助，我們的行李推車你可以使用。

❷ Did you valet park your car?
你有沒有做代客泊車？

❸ How long are you staying?
你要在這裏住多久？

❹ Will you be checking out tomorrow?
你明天會退房嗎？

❺ Do you need one or two keys for your room?
你需要有你的房間一個或兩個鑰匙？

❻ I'm afraid you can't check in until 2 pm.
我想你在下午 2 點前是無法入住。

❼ Is room service still available since the restaurants are closed?
因為餐廳已經關了，客房服務仍然可用嗎？

❽ How late are the pool and the exercise room open tonight?
游泳池會開到多晚呢，還有健身室今晚有開嗎？

❾ The WiFi passcode is written down here on the key envelope for you.
無線網路的密碼寫在給你的鑰匙的信封上。

❿ Please call the front desk if you have any problem.
如果你有任何問題，請打電話給櫃檯。

Speak Up!
說出來！
MP3 066

Dialogue 01 對話

Desk Clerk: How did you arrive today? Taxi, bus, or car?
櫃檯服務員：你今天是怎麼到達的呢？是坐計程車、公車、或汽車？

Guest: I drove and parked in your garage.
顧客：我有開車，也把車停在你們的車庫裡。

Desk Clerk: If you give me your parking pass, I will validate it and you will receive a 25% discount off of parking while you are here.
櫃檯服務員：如果你給我你的停車證，我可以驗證一下，你住在這裡的時間內你就可以獲得 25% 的停車折扣。

Dialogue 02 對話

Desk Clerk: I will need a deposit to hold the room if you are arriving late.
前台服務員：如果你會晚到，我需要有訂金來保留你訂的房間。

Guest: Certainly. We may be early, but I'm worried about missing a flight or something happening.
顧客：當然可以。我們可能早到，但我是很擔心錯過航班或有什麼事發生。

Desk Clerk: Once you give me a deposit, we will hold the room until you arrive- regardless of how late it is. The deposit will be deducted from the cost of the room at check out.
前台服務員：一旦你給了我訂金，無論是多麼晚我們都會把房間保留到你到達。在要退房時，這個訂金會從房間的費用中扣除。

Dialogue 03 對話

Guest: How do we get to our room from here?
顧客：我們如何從這裡到我們的房間呢？

Desk Clerk: Take the elevator to the fifth floor and turn right. It should be on the left-hand side.
櫃檯服務員：坐電梯到五樓，然後右轉。房間應該是在左手邊。

Guest: Where is breakfast served?
顧客：早餐是在哪裡呢？

Desk Clerk: On the main floor between 7 am and 10 am. It's complimentary.
櫃檯服務員：在一樓，從上午 7 點到 10 點之間。這是免費的。

Job Wisdom
職業補給站

While working the Front Desk, you are the brains of the hotel and the first line of customer service. Your attitude will make a difference to guests who arrive tired and irritable. This position requires you to be a problem-solver. If you can't provide a solution, get a manager to help you. However, your first requirement is to provide exceptional customer service and keep the guests your #1 priority. Start with your dress. Be presentable and neat, eager to help, with a smile on your face. Know the hotel facilities and give clear and precise directions. Help each guest to feel special and you can see the frustration and exhaustion disappear from their face. Don't take it personally when guests are grouchy or miserable. In the morning, after a good night's sleep, they will appreciate your efforts. You will need to know the reservation and billing system so you can check people into their rooms and check them out when they leave.

　　在櫃檯工作時，你就是酒店的大腦，也是第一線的客戶服務。你的態度對疲倦和煩躁的客人來說會造成很大的作用。這個職位要求你來當一個問題的解決者。如果你不能解決問題，就要請經理來幫助你。但你的第一個被要求做到的是要提供出色的客戶服務，並把你的客人當作第一優先。首先，從你的衣服開始。你的穿著是要看起來很像樣也要整潔，你要很熱心地幫助客人也要面帶笑容。你要了解飯店的設施，並給予清晰明確的方向。你要幫助每一位客人讓他們感到特別，你也應該可以看出他們臉上的無奈和疲憊。當客人不高興或痛苦不堪時，不要覺得這是衝著你而來。當他們有一夜的好眠後，在早上他們就會欣賞你的努力。你需要知道預訂和計費系統，這樣你可以順利地讓客人住進自己的房間，當他們離開時，你也可以幫他們做退房的手續。

Part III 旅館英語

Unit 01 Front Desk 櫃台

Conversations

不停住對話 MP3 067

A guest is requesting a wakeup call at the front desk.
一位顧客正在問櫃檯有關晨喚服務。

Guest	I need a wake-up call for 4 am in the morning tomorrow. Can you make sure I'm called on time? I have a very important meeting to get to and I <u>can't be late</u>.	我需要明天凌晨 4 點的晨喚服務，你是否能確保會準時叫我？我有一個非常重要的會議不能遲到。
Front Desk	What room number is that?	請問你的房間號碼是什麼？
Guest	546. You won't forget, will you?	546，你不會忘記吧？
Front Desk	<u>We won't forget</u>. An actual **human** person will call you three times and if you don't respond, we can send up a security person to make sure you're awake.	我們不會忘記的，我們會實際有人會打電話給你三次，如果你不回應，我們會派送一個安全人員來確保你有起床。

Guest	Can you do that? I hate those **automated** voices. Once I got a wake-up for the guest who stayed in the room before me. <u>All I can guess</u> is that he didn't **make his appointment** either since the wake-up call was a day late!	你可以這樣做嗎？我很討厭那些自動化的聲音，有一次電話打來的是要喚醒之前住同一個房間的客人，我只能猜測的是，他應該也沒有赴約，因為晨叫服務的電話是晚了一天！
Front Desk	I am making a note. That's a 4 am call for room 546. You can also use the regular alarm clock in the room.	我會寫下來的，是 546 房間要求 4 點晨叫服務，你也可以用房間內的定時鬧鐘。
Guest	Hotel alarm clocks are the most **complicated** mechanical devices known to man.	飯店內的鬧鐘是人類已知的最複雜的機械裝置！
Front Desk	That's why we offer wake-up service. We know how critical it is for you to make your meeting and how hard it can be to wake up when you're fighting jet lag as well.	這就是為什麼我們有提供晨喚服務，我們知道出席會議是有多麼的重要，而且同時在調時差是有多難！
Guest	<u>That's the truth</u>! My body still thinks it's yesterday morning!	這是真的！我的身體仍然在昨天早上的時間！

Part II 旅館英語

Words
單　字

* human /ˈhumən/　*adj.* 人類的
* automated /ˈɔtəmetɪd/　*adj.* 自動的

∗ appointment /əˋpɔɪntmənt/　*n.* 任命；選派；約定

∗ complicated /ˋkɑmpləˌketɪd/　*adj.* 複雜的

∗ truth /truθ/　*n.* 真理；真相

Grammar
文法片語
·········

1. can't be late 不能遲到

　★小提點：形容詞〈late〉「遲到的」。

　　例一：We are going to be late. 我們快要遲到了。

　　例二：〈Don't be late.〉不要遲到，有禮貌的說法是〈Please don't be late.〉請不要遲到。

　　例三：〈We had a late start.〉我們起步比較晚。

2. We won't forget. 我們不會忘記的

　★小提點：〈won't〉是〈will not〉的縮寫「將不會」，這是很口語化的用法。動詞〈forget〉忘記。

　　例一：Don't forget to check in by 1:00 in the afternoon. 不要忘了在下午一點前辦住入手續。

　　例二：We will not forget the hospitality of Taiwanese people. 我們不會忘記台灣人的熱情。

　★小提點：形容詞〈forgetful〉就變成是「健忘的」。

　　例三：〈I became very forgetful.〉我越來越健忘。

3. All I can guess is that... 所有我可以想到的……

　★小提點：動詞〈guess〉是「猜測」或「假設」，這個和〈suppose〉有同樣的意似。

　　例一：〈I guess so.〉和〈I suppose so.〉意思完全一樣，都是「我想也是」。

　　例二：〈Guess what?〉猜猜看？這是常講的口語用法，用這句時是有點要引起對方的注意。

　★小提點：〈guess〉也可以當名詞。〈Take a guess〉猜猜看。

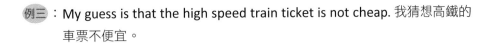

例三：My guess is that the high speed train ticket is not cheap. 我猜想高鐵的車票不便宜。

4. That's the truth. 那是真的

★小提點：名詞〈truth〉「真理；真相」，這裡是指特定的真理，前面要加冠詞〈the〉，所以正確用法是〈the truth〉。

例一：To tell you the truth, I really don't like the Stinky Tofu. 坦白的說，我真的不喜歡臭豆腐。

★小提點：這個片語也不錯〈the naked truth〉，〈naked〉直接意思是「沒有穿衣服，可以解釋成「赤裸裸的」，所以〈the naked truth〉就是「赤裸裸的真相」。

例二：Please tell me the naked truth, I can take it. 請告訴我完全的真相，我可以承受的。

Short Sentences
不尷尬短句

❶ Do you need a morning call tomorrow?
需要提供晨喚服務嗎？

❷ We offer copy and fax services.
我們有提供影印與傳真的服務。

❸ We do have morning call service.
我們確實有提供晨叫服務。

❹ For laundry service, dial 3 and you will get housekeeping.
如果需要洗衣服務，撥打 3，你會接到清潔服務。

❺ If you need clothes cleaned by tomorrow, we offer express laundry service.
如果你需要你的衣服在明天前洗好，我們有提供快洗服務 。

❻ We can guarantee your shirt be cleaned before 7 am but there is an extra fee.
我們可以保證在早上 7 點之前你的襯衫就會洗好，但是有額外的費用。

❼ We have a 24 hour laundry service available to our guests.
我們有提供給我們的客人 24 小時的洗衣服務。

❽ All our nannies are licensed.
我們所有的保姆都是有執照的。

❾ Would you like me to connect you with our concierge for nanny service?
你要不要我幫你轉我們的禮賓人員來接洽保姆服務？

❿ You should be able to get free internet access in your hotel room.
你在飯店房間內應該能夠免費上網。

Speak Up!

說出來！ MP3 068

Dialogue 01 對話

Guest: I have a suit jacket that I needed cleaned before tomorrow morning. Is that possible?
客人：我有一件西裝外套需要在明天早上之前清洗好，這可能嗎？

Front Desk: Of course. I will send Housekeeping up to your room to pick it up immediately. It will cost a bit more to have it done on such notice. Is that ok?
櫃檯：當然，我會請房務部馬上到你的房間拿衣服，這麼短的時間內要把衣服洗乾淨需要付一些多餘的費用，這樣可以嗎？

Dialogue 02 對話

Guest: I heard you offer laundry service. Is that true?
客人：我聽說你們有提供洗衣服務，這是真的嗎？

Front Desk: Yes it is. There is a plastic bag in your room. Just place the items you wanted laundered in it and I will send housekeeping up to pick it up.
櫃檯：是的，你的房間內有一個塑膠袋，只要把你想要送洗的東西放在袋子裡，我就會請房務部去拿。

Dialogue 03 對話

Guest: I'm really desperate! My nanny got sick at the last moment and cancelled, but I have to go to an important meeting tomorrow. Does your hotel offer childcare?

客人：我是真的很絕望！我的保姆在最後時刻生病了不能來，但我明天必須去參加一個很重要的會議，請問你的飯店是否有提供托兒服務？

Front Desk: We have a Hotel Nanny program that will help. You reserve the day and time you want with our concierge and the nannies are good with all ages of children.

櫃檯：我們是有一個飯店保姆服務可以幫你，你可以和我們的禮賓服務人員講你需要的日期和時間，我們的保姆可以看照各年齡層的孩子。

Job Wisdom 職業補給站

Hotels are known for either having the wake-up call come at the wrong time or the wrong day, or not at all. Once in a while the automatic system doesn't cancel a wake-up call and it will ring the room the next day, awaking a guest who didn't request the call. For the business traveler who is suffering from jet lag, it can be a major issue. Not getting the call in a timely manner could mean that they miss an important meeting, have to go unprepared and not shower, or even miss their plane. Being meticulous and organized will help resolve some of these issues and will make a difference with providing a service needed by your guests. Make sure you know the wake-up system and enter each request as soon as it comes in. Verify the room number and the time as well so that you can avoid calling the wrong room or calling at the wrong time.

飯店的晨喚服務弄錯時間或日期是眾所周知的，或根本沒有做到應有的晨喚服務，有時候自動系統沒有自動取消晨喚服務，然後會在第二天響起，把沒有要求晨喚服務的客人給叫醒。對於在調時差的商務旅客來說，這真是一個大問題，沒有在預訂的時間內得到晨喚服務可能意味著他們錯過一次重要的會議，因為時間的錯誤，他們也必須措手不及的出席會議，沒有洗澡，甚至錯過他們的飛機。當你提供服務給需要的客人時，你在工作上的細心和有組織的能力將可以幫助解決其中的一些問題，你要確保你了解晨喚服務的系統，當有人申請服務時，你要盡快的輸入資料。也要好好的確認房號和時間，這樣能夠避免呼叫錯誤的房間或呼叫錯誤的時間。

Part Ⅲ 旅館英語

Unit 01 Front Desk 櫃台

3.1.5 Introducing the Stores Around the Hotel 周圍店家介紹

Conversations
不停住對話 　MP3 069

A guest asks for help at the Front Desk for a way to **occupy** herself.
一位顧客詢問櫃檯有關打發時間的方式。

Guest	My husband is at a meeting and I have to kill time for an hour before we meet for dinner. Is there anything to do here besides the pool and the exercise room? I don't want to get **sweaty** before dinner.	我的先生在開會，在我們見面吃晚餐前，我需要打發一個小時的時間。除了游泳池和健身室？這裡有什麼可以做的呢？我不想在晚飯前流很多的汗。
Front Desk	We have several **designer** boutiques on the grounds. Maybe you would like to shop at one of them. There is one that **caters** to high end women's brands as well as a jewelry store that has pieces you might like	我們有幾個設計師的精品店。也許你會想去逛逛其中的一個店。有一個是專門賣高級的女裝品牌，也有一家珠寶店，你可能會喜歡他們的產品。
Guest	Is there a men's shop?	有沒有賣男性衣服的店呢？
Front Desk	There is. It's right next to the Woman's clothing boutique. Let me get you a map. (Pulls out map)	有的。就在女性服裝精品店的旁邊。讓我給你一張地圖。（拿出地圖）

Guest	What's this shop? (points to spot on the map)	這是什麼店？（指著地圖上的一個地方）
Front Desk	That's our Wine Lounge. It's the perfect place to order a glass of wine and linger for a while. It's across from the handbag shop which just got in this season's purses. There is the gift shop as well.	這是我們的酒吧。這是一個完美的地方讓你點一杯酒和打發時間。這個就在皮包店的對面，他們剛進了本季的錢包。那裡也有一間禮品店。
Guest	I will visit it before we leave. What about skin care products? I left my moisturizing cream at home.	在我們離開之前我會去看看。有賣護膚品的地方嗎？我把我的保濕霜留在家裡忘了帶。
Front Desk	Next to the Wine Lounge is a high end skin care product store and the women there would be delighted to help you find the right moisturizer for your skin.	在酒吧旁邊有一個高級的護膚品店，店裡的服務人員會很樂意幫助你找到適合你的皮膚的保濕產品。

Part II 旅館英語

Words 單字

* occupy /ˈɑkjəˌpaɪ/   v. 佔用；占領
* sweaty /ˈswɛti/   adj. 流汗的；吃力的
* designer /dɪˈzaɪnɚ/   n. 設計師；設計者
* cater /ketɚ/   v. 承辦伙食；滿足；迎合
* product /ˈprɑdəkt/   n. 產品；成果；作品

Grammar
文法片語

1. It's the perfect place to... 這是一個完美的地方用來⋯⋯

 ★小提點：形容詞〈perfect〉「完美的」。

　例一：〈perfect timing〉時間正好，〈perfect food〉完美的食物。

 ★小提點：當你對事情的結果或發展很滿意的時候，可以說〈It is perfect!〉「太完美了！」，在讚美一個人很完美時可以這樣說〈You are perfect.〉「你太完美了！」，有時你做錯事時，你也可以為自己找台階下說〈I am not perfect.〉「我不是完美的人。」

 ★小提點：〈perfect+for sth〉對⋯⋯來說是很好的方式

　例二：Nina's house is perfect for parties. 妮娜家超適合辦派對的。

2. What about... 那麼⋯⋯如何呢？

 ★小提點：很普遍的客套話用來詢問對方的意見。後面可以直接接名詞。

　例一：I like this idea. What about you? 我很喜歡這個想法，你覺得呢？

 ★小提點：也可以用來做建議性的問句，語氣和〈Would you like...?〉很類似，是非常客氣地在問對方。

　例二：What about a cup of tea? 要不要來一杯茶？

　例三：What about taking the bus to downtown? 要不要坐公車到市中心？

3. I left my... at... 我把⋯⋯放在⋯⋯

 ★小提點：動詞〈left〉是〈leave〉「離開」的過去式，〈I left my keys at home.〉直譯是「我把我的鑰匙放在家裡」，意思就是「我忘了帶鑰匙」。

　例一：He left the hotel in the morning. 他在早上就離開了飯店。

　例二：She left you a message. 她有給你留言。

 ★小提點：〈left〉和〈over〉加在一起成為一個字〈leftover〉是「剩菜」的意思。

4. be delighted to... 會很高興的做⋯⋯

 ★小提點：過去分詞〈delighted〉「歡喜的；高興的」，原形動詞是〈

delight〉但是通常在句子裡會用過去分詞〈delighted〉，〈be delighted to〉後面直接加原形動詞。

例一：I am delighted to be here. 我很高興能來這裡。

例二：The manager is so delighted to see the visitors. 那個經理很高興看到那些訪客。

Short Sentences
不尷尬短句

❶ It is about 10 minutes walk from the hotel to the biggest night market in Taichung called Feng Chia Night Market.
離飯店走路 10 分鐘就是台中最大的夜市逢甲夜市。

❷ It only takes 5 minutes to walk from the hotel to the MRT.
從飯店走路 5 分鐘就有捷運站。

❸ There is a department store next door to our hotel and you can go shopping there.
我們飯店的隔壁是百貨公司，可以去逛逛街。

❹ There is an aboriginal handicrafts shop downstairs in the hotel.
飯店的樓下有賣原住民手工藝品的店。

❺ The post office is about 2 blocks from our hotel.
郵局離飯店有兩條街的距離。

❻ I can show you where the stationary store is on the map.
我可以在地圖上告訴你文具店在那裡。

❼ The Sunglasses Shop is right next to the tea shop.
眼鏡店就在茶葉店的旁邊。

❽ If you go to the first intersection outside the hotel, you'll see the coffee shop right away.
如果你在飯店外到第一個路口，你就會馬上看到咖啡廳。

❾ Right outside the hotel there is a candle store and a designer handbag store as well as a high end women's boutique.
在飯店外就有一個蠟燭店，還有名牌包包店以及高級的女裝精品。

Part Ⅲ 旅館英語

Speak Up!
說出來！ MP3 070

Dialogue 01 對話

Front Desk: Have you tried the spa next to our hotel?
櫃檯：你有沒有去我們飯店旁邊的 spa ？

Guest: Not yet. What kind of services do they offer?
顧客：還沒有。他們有提供什麼樣的服務？

Front Desk: They have the full menu of services from massages to pedicures. You should try it.
櫃檯：他們有從按摩到足療的全套服務。你應該試一下。

Dialogue 02 對話

Guest: Does the convenience store carry local products for souvenirs? Maybe I could find something special for my mother there.
顧客：在角落的便利店是否有賣當地的紀念品？也許我可以在那裡找到一些特別的東西給我媽媽。

Front Desk: Does she like art? The little art shop around the corner has local artists and they will ship things home so you don't have to carry them back on the plane.
櫃檯：她喜歡藝術嗎？在拐角處的小藝術品店有本地藝術家，他們會把東西寄到你家，這樣你就不必上飛機時自己帶。

Dialogue 03 對話

Guest: I promised my wife I'd bring back something special for her. Do you have any suggestions?
顧客：我有答應過我的妻子，我會帶回一些特別的東西給她。你有什麼建議嗎？

Front Desk: Why don't you visit the boutiques right next to the hotel? They have a variety of special items so you'll find something your wife will love.
櫃檯：你可以看看飯店旁邊的精品店？他們有各種特殊的產品，你會找到你的妻子一定會喜歡的東西。

Know the stores in your hotel and surrounding your hotel. Take time to walk around them and check out their most recent acquisitions so that you can make appropriate suggestions to your guests who seek your advice. Not only is it good customer service, but it will be appreciated by the owners of the small shops who need the business. Having shops on the grounds of the hotel can save the guest time finding a store and shopping when they have a busy schedule. Know which shops will ship products for your guests and which ones won't. You don't want to say a store will do something only to have the guest find out that's not true later on. Many of the high end boutiques sell something unique that your guest can only buy at that location. By sharing that information with your guests, they will know what to look for when they enter the store. If your boutiques are only found at your hotel, make sure you share that information as well. That way the guest won't think that they'll find the same products at a different boutique when they are out shopping at the mall or when they get home.

　　你應該要知道飯店內的商店和周邊的店。花一點時間去看看這些店，並看看他們最近的進貨，這樣當你的客人在徵求你的意見時，你就可以做出適當的建議。這不僅僅是良好的客戶服務，商店的老闆也需要客人來買，他們對你的推薦也會不勝感激。當客人有繁忙的行程時，飯店裡的商店可以節省客人找商店購物的時間。你應該要知道哪些店可以為你的客人做產品運送的服務和哪些店沒有這樣的服務。你不會想讓客人覺得你說的與實際的不同。有許多高檔的精品店會賣一些獨特的產品，你的客人也只能在特定的商店買。與你的客人分享這些信息，當他們進入商店後他們會知道要如何找他們要的東西。如果你的精品店的產品只有在你的飯店內才有賣，你要確保告訴客人這些信息。這樣當他們外出在商場購物或當他們回家後，客人就不會認為他們會在不同的精品店找到相同的產品。

Unit 01 **Front Desk** 櫃台

Conversations

不停住對話 MP3 071

A guest had a letter delivered to the hotel before he arrived.
一位客人在他到達飯店之前有一封他的信件被送達。

Guest	Hello. I am expecting a letter for Sam Jones. I understood it arrived and you are holding it for me.	你好。我在等一封來自山姆 • 瓊斯的信。我知道這封信已經到了而且你們有幫我留著。
Desk Clerk	Let me check. Do you know if it has the date of your arrival on the **envelope**?	讓我看看。你知不知道這信封上面是否有寫你的到達日期？
Guest	It should. I got notice that it arrived two days ago. When I e-mailed the hotel to ask about this, they said you would keep it for me until I arrived.	應該是有。我有收到通知說這封信在兩天前被送達。當我發電子郵件給飯店詢問有關這封信時，他們說在我到達前，你們會為我保留著。
Desk Clerk	They are right. It should be right here. I remember signing for it. It came Fed Ex if I remember **correctly**. Oh, here it is.	他們說的是對的。應該是在這裡。我記得有簽收過這封信。如果我沒記錯的話，這是透過聯邦快遞公司寄來的。啊，在這裏。

Desk Clerk	Would you mind signing for it for me? Thank you.	你可以在這裡簽名嗎？謝謝你。
Guest	Whew! I was worried a minute.	呼！剛剛真的是很擔心。
Desk Clerk	Our guests do this <u>all the time</u>. Sometimes when they are hosting a **convention** here, all their materials are shipped ahead of time and we hold them.	我們的客人常常會做這種事。有時，當他們在這裡主持一個會議，他們所有的資料都提前寄來，我們會幫他們保留。
Guest	I will remember that next time <u>instead of</u> bringing an **extra** suitcase.	我下一次會記得，也就不用帶另外一個手提箱來。

Words 單字

* envelope /ˈɛnvəˌlop/　*n.* 信封
* correctly /kəˈrɛktlɪ/　*adv.* 正確地
* convention /kənˈvɛnʃən/　*n.* 會議
* extra /ˈɛkstrə/　*adj.* 額外的
* access /ˈæksɛs/　*v.* 進出；拿取

Grammar 文法片語

1. I e-mailed someone 我有發郵件給某人

　★小提點：動詞〈email〉發郵件，〈e-mail〉是原始的用法，這裡的〈e〉指的就是〈electronic〉「電子的」，也就是〈electronic mail〉。也可以

做名詞使用。

例一：Please email me about the hotel website. 請發給我電子郵件告訴我有關飯店的網站。

例二：We keep in touch by email. 我們會透過電子郵件保持聯絡。

2. They are right. 他們是對的

★小提點：形容詞〈right〉「正確」，〈They are right.〉「他們是對的。」是很肯定的說法，當然也可以更加強語氣地說〈They are absolutely right.〉「他們是絕對正確的。」

例一：Maybe you are right. 你或許是對的。（但這是不確定的口語）

例二：I think you are right. 我認為你是對的。

例三：I don't think you are right. 我不認為你是對的。

3. all the time 一直；時時刻刻

★小提點：〈all the time〉通常是一段時間內，可以是現在的一段時間，也可以是過去的一段時間。

例一：Thank you for helping me all the time. 謝謝你一直都在幫我。

例二：I am busy all the time. 我一直都很忙。

4. instead of 取代

★小提點：副詞〈instead〉替代，副詞片語〈instead of 〉後面加動名詞或名詞。

例一：Instead of taking the bus, we walked. 我們沒有坐公車而是走路。

例二：We had noodles for lunch instead of rice. 我們中午是吃麵不是吃飯。

Short Sentences
不尷尬短句

❶ You can get the room card at the front desk.
你可以在櫃檯拿到房卡。

❷ You can leave your room card and room key at the front desk.
你可以把房卡和房間鑰匙交給櫃檯。

❸ You can fill out the mail service information on our website.
你可以在我們的網站上填寫郵件服務的資料。

❹ If you lost the room card, you will be charged a fee.
如果遺失了我們的房卡，你會需要付一些費用。

❺ Our hotel has delivery service to the airport. You can pick up your package at the ABC Information Desk in the first terminal.
我們的飯店有宅急便到機場的服務。取貨地點在第一航廈 ABC 櫃台。

❻ Guest doesn't need to be present when the delivery service picks up the package.
快遞來收包裹時旅客不必在現場。

❼ We can help our guests mail their postcards.
我們可以幫旅客代寄明信片。

❽ We can help you ship around the world.
我們可以幫你運送到世界各地。

❾ There is a lost and found room at the corner where you might find your jacket.
你或許可以在轉角處的失物招領室找到你的夾克。

❿ Why don't you check back in an hour and I'll ask housekeeping if they found your backpack in the meantime?
你要不要一小時後再來看看，我會問房務部看看他們在此期間是否有找到你的背包？

Speak Up! 說出來！ MP3 072

Dialogue 01 對話

Guest: I lost a sweater. I think I left it in the exercise room, but when I returned to get it, it was gone.

顧客：我丟了一件毛衣。我想我把毛衣放在健身室，但我回去找時已經不見了。

Desk Clerk: Maybe housekeeping found it. Let's check lost and found. What color was it?

櫃檯服務員：也許房務部有發現了它。讓我們來看看失物招領處。是什麼顏色呢？

Dialogue 02 對話

Guest: I had my room key when I went to the gym this morning, but I can't find it anywhere and my ID is in my room.

顧客：我今天早上我去健身房時還帶有我房間的鑰匙，但我現在都找不到在哪裡。我所有的 ID（身份證件）都在我的房間裡。

Desk Clerk: I can give you a new key if you'll let Security escort you to your room where you can show him your ID.

櫃檯服務員：我可以給你一個新的鑰匙，如果你讓保全護送你到你的房間，你可以給他看你的 ID。

Dialogue 03 對話

Guest: My room key isn't working. I put it in and the light doesn't flash green.

顧客：我房間的鑰匙不能用。我把它插進去但是燈沒有閃爍綠色。

Desk Clerk: Did you insert it towards the green arrow?

櫃檯服務員：你有依綠色的箭頭指示插進去嗎？

Guest: I did.

顧客：有的。

Desk Clerk: Let me get you a new one. By the way, you aren't carrying it next to a magnet are you? Like on your phone or tablet case? The magnet will erase the code.

前台服務員：我可以給你一個新的。順便說一下，你有沒有把鑰匙放在磁鐵的旁邊呢？像是放在你的手機或平板電腦旁邊？磁鐵會把代碼消除。

In a hotel that holds lots of conferences and conventions as well as hosts many international business guests, there will be a variety of issues with mail services. Packages won't arrive on time, won't be labeled clearly, won't have the arrival date of the guest on them, and may be lost in the shuffle of all the packages. This is very upsetting to the guest who is depending on receiving her package before she gives a key note speech or an important presentation. If you can help solve the issue in a timely manner, it shows a degree of caring that goes beyond the typical professionalism. It's service at its finest. But there are some things you can't solve. If the package isn't there, you can't make it be there. You can express regret and offer a suggestion. You can contact the local copy service place to see if they can do an emergency order for you as well. Don't be afraid to think outside the box and try something. Even if it doesn't work out, it's better than giving up. Put yourself in your guests' shoes.

在舉辦有大型講座和會議以及接待許多國際商務客人的飯店會有各種各樣與郵件服務有關的問題。這些問題包括有，包裹沒有準時到達，沒有清楚地標示，沒有在客人所寫的日期抵達，或者在過程中可能會丟掉所有的包裹。這對客人來說是會讓他們感到非常生氣的，因為他們在等待包裹的資料有準備演講或做重要發表的資料。如果你能幫助及時解決這個問題，這會顯示出超越典型敬業精神上一定程度上的關懷。這也是把服務發揮到最好的程度的一種表現。但也有一些事情你是解決不了。如果包裹不存在，你也無法讓包裹存在。你可以表示遺憾，並提供建議。

Conversations

不停住對話 MP3 073

A Guest inquires at the Front Desk about parking.
一為顧客在櫃檯詢問關於停車的事。

Front Desk	Good morning. How may I help you today?	早。我如何幫你呢？
Guest	The website said you have parking and I was wondering how much it costs. My business partner is joining me tomorrow and we're trying to **decide** if he should rent a car at the airport when he arrives.	網站説你有停車場，我想知道停車的費用是多少。明天我的商業合夥人會來，我們想知道當他到達時是否應該在機場租一輛車。
Front Desk	We do have parking. Our valet parking is $9 a day or you can park yourself for $6. Valet parking is added **directly** to your bill which you can pay when you check out.	我們確實有停車場。我們的代客泊車是一天 $9 美元或者你可以自己停放則是 $6 美元。代客泊車是直接加到你的帳單，你可以在退房時支付。
Guest	Do we have to pay every time we enter the garage?	我們每一次在進入停車場時就要付費嗎？

Front Desk	No. Bring your parking ticket to the front desk and we will sign it giving you **unlimited** access for the day.	不用的，把你的停車票拿到前台，我們會簽署這樣可以讓你一整天無限制地的進出。
Guest	I have to do it every day? That seems **inconvenient**.	我每天都要這樣做嗎？這似乎很不方便。
Front Desk	We can give you a pass for the length of your stay, <u>if you like</u>.	如果你要的話，我們可以給你在你停留時間的通行證。
Guest	Do you have a discount for staying the entire week? That seems very **expensive** to me.	你對住一整個星期有沒有打折呢？對我來說這似乎是非常昂貴的。
Front Desk	We don't. I'm sorry. Parking in the city is very expensive. <u>You might want to consider</u> not renting car.	對不起，我們沒有打折，在城市裡停車是非常昂貴的。你可能要考慮不要租車。

Part III 旅館英語

Words
單　字

* decide /dɪˋsaɪd/　*v.* 決定
* directly /dɪˋrɛkli/　*adv.* 直接地
* unlimited /ənˋlɪmɪtɪd/　*adj.* 無限的；不受限制的
* inconvenient /ˏɪnkənˋvinjənt/　*adj.* 不便的；有困難的
* expensive /ɪkˋspɛnsɪv/　*adj.* 貴的

Grammar
文法片語

1. Do we have to...? 我們一定要……?

★小提點：〈have to〉有「一定要；不得不」的意思，這是強烈語氣的用法，告訴對方是沒有選擇性的。

例一：We have to come back by 10:00. 我們一定要在 10:00 前回來。

例二：You have to finish your breakfast. 你一定要吃完早餐。

★小提點：must 是指說話的人自己覺得必須做；而 have to 則指其他人認為該這麼做。

例三：I must buy flowers for my mother. 我一定要買花給我媽媽。（我自己有意這麼做。）

例四：I have to buy flowers for my mother. 我一定要買花給我媽媽。（基於別人要求，所以我必須這麼做。）

2. If you like 如果你要的話……

★小提點：這是很口語的用法，看說話者的語氣，可以很客氣的表達「如果你想要的話」，也可以很不客氣的表達〈If you like〉可以是「隨你便！」，「你想要怎樣就怎樣吧」。

例一：We can visit the mall if you like. 如果你要的話，我們可以去商場逛逛。

例二：If you like, we can stop by the coffee shop. 如果你要的話，我們可以去咖啡廳坐一下。

例三：You can open the window if you like. 如果你要的話，你可以打開窗戶。

3. You might want to... 你可能要……

★小提點：〈might〉有推測或可能的意思，不是表示時態，〈might〉是助動詞所以後面要加原形動詞。

例一：You might want to think about it again. 你可能要再想想看。

例二：You might want to stay here tonight. 你可能今晚要住這裡。

★小提點：否定〈You might not want to...〉「你可能不會想要……」，這是有禮貌的建議對方不要做某件事。

例三：The weather is bad so you might not want to go out. 天氣不好所以你可能不會想要出門。

Short Sentences
不尷尬短句

1. The hotel has an underground parking garage.
   本飯店設有一個地下停車場。

2. There is a car rental company nearby the hotel.
   本飯店附近有一家汽車租賃公司。

3. We charge 25 USD daily for on-site parking.
   我們的停車場是一天 $25 美金。

4. Self-parking is based on availability.
   自己停車的話是有空位才能停。

5. The parking rates are subject to change.
   停車費用是會變動的。

6. There is a free shuttle bus to the airport.
   有到機場的免費接駁車。

7. The hotel also provides a tourist bus service.
   飯店另有提供包車旅遊服務。

8. You can consider about renting a scooter or a bicycle.
   你可以考慮租機車或腳踏車。

9. Do you have your international drivers license?
   你有國際駕照嗎？

10. Please show a drivers license for auto rental.
    租車請出示駕照。

Part Ⅲ 旅館英語

Speak Up!
說出來！

MP3 074

Dialogue 01 對話

Guest: I need a car reserved for tomorrow.
顧客：我需要預約明天的汽車。

Front Desk: Do you want taxi service or car rental?

前台：你要計程車服務或租車？

Guest: I would prefer to rent a car. I have several places I need to be and I don't want to keep looking for a taxi.

顧客：我是寧願租一輛車。我需要去幾個地方，我不希望一直在找計程車。

Front Desk: I can't make a car reservation for you, but here is the phone number you can call.

前台：我無法幫你做租車子的預約，但你可以打這個電話。

Dialogue 02 對話

Guest: There are six of us who want to go to dinner tonight. Can you call a taxi service for us? Our dinner reservation is for 6:30 at Tommi's. Is that enough time?

顧客：我們有六個人想要今晚一起去吃飯。你可以幫我們叫計程車服務嗎？我們的晚餐的預訂是 6:30 在托米餐廳，這樣有足夠的時間嗎？

Front Desk: I can. I think you will need at least two. Traffic is fairly heavy at 6 pm, but Tommi's isn't that far from our hotel.

前台：我是可以這樣做的。我想你會需要至少兩輛車。下午 6 點的交通是相當擁擠的，但托米餐廳離我們飯店不是那麼遠。

Dialogue 03 對話

Guest: I need my car tomorrow at 7:30 am.

顧客：我明天上午 7:30 要用我的車。

Valet: Let me make a note so the morning shift will be prepared. Do you have your valet card with you?

代客停車員：讓我記下，這樣的早班會有所準備。你有你的代客停車卡嗎？

Guest: Here it is.

顧客：在這裡。

Valet: Ok, so car #43562 will be waiting for you at 7:30 out front.

代客停車員：好了，車號 # 43562 會在 7:30 在大門前等著你。

Valet parking a customer's car is an act of respect for the guest. If it is his/her personal car, it is one of their most expensive assets and a good Valet treats all cars carefully. There are some very specific DON'TS: Don't roll down the windows, don't change the radio station, don't move anything, don't drive the car for any reason other than to park it and retrieve it, and don't lose the keys! When a car pulls up to Valet parking, always let female guests out of the car first. It may be old fashioned, but it's still a sign of respect. If you are valet parking at a hotel, be prepared to run things up to the room that the guest has forgotten. It may happen several times a shift. Some guests will be surprised at the cost of parking their car at a hotel. It can run as high as $40 a night in some cities. Explaining the cost upfront will help them decide about bringing their car or using public transportation. You may have special discounts you can offer as well at your discretion.

代客泊車客戶的車是對客人表現尊重的行為。如果這是他 / 她的私人車，這會是他們最昂貴的資產之一，一個良好的代客泊車員應該要很認真的對待所有的汽車。有一些非常具體的注意事項應該不要做的：不要搖下車窗，不要改變電台，不移動任何東西，除了停車和還車給客人外，不要以任何理由開客人的車，當然也不能丟了鑰匙！當一輛車開給代客泊車員時，泊車員總是應該讓女乘客先下車。這可能是老式的禮貌，但仍然是尊重的表現。如果你是飯店的代客泊車服務員，如果客人忘記車上的東西，你要準備好能把東西送到房間。這樣的事在值班時可能會發生好幾次。有些客人對飯店停車的費用感到驚訝。在一些城市一個晚上的停車甚至會高達 40 美元。你要對客人說清楚費用，這樣的資訊可以幫助客人決定要自己開車或者利用公共交通。如果你有權可以決定提供特別的折扣，你也應該看情形提供折扣給客人。【註：美式作法】

Unit 01 **Front Desk** 櫃台

Conversations
不停住對話 MP3 075

Guest needs to make an international phone call.
顧客需要撥打國際電話。

Front Desk	How may I help you today?	我如何幫助你呢？
Guest	I will need to make an international phone call later tonight. How can I do that?	我今天晚一點需要撥打國際電話。我該怎麼打呢？
Front Desk	You can use the IDD phone. Dial 00 before the number and you will be connected right away. Dial 00- the area code- and then the local number.	你可以用 IDD 電話，在號碼前加撥 00，你就會馬上被接通。撥 00 一地區代碼一然後本地號碼。
Guest	Are there any <u>surcharges on the call</u>?	這樣的電話有沒有任何附加費用？
Front Desk	You will incur some taxes and long distance charges that will show up on your bill when you check out.	你需要付一些稅和長途電話費，當你退房時這會顯示在你的賬單上。

Guest	<u>Is there a way to</u> prepay the expenses?	有沒有辦法可以預付費用？
Front Desk	There are also IDD phones in our lobby as well that you can use with the IDD phone cards. They are quite **private** and convenient and perfect <u>if you wish to</u> prepay the call.	在我們的大廳裡有 IDD 電話，你也可以用 IDD 卡使用這些電話。如果你想要預付電話費的話，這是是相當私人、方便和完美的。
Guest	IDD?	IDD 是什麼？
Front Desk	International Direct Dialing. Make sure you use the **complete** number starting with 00 first or it won't work.	國際直撥電話。請確保你要一開始先打完整的 00 數字，不然無法接通。
Guest	So I dial 00- then the area code- and then the number?	所以我先撥 00 - 然後是區號，然後是電話號碼？
Front Desk	That's correct. Call the front desk if you <u>encounter</u> any difficulties, ok?	這是正確的。如果你遇到任何困難你可以打電話給櫃檯，好嗎？

Part III 旅館英語

Words 單　字

* international /ˌɪntɚˈnæʃənəl/　*adj.* 國際的
* surcharge /ˈsɝˌtʃɑrdʒ /　*n.* 額外付費
* private /ˈpraɪvɪt/　*adj.* 私人的
* complete /kəmˈplit/　*adj.* 完成的
* encounter /ɪnˈkaʊntɚ/　*v.* 遇到

Grammar
文法片語

1. surcharge on the call 打電話的附加費用

★小提點：這裡的重點是介係詞〈on〉「在……上面」，對什麼的東西收取費用時可以用〈on〉，如〈on a credit card〉用信用卡付款。

例一：How much is the fee on the late payment? 延遲付費的費用是多少呢？

例二：How much is the interest on the loan? 貸款的利息是多少呢？

2. Is there a way to... 有沒有什麼方法能……？

★小提點：通常我們知道的〈way〉是「道路」，但是〈way〉可以當做可數名詞是「方法」。

例一：〈No way!〉「沒有辦法的啦！絕不！」和〈It is not possible.〉「這是不可能的。」有同樣意思。

例二：Another way to go to Taipei is taking the bus. 去臺北的另一個方式是坐巴士。

3. If you wish to… 如果你希望要……

★小提點：以〈If〉所帶出的句子表示有條件的，通常是連接兩個句子，其中一個句子是「如果……」在講條件，另外一個句子講的是結果。

例一：If you wish to go to the night market, I can go with you. 如果你想要去夜市，我可以跟你一起去。

例二：If you give us a better discount this time, we will come again. 如果你給我們好的折扣，我們還會再來。

★小提點：〈wish〉也可以用來當做是無法實現的期望，因為是不可能的期望，後面的動詞用過去式。〈I wish you were here.〉「我希望你在這裡。」，〈I wish I had more money.〉「我希望我有更多的錢。」，〈I wish I knew about it.〉「我希望我知道這件事。」

4. encounter any difficulties 遇到任何問題〈encounter〉動詞，常是面臨問題、困難。

例一：They encountered serious problems when someone left the team. 當他們有成員要退出，他們面臨很嚴重的問題。

例二：We encountered problems early in the project. 我們在計畫的一開始就遇到了問題。

Short Sentences

不尷尬短句

❶ We don't charge for internet access.
我們對上網是沒有收費的。

❷ All our hotel rooms have free Wi-Fi.
我們所有的房間都有免費無線。

❸ Here is the hotel password to login into the internet.
這裡是飯店登錄到網路的密碼。

❹ Our lobby and public areas have complimentary wireless.
我們的大廳和公共區域都有免費無線。

❺ There is wireless in the meeting room and phone for international calls.
會議室有無線網路，也有可以打國際的電話。

❻ If you need to do Skype during the meeting, you better set it up ahead of time and test it.
如果你需要在會議期間用的 Skype，你最好提前準備好和做一下測試。

❼ All guest rooms have flat screen TVs & iPod docking station.
所有客房都配有平面電視和 iPod 音樂基座。

❽ There is a public phone in the lobby, but it is for local calls only.
大廳有公用電話但是只能打國內。

旅館英語 Part III

Speak Up!

說出來！ MP3 076

Dialogue 01 對話

Guest: I'd like to leave a message for a guest, but I forgot my phone.
顧客：我想對某個客人做留言可是我忘了帶手機。

Front Desk: That's fine. What's their name?

櫃檯：沒問題的。他們的名字是什麼？

Guest: Bill Thomas. I want him to meet me at the café at 7:30 instead of 7.

顧客：比爾·托馬斯。我要他和我在咖啡廳見面的時間是在 7:30 而不是 7 點。

Front Desk: I will give him the message note as soon so he checks in.

櫃檯：只要他一辦住入手續，你的留言就會在他這個字條留言。

Dialogue 02 對話

Caller: I'd like to be connected to room #342.

來電者：請幫我接 # 342 房間。

Receptionist: No problem. Wait a minute. Who may I say is calling?

接待員：沒問題。等待一分鐘。你是哪位？

Caller: Mr. Thomas.

來電者：托馬斯先生。

Receptionist: I have a call for Room #342 from a Mr. Thomas. Will you take it?

接待員：有一通給 # 342 托馬斯先生的電話。你要接嗎？

Room Guest: Yes please.

飯店顧客：是的，請幫我接通。

Dialogue 03 對話

Guest: This is Room #564. Is there a special password code for the Wi-Fi? I can't seem to log on.

顧客：這是 # 564 房。是否有特殊的密碼才能用無線網路呢？我似乎無法登錄。

Front Desk: Yes there is. It should be written on your key card case. Do you see it?

櫃檯：是的，有。應該寫上放在鑰匙卡袋上面。你有看到嗎？

Guest: I tried that code and it doesn't work. Is there another one?

顧客：我有試過那個密碼，但是不行。還有其他的密碼嗎？

Front Desk: No, that's the only one. Maybe it was written incorrectly. Let me give it to you again.

櫃檯：沒有，那是唯一的密碼。也許是寫錯了。讓我再給你一次。

Job Wisdom
職業補給站

Go the extra mile. That's the mantra for excellent service in the service industry. It may require explaining something a couple of different ways until the guest understands what you are saying or doing something twice so the guest is reassured that his problem is solved. When you have a foreign traveler who's not traveled a lot, little things like making a long distance phone call or getting the WiFi to work add to the stress of the experience. When you relieve that stress, they are able to relax and enjoy the rest of the trip.

多走一英里。這就是在服務行業優良服務的口頭禪。有可能你需要用不同的方式解釋同樣的事一直到客人理解你說的話，或者你要把事情做兩次才能讓客人相信他的問題有被解決了。當你有一個外國旅客本身不是常常旅行，小事情像打長途電話或上 Wi-Fi 的網路都是會對他們的旅行經驗增加壓力的。如果你可以幫忙減輕這樣的壓力，他們對接下來的行程就能夠感到比較放鬆和享受。

Part II 旅館英語

Conversations

不停住對話   MP3 077

Guest is checking out.
顧客正在退房。

Receptionist	Are you ready to check out? What room were you in?	你準備好要退房了嗎？你是在哪一個房間呢？
Guest	We were staying in Room #232. We aren't **quite** ready to check out. We overslept and will be a few minutes late checking out. I thought I would come down and **review** the bill at least.	我們住的房間是＃232。我們還沒有準備好要退房。我們睡過頭了，所以會遲到幾分鐘退房。我是想說下來至少看一下賬單。
Receptionist	You're fine! You missed the big rush and a few **extra** minutes won't hurt.	沒問題的！你避開了忙碌的時間，多餘的幾分鐘是無害的。
Guest	I'm sorry about that. I know you want to get your staff in to clean for the next guests.	我感到很抱歉。我知道你想讓你的員工為下一個客人做好清潔準備。
Receptionist	That's usually true. Will you be putting this on the credit card you reserved the room with?	你說的沒錯。你要用你預約房間時的那一張信用卡付款嗎？

Guest	Yes. There are a few charges <u>on the bill</u> I didn't **expect**.	是的。有幾個費用是我沒有想到的。
Receptionist	One is for room service and the other one is the Valet parking charge.	一個是客房服務，另一種是代客泊車收費。
Guest	I forgot they put the Valet parking on the bill.	我忘了他們會把代客泊車加在賬單裡。
Receptionist	Do you wish to finish checking out and <u>drop off</u> the keys when you leave or do you want to wait until you are **completely** out of the room.	你想要現在就完成退房的手續，在離開時將鑰匙交回即可，還是要等到完全準備好要離開房間時再退呢？
Guest	We should be nearly out so let me go ahead and pay. I'll drop off the keys on my way out.	我們應該是差不多了，所以讓我就繼續完成退房也同時付費。我會在離開時就會把鑰匙還回。
Receptionist	Thank you for staying with us last night.	謝謝你昨天晚上住這裡。

Part II 旅館英語

Words 單 字

* quite /kwɑɪt/   *adv.* 相當地
* review /rɪˋvju/   *v.* 審查
* extra /ˋɛkstrə/   *adj.* 額外的
* expect /ɪkˋspɛkt/   *v.* 期待
* completely /kəmˋplitlɪ/   *adv.* 完全地

Grammar
文法片語

1. You're fine. 你是沒問題的

★小提點：形容詞〈fine〉好的，〈You are fine.〉直譯是「你是好的。」但是這句話通常用在告訴對方「沒有問題的。」，如果有人遲到了向你道歉，你覺得是沒有問題的，就可以用這句回答。如果有人不小心撞到你之後向你道歉，你覺得沒有大礙，也可以用這句回答。〈You are fine.〉等於是〈Don't worry about it.〉「不用掛在心上。」，如果有一群人在大廳講話很大聲，經理對你說抱歉，你如果覺得吵鬧聲對你來說是無所謂，你可以說〈They are fine.〉，如果你的孩子打擾到別人，你向對方道歉，對方覺得不是什麼大事，可能會說〈She is fine.〉。

2. You missed it. 你錯過了

★小提點：動詞〈miss〉錯過，通常錯過什麼事很明顯是已經發生了，所以〈You missed it.〉一定要用過去式。

例一：We missed the bus. 我們錯過巴士了。

例二：She got up too late and missed the train. 她起得太晚錯過火車了。

3. on the bill 在賬單上

★小提點：名詞〈bill〉賬單，通常前面的介係詞要用〈on〉，其他類似用法有，〈on the credit card〉用信用卡付款，〈on the payment〉在付款裡，〈on the receipt〉在收據裡，〈on the check〉在支票裡。

例一：I added the tip on the bill. 我把小費加在賬單上了。

例二：This purchase will show on your credit card statement next month. 這筆購買會顯示在你的下個月信用卡明細上。

4. drop off 送下車；放在

★小提點：〈drop off〉可以指開車送人下車，〈drop off the friend〉「送朋友下車」，也可以指把東西放在某個地方〈drop off the book〉「把書放在某個地方」，另一個形態是〈drop+N+ off〉，〈drop the key off〉「把鑰匙在某個地方」。

例一：Can you drop us off at the hotel? 你可不可以讓我們在飯店下車？

例二：We will drop the books off at the library. 我們會把書還回圖書館。

Short Sentences
不尷尬短句

❶ You must check out before noon or you will be charged for the next day.
你必須在中午之前退房不然你需要付另一天的費用。

❷ Does this total include the service fee?
這個總額有包括服務費嗎？

❸ There is no service fee.
這是沒有服務費的。

❹ There two sales taxes, one is national and the other one is local.
這有兩種銷售稅，一個是國家的，另一種是當地的。

❺ You can pay by cash, credit card or traveler's check.
你可以用現金，刷卡或旅遊支票付費。

❻ Would you like to apply for our hotel credit card? You will receive a 10% discount for today.
你要不要申請我們飯店的信用卡？你今天會有 10% 的折扣。

❼ We have a promotion now for a dinner package.
我們現在有一個包含晚餐的促銷。

❽ If you plan to make a reservation next week, don't forget to ask for our promotional code.
如果你打算在下週做預約，別忘了詢問我們的促銷代碼。

❾ This price does not include taxes.
此價格是沒有含稅的。

❿ This seasonal offer does not apply to groups of 6 or more.
這個季節性優惠不適用於 6 個人以上的團體。

Part II 旅館英語

Speak Up!

說出來！ MP3 078

Dialogue 01 對話

Front Desk: How was your stay with us?
櫃檯：你在這裡住的如何呢？

Guest: We were disappointed that the pool was closed. We were looking forward to swimming.
顧客：我們對游泳池的關閉感到失望。我們是很期待游泳。

Front Desk: I'm sorry about that, but maintenance found a leak in it and we're having to renovate the entire pool. It will be closed for six weeks at least.
櫃檯：我感到很抱歉，但維修部發現有漏洩，結果我們發現是需要翻修整個游泳池。至少有六個星期會是關閉的。

Dialogue 02 對話

Guest: I thought the room rate was $199 a night. Why is the bill so high?
顧客：我以為房間的價格是一晚 $199 美元。為什麼花費這麼高？

Front Desk: There are taxes on it. There is the regular tax and then the city added an entertainment tax recently so that makes the room $220.
櫃檯：這是有加稅在裡面的。還有就是一般的稅，然後這個城市在最近又加了娛樂稅，這樣使房間的價格是 $220 美元。

Guest: I knew there were taxes, but that still seems high.
顧客：我知道是有加稅，但似乎仍然很高。

Front Desk: I know. That's why our management lowered the standard rate on your room and offered it at that special price. It's usually $250 a night.
櫃檯：我知道。這就是為什麼我們的管理部有降低了你的房間的標準價，並提供了特殊的價格。這個房間通常是一晚 $250 美元。

Check out time! That's when you'll hear all kinds of complaints-mostly about things you could have fixed at the time if you'd known or about things you have no control over; like taxes. You can't make the pool open when it's broken or make guests be quiet when they are on the floor. But keep smiling. This is the last contact your guests will have your hotel and the impression they leave with will impact their decision to return or to suggest others visit. Having return guests are critical to the bottom line of the hotel's financing. They are walking advertisements for your place of business so let them leave feeling good about their visit and your brand. Offer them some coffee or water for the road, maybe a cookie or fruit if the breakfast bar is closed. When a guest puts you in a difficult position that you can't solve, ask for help from the manager. Offer them a discount on a future visit to appease them if possible. This will ensure that they'll visit again and will make them feel heard.

退房時間！這時候，你會聽到各種不同的抱怨，大部分的事情是你可以在當下時間解決的，但是還是有你早知道的事或了解卻無法控制的事，如稅收。像是游泳池損壞你不能讓游泳池開放，或讓在樓層的客人保持安靜。但你還是要保持微笑。這是你的客人最後一次和你的飯店做接觸，他們留下的印象會影響他們決定再光臨或建議他人來這裡。回流客人是飯店財務利潤的關鍵。他們是你的營業場所的活廣告，所以要讓他們在離開時對飯店有良好的印象。你可以在他們在離開時提供一些咖啡或水，如果早餐吧已經關閉，你也許可以提供餅乾或水果。當客人讓你為難而你解決不了情況時，你可以要求經理的幫助。如果可以的話，為未來的回流提供一些折扣來讓他們高興。這將確保他們會再次來住，並會令他們感到他們的心聲有被聽到。

Unit
01

Front Desk
櫃台

3.1.10   Foreign Currency Exchange 外幣兌換

Conversations
不停住對話   MP3 079

Guest wants information about using her Traveler's Checks in Taiwan.
顧客在詢問有關在台灣使用旅行支票的資訊。

Guest	I was told that many places in Taiwan won't accept my Traveler's Checks and that I should exchange them. Is that right?	有人告訴我，在台灣很多地方不會接受我的旅行支票，我應該換掉的。是這樣嗎？
Front Desk	That is correct. Most Taiwanese people don't use Traveler's Checks. You may use them here at the hotel and at some other places, but make sure you ask first. The best bet would be to exchange them for cash. You can do that either at the hotel or at the American Express Office on Tunhua N Road.	這是正確的。大部份的台灣人不使用旅行支票。你可以在這個飯店或其他地方使用旅行支票，但要先問問看。最好的辦法是把這些兌換為現金。你可以在飯店做兌換，也可以在位在敦化北路的美國運通辦事處做兌換。
Guest	How is the exchange rate currently?	目前的匯率是怎樣呢？

Front Desk	It changes **frequently** so <u>it's hard to say</u>. It's usually slightly higher for Traveller's Checks, but there is a **commission** fee. ATMs won't work for cashing your checks, but they work well for withdrawing cash. 7/11 has good machines that have English options and they are safe as well.	匯率是常常變換的,所以很難説。通常旅行支票的匯率會略高,但是有手續費。自動取款機不會為你兌現支票,要提取現金卻是很棒的。7/11是有好的自動取款機也有英文選項,也是安全的。
Guest	Can you cash my checks here then?	你能在這裡兌現我的支票嗎?
Front Desk	I can't, but I will get the Front Desk Cashier. It is a service we offer our guests and he will know the current exchange rate as well.	我不能這樣做,但我會請前台收銀員幫你。這是我們提供給客人的一種服務,他會知道現在的匯率。

Part II 旅館英語

Words

單　字

* exchange /ɪksˋtʃendʒ/　*v.* 交換
* correct /kəˋrɛkt/　*adj.* 正確的
* currently /ˋkɝəntlɪ/　*adv.* 目前地
* frequently /ˋfrikwəntlɪ/　*adv.* 經常地
* commission /kəˋmɪʃən/　*n.* 佣金;手續費

Grammar
文法片語

1. Is that right? 是這樣嗎？這樣對嗎？

  ★小提點：〈right〉在這裡是形容詞「正確地」，說這句時如果只是單純的問句，說話者會期待對方的回答是〈yes〉或〈no〉，如果說話者語氣不確定，有可能是在懷疑對方對不對，也可以等於〈Are you sure?〉「你確定嗎？」

  例一：Is that true? Is she right? 那是真的嗎？她是對的嗎？

  例二：Are you right about that? 你對那個有確定嗎？

2. best bet 最好的辦法

  ★小提點：〈best〉最好的，〈bet〉打賭，〈best bet〉是一種強烈的建議，說話者要表達的是，如果要實現你想要的結果，最好按照我的建議。

  例一：Our best bet would be to call again this afternoon. 我們最好的辦法是下午再打來。

  例二：If you want real local food, your best bet is to try the night market. 如果你真的要吃當地的食物，最好的方式就是去夜市。

  ★小提點：打賭〈bet〉也可以單獨用在句子，〈Don't bet on it.〉「那可不一定。」〈Want to bet?〉「要打賭嗎？」〈You bet.〉「就這麼決定了」。

3. Either...or... 不是……就是……

  ★小提點：〈either〉後面接單數，表示有兩個選擇要對方選其中一個。

  例一：We can take either the regular train or the high speed train. 我們可以搭一般的火車或搭高鐵。

  例二：You can have coffee either here or at the coffee shop. 你可以在這裡喝咖啡或者去咖啡廳。

4. It's hard to say. 很難說

  ★小提點：形容詞〈hard〉「困難」，有兩種情形可以用這個句子〈It's hard to say〉，不確定好不好的時候可以用這個句子，或者內心的有複雜的感受時也可以用這個句子。

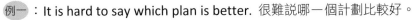

例一：It is hard to say which plan is better. 很難説哪一個計劃比較好。

例二：It is hard for me to say goodbye to Taiwan.　對我來説很難跟台灣説再見。

★小提點：〈It is too hard to say.〉「太困難了而無法説出」，這句和〈It's hard to say〉有很類似的用法。

Short Sentences

不尷尬短句

❶ Make sure you save the receipts so you can exchange unused NT dollars before you depart.
確保保存收據，這樣在你離開之前你可以兌換沒使用的台幣。

❷ What is the US currency rate now?
現在美金的匯率是什麼？

❸ We have a free currency converter on our website.
我們的網站上有一個免費的貨幣換算站。

❹ By the way, what other currencies do you accept for payment?
順便問一下，你們接受哪些可以支付消費的貨幣呢？

❺ We do not accept cash payment in Korean Won. US Dollars or Euros only, please.
我們不接受韓元的現金付款。我們只接受美元或歐元。

❻ I'm sorry we don't do the Indonesian rupiah exchange here.
很抱歉我們這裡沒有印尼幣的兌換。

❼ You don't have to go to banks to do currency exchanges.
你不一定要去銀行做外幣兌換服務。

❽ Usually there is a fee when you try to exchange money to a different currency.
通常當你要兌換貨幣時是要付費用的。

❾ You can exchange RMB（Ren Min Bi）now in Taiwan.
你現在可以在台灣兌換人民幣。

❿ I will pay in American dollars.
我將用美金付款。

Speak Up!
說出來！ MP3 080

Dialogue 01 對話

Customer: I'm not staying at this hotel, but was wondering if I could use your exchange services?

顧客：我不是住在這家飯店，但不知道是否可以用你的兌換服務？

Cashier: I will need to talk to my manager. Do you have your passport and the address where you are staying with you?

收銀員：我需要問一下我的經理。你有你的護照和你住哪裡的地址嗎？

Customer: I do. I would really appreciate it. I have a business meeting here today and am too busy to find a bank.

顧客：有的。我會很感激。我今天在這裡有一個商務會議，但是我太忙了沒有時間去找銀行。

Manager: Let me see your identification please. If it looks good, I will approve the transaction.

經理：請讓我看看你的證件。如果看起來可以，我會批准交易的。

Dialogue 02 對話

Guest: I need to exchange $100 US into NT dollars.

顧客：我要把 $100 美元換成新台幣。

Cashier: Certainly. Do you have your passport with you?

收銀員：當然可以。你有帶你的護照嗎？

Guest: Sure. Here.

顧客：當然。在這裡。

Cashier: What room are you staying in?

收銀員：你住在什麼房間？

Guest: #231.

顧客：# 231。

Cashier: I will need you to sign some paperwork and the exchange will be complete.

收銀員：我會需要你簽署一些文件，這樣就可以完成交易。

When working as the Front Office Cashier, be very careful while filling out paperwork, determining the rate of exchange, and making the transaction. There are many ways to make a mistake if you get distracted or don't focus on the task at hand. Know your company's routine and expectations as well as fees and commissions so that you can give your clients wise advice. If your company's policy is to only operate for guests, be prepared to give the non-resident person suggestions on places that will help them with their transaction. Traveler's Checks are generally viewed as acceptable everywhere and it may be a shock to the tourist who came prepared with them that they're not common or accepted many places in Taiwan. It will help if you can direct them to the American Express Office and know when it's open. At least give them the address and contact information so they can talk to the office about their choices. Most major Taiwanese hotels accept Traveler's Checks so your hotel should have a policy and procedure about them in place already.

當你在前台做收銀的工作時，你必須非常小心的填寫文件，同時確定交換的匯率，並完成交易。如果你出神或不專注於手邊的任務時，有許多細節就會讓你出錯。了解公司例行程序及期望就和費用和手續費一樣重要，這樣你可以給的客戶做明智的建議。如果公司的政策規定只能為住進的飯店客人做交易，你就應該準備好可以提供意見給非住客有關可以交易的地方。旅行支票通常被視為是到處都可以被接受的，對帶旅行支票的旅客來說，如果在台灣有很多地方不普遍或不接受旅行支票的話，對他們來說可能是一個衝擊。如果你可以幫他們直接找到美國運通公司和知道營業時間，這是會幫他們很大的忙。至少可以給他們地址和聯繫信息，以便他們可以跟該辦公室的人討論關於他們的選擇。大多數主要的台灣飯店都會接受旅行支票，所以你的飯店應該都有旅行支票的政策和程序。

Part Ⅲ　旅館英語

Conversations
不停住對話 MP3 081

Tourists want help planning a tour.
遊客希望櫃檯幫助規劃一個旅遊。

Guest 1	We want to see <u>as much as **possible** in a short time</u>.	我們希望在很短的時間內盡可能看到很多地方。
Concierge	We have all kinds of options for tours and day trips. You can even do short overnight trips.	我們有各種的旅遊和一日遊的選擇。你甚至可以做短程過夜的行程。
Guest 2	First we want to see Taipei's **historic** areas.	首先，我們希望看到台北的歷史區。
Guest 1	And a night market. I heard they are **incredible**.	和夜市。我聽說那裡很棒。

Concierge	What about a 3 hour tour that includes The National Palace Museum, The Martyr's Shrine, Chiang Kai Shek Memorial Hall, a temple, and some shopping? You will see the largest <u>collection</u> of valuable Chinese Art, Ming Dynasty architecture, and the city with an English speaking guide for about $38 each. <u>It will pick you up</u> here at the hotel and return you when you are finished.	要不要考慮 3 個小時的遊覽，這有包括國立故宮博物院、忠烈祠、中正紀念堂、一座寺廟和一些購物？你會看到很多有價值的中國藝術的收藏，明代建築，還有遊覽城市，這樣加一個英語導遊大約一個人是 $38 美金。他們會來飯店接你，結束後會把你帶回來。
Guest 1	What about the night market?	那夜市呢？
Concierge	One of our guests' favorite tours is the Night tour of Taipei. It's 3 and half hours long and includes a Mongolian BBQ dinner, a walk through Huaxi Street market, a visit to Longshan **temple** and a trip to the top of Taipei 101 for about $52.	我們有一個客人最喜歡的行程是叫台北夜之旅。這是 3 個半小時，有包括一個蒙古烤肉晚餐，逛逛華西街夜市，和參觀龍山寺，並到台北 101 的觀景台，這樣是 $52 美元。

Part II 旅館英語

Words 單字

* possible /ˈpɑsəbəl/　*adj.* 可能的
* historic /hɪsˈtɔrɪk/　*adj.* 歷史的
* incredible /ɪnˈkrɛdəbəl/　*adj.* 難以置信的
* collection /kəˈlɛkʃən/　*n.* 收藏
* temple /ˈtɛmpəl/　*n.* 廟

Grammar
文法片語

1. as much as possible 儘可能地很多

★小提點：這個文法形態是〈as...as possible〉「儘可能地……」，〈as soon as possible〉儘可能地快，〈as long as possible〉儘可能地長時間，〈as fast as possible〉儘可能地速度快。

例一：I try to avoid spicy food as much as possible. 我會儘量避免刺激性食物。

例二：We are late so we need to check in as soon as possible. 我們來晚了，因此我們需要儘快辦理入住手續。

2. in a short time 很快的；一會兒

★小提點：〈in a short time〉的直譯是「在很短的時間內」，類似的用法有〈in a minute〉在一分鐘內，〈in a moment〉一會兒。

例一：The front desk found a room for us in a short time. 櫃檯在很短的時間內就幫我們找到房間。

例二：You will get sun burned outside in a short time in summer. 夏天你在外面很快就會被曬傷。

3. collection of... ……的收藏

★小提點：名詞〈collection〉收藏，通常指的是有一定數量的收集，後面接介係詞〈of〉「由……組合的」

例一：The museum has a collection of hundreds of new age paintings. 那個博物館裡有收藏數以百計的新時代畫作。

例二：She has a collection of postcards and tickets from her travel. 她從她的旅行中收集了很多的明信片和票根。

4. It will pick you up here at the hotel. 他們會來飯店接你

★小提點：〈pick up〉有很多含意，其中有「將人或東西接到車子裡的意思」。

例一：I will pick up my luggage tomorrow. 明天我會去載我的行李。

★小提點：另外還有「無意間學會某樣語言或技能」的意思。

例二：Growing up with a Vietnamese nanny, she picked up some phrases and words in Vietnamese. 由越南籍保姆帶大，她無形中學會了一點越南文的句子和單字。

Short Sentences
不尷尬短句

❶ This travel package already includes accommodations.
此旅遊套票已包括住宿。

❷ You can make your own hotel arrangements as well.
你也可以自己安排你要住的飯店。

❸ I can go over those travel options for you, if you like.
如果你要的話，我可以和你一起看看這些旅遊的選擇。

❹ You can request an English speaking guide if you need it.
如果你需要的話，你可以要求一位英語導遊。

❺ There is a day tour bus that goes to several sites for $45.
有個白天旅遊巴士會去幾個站點，價格是 $45 美元。

❻ There are lots of online vacation packages and deals that meet your budget and travel needs.
網路上有很多適合你的預算和旅遊需求的度假套裝行程和促銷。

❼ Many vacation packages are all inclusive including flight, hotel and car rental.
很多的渡假套裝行程都是整套的包括有航班、飯店和汽車租賃。

❽ Some travel agencies make exclusive offers and deals on their website.
有一些旅行社會在他們的網站有獨家的優惠和促銷。

Part II 旅館英語

Speak Up!

說出來！

MP3 082

Dialogue 01 對話

Guest: I heard that there is a Tourist Shuttle Bus that I can take to main attractions. Can you tell me more about it?

顧客：我聽說有一個旅遊觀光巴士會去一些主要景點。你能告訴我更多一點的資訊嗎？

Concierge: Let me give you this pamphlet that gives you all those details. What do you think you'd like to see?

禮賓服務：讓我給你這本小冊子，這裡有所有你需要的細節。你想看到什麼？

Guest: I want to go to Yingge to buy some pottery to take home.

顧客：我想去鶯歌買一些陶器帶回家。

Dialogue 02 對話

Guest: We have a long weekend and would like to take an overnight trip to Sun Moon Lake. What would you suggest?

顧客：我們還有很長的週末假期，想藉此到日月潭過夜旅行。你有什麼建議呢？

Concierge: The easiest way to do it is with an English speaking tour that picks you up here at the hotel and returns you here. They provide overnight accommodations that are quite nice and suggest good places to eat as well.

禮賓服務：最簡單的方法是參加有英文導遊的行程，他們會來飯店接你，也會把你帶回這裡。他們有提供過夜住宿，這是是相當不錯的，他們也會建議吃的地方。

Dialogue 03 對話

Guest: Where is your favorite place to visit if you have free time?

顧客：如果你有空閒的時間，哪裡是你最喜歡參觀的地方呢？

Front Desk: Me? I love Tamsui. It is on the delta where the river meets the sea so you can see the water and is full of fun things to do.

櫃檯：我嗎？我很喜歡淡水。它位於入海口的三角洲上，所以你可以看到水，也有充滿樂趣的事情可以做。

The best thing you can do to help your guests make wise decisions is to travel on the tours you're recommending they take. Personal experience carries a lot of weight and you will know not to recommend a trip that requires walking a lot of stairs to someone who has difficulty navigating them. It will also give you a new perspective on Taiwan and give you a chance to practice your English when you go with an English Speaking group. Sometimes tour companies will offer hotel workers reduced rates when they travel with them so that they can sell more trips in the future. It doesn't hurt to ask the companies you are suggesting for that perk. Your travel will help them. Keep current on changes in the tourism industry. Make sure you have brochures in English whenever possible as well.

你可以做到幫助你的客人做出明智的決定的最好方法就是你自己去經歷一下你所建議給他們的行程。個人的經歷是很有份量的，在經歷後你就會知道，你不會對走路有困難的人建議需要走很多樓梯的行程。當你和講英語的旅行團一同出遊時，這會讓你有機會換一個角度看台灣，也有機會練習英語。有些旅遊公司會提供較低的費用給飯店工作人員，因為飯店工作人員參加旅遊公司的旅遊會讓他們可以在未來推銷更多的行程。跟旅遊公司建議你的目的是無害的。你參加他們的旅程將對他們的生意有幫助。

你要掌握不斷變化的旅遊業資訊。你也要確保盡可能有英文的導覽小冊子。

3.2.1　Hotel Facilities 飯店設施

Conversations

不停住對話 　MP3 083

Guest is asking Front Desk about things to do in or around the hotel.
顧客在問櫃檯有關可以在飯店內或周圍做的事情。

Guest	I noticed you had a marina <u>attached to</u> the hotel. Is it possible to rent a boat there?	我注意到你們有連接到飯店的碼頭。是否可以在那裏租一艘船呢？
Front Desk	You can not only rent a boat, but we offer **sailing**, fishing, scuba diving, and boat maintenance as well. Plus we do eco-**excursions** that introduce you to the local habitats.	你不但可以租一艘船，但我們提供帆船，釣魚，潛水，也有船隻保養。還有，我們做生態遊覽可以向你介紹當地的棲息地。
Guest	My wife doesn't like the water. What can she do while we go fishing?	我妻子不喜歡水。當我們去釣魚時，她可以做什麼呢？
Front Desk	We have bike rentals as well and the tennis court is nearby. She can walk there in <u>less than</u> 5 minutes.	我們有自行車出租服務，網球場也就在附近。她可以在不到 5 分鐘內步行到那裡。

Guest	She said something about a massage.	她有提到一些關於按摩的事。
Front Desk	I would be happy to schedule a massage for her with one of our **professional** masseuses in the Spa. There are some **aerobic** classes she can take too. I will give you a list of the times and the location for the classes for you to give her.	我會很樂意為她與我們的專業按摩師安排在水療部做按摩。她也可以上一些有氧課程。我會給你時間表和上課的地方,這樣你可以讓她看看。
Guest	That would keep her busy, but my mother is with us and she has trouble walking.	這將會讓她很忙,但我的媽媽和我們在一起,她行走有困難。
Front Desk	There is handicap access to all our facilities.	我們所有的設施都有無障礙通行的設計。

Part III 旅館英語

Words

單　字

* sailing /ˈselɪŋ/　*n.* 航行
* excursion /ɪkˈskɚʒən/　*n.* 遊覽;短程旅行
* professional /prəˈfɛʃənəl/　*adj.* 職業的;專業
* aerobic /ɛˈrobɪk/　*adj.* 有氧的

Grammar
文法片語

1. It is attached to...　連接到……

　　★小提點：動詞〈attach〉「連接」，這裡是用被動語態〈be attached〉，可以解釋為「被連接到」。

　　例一：The light is attached to the ceiling. 這個燈是安裝在天花板上。

　　例二：The pool is attached to the hotel. 這個游泳池有連接到飯店。

2. less than 少於

　　★小提點：〈less〉是〈little〉的比較級，後面接不可數名詞。和這個片語相同的是〈fewer than〉「少於」，〈fewer〉是〈few〉的比較級，後面接複數可數名詞。

　　例一：Everything in that shop is less than NT 100 dollars. 這個商店裡的每件產品都是低於台幣 100 元。

　　例二：I had less coffee than she did this morning. 今天早上我喝的咖啡比她喝得少。

　　★小提點：相反片語是〈more than〉「多於；超過」，〈I can't stay in Tainan more than 3 days.〉我不能在台南停留多餘三天。

3. a list of…　……的清單

　　★小提點：名詞〈list〉「目錄；列表」，片語〈a list of〉指列出幾件某某事，後面加名詞。

　　例一：His wife gives him a list of items to buy at the grocery store. 他的太太給他要在商店買東西的清單。

　　例二：The hotel has a list of various summer positions. 這個飯店有不同暑假職位的機會。

4. She has trouble walking.　她在行走上有困難

　　★小提點：名詞〈trouble〉「煩惱；困境」，在表示事情有困難時的句型是〈S+V+ trouble in +V+ing〉，很多時候是把〈in〉省略。

　　例一：She has trouble getting around downtown Taichung. 她在台中市中心逛的時候遇到一些問題。

例二：We have no trouble finding this hotel. 我們沒有問題的找到這個飯店。

★小提點：介係詞片語〈in trouble〉「有麻煩了」，〈We are in trouble.〉「我們有困難」，〈We are in deep trouble.〉「我們有很大的困難。」，〈We are obviously in trouble.〉「我們很明顯的有困難。」。

Short Sentences

不尷尬短句

❶ All our rooms are sound proof and have filtered fresh air.
我們所有的客房都有隔音，並有過濾的新鮮空氣。

❷ Our staff is multi-lingual. Which language would you prefer?
我們的員工都是多語言。你希望有哪種語言？

❸ We have several restaurants in the hotel.
我們在飯店裡就有幾個餐館。

❹ Our lounges offer a variety of simple snacks and munchies for someone who doesn't want a full meal.
我們的休息室有提供各種簡單小吃和零食，這是給不想要吃全餐的顧客使用的。

❺ The fitness and recreation rooms stay open 24 hours a day.
健身和娛樂室是全天 24 小時開著的。

❻ Our guests can receive a 10 % discount on Monday for spa service.
我們的客人可以在星期一享受水療服務的 10%的折扣。

❼ The Banquet Room is reserved for a wedding.
宴會廳有被一個婚禮預定了。

❽ There is a dance party in the ballroom tonight.
今晚的宴會廳有一個跳舞晚會。

❾ There is a bar next to the lobby in the hotel.
飯店內大廳的旁邊就有一個酒吧。

❿ Our Business Center can handle all of your business needs from color copying to faxing to packing and shipping items.
我們的商務中心可以處理所有你的業務需求，包括彩色複印、傳真、包裝和運輸東西。

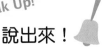

Speak Up!

說出來！ MP3 084

Dialogue 01 對話

Lead Housekeeper: There are six of the private cabanas on the deck of the pool rented out tonight for private candlelit meals.
房務部主管：今晚在泳池甲板有租出去六個池邊小屋是要做私人燭光晚餐的。

Housekeeper: What time do you want them set up by?
房務部人員：你希望什麼時候東西都擺設好？

Lead Housekeeper: 3 asked for dinner at 8 and the other 3 are after that, but you can set up all 6 settings at the same time.
房務部主管：有 3 個池邊小屋要求在 8 點吃晚餐，其他 3 個池邊小屋是在 8 點後，但你可以把 6 個池邊小屋在同一時間擺設好。

Dialogue 02 對話

Guest: I need a local secretary for a few hours while I'm here. Can you recommend one for me?
顧客：當我在這裡時，我需要幾個小時的本地秘書。你能幫我推薦一個嗎？

Front Desk: Certainly. That's easy. Our Business Center has professional secretaries who can also translate if you need them to and you can hire them by the hour or by the day.
櫃檯：當然可以。這是很簡單的。我們的商務中心擁有專業秘書，他們也可以做翻譯，如果你需要他們，你可以按小時或按天僱用他們。

Dialogue 03 對話

Guest: I will need a crib during our stay. What kind of cribs do you have and will they cost extra?
顧客：在我們的停留期間我會需要一張嬰兒床。你有什麼樣的嬰兒床，需要額外的費用嗎？

Reservationist: You can reserve a full size wooden crib for $10 a day.
接待員：你可以預留一個全尺寸木製嬰兒床，每天是 10 美元。

Facilities and amenities vary according to hotel and the quality of the hotel. While a high end hotel might offer a multi-lingual staff and a full Business Center, a mid-price hotel's Business Center may be a couple of computers and a copy machine. Almost all hotel rooms include small appliances such as a clock radio, TVs with remotes, hair dryers, irons and ironing boards, coffee pots and coffee and tea accessories. Charging stations, wall mounted large screen TVs and DVD/Blu-ray players are becoming more common as well. It doesn't matter if you work for a hotel with its own golf course or a hotel that offers a simple night's rest. Both require the same high quality of service for their guests. All guests, no matter how much they are spending for their stay, deserve to be given respect and professionalism from the staff.

　　根據飯店和品質，其設施和設備會有所不同。高端飯店可能會提供多語種的工作人員和一個完整的商務中心，而一個中等價位的飯店的商務中心可能就只有幾台電腦，和一台印表機。幾乎所有的飯店客房都會有包括小家電，如時鐘收音機、有遙控器的電視、吹風機、熨斗和燙衣板、咖啡壺、咖啡和茶配件。充電站、壁掛式大屏幕電視和 DVD/ 藍光播放器也都變得越來越普遍。但是無論你所工作的飯店是擁有自己的高爾夫球場或只是提供了一個簡單的夜間休息，這兩種類型的飯店都還是需要為他們的客人提供同樣高品質的工作。所有的客人，不管他們付多少住宿的房費都是值得得到工作人員的尊重和高度專業的服務。

Conversations

不停住對話 MP3 085

The Front Desk Clerk is helping a guest locate the laundry area.
櫃檯人員在幫助客人如何找到洗衣區。

Guest	I'd like <u>to ask you about</u> laundry.	我想請教你一下有關洗衣服的事。
Front Desk	We can send your laundry out, but it will take 24 hours for it to **return** or you can do it yourself.	我們可以把你的衣服送洗，但是需要 24 小時才能送回來，或者你可以自己洗。
Guest	You have a place where <u>I can do it myself</u>? I don't want to wait 24 hours. I need my dress pants tonight.	哪裡我可以自己洗衣的地方嗎？我不想等待 24 小時。我今晚就需要我的正式褲子。
Front Desk	It's in the **basement** and you'll need **change**.	那是在地下室，而且你需要零錢。
Guest	How much are the machines?	洗衣機需要多少錢呢？
Front Desk	It will <u>cost</u> you a couple of dollars to wash and **dry** a load.	清洗和烘乾一桶衣服將花費你一些錢。

Guest	That's not bad. I only have one load. Where did you say it is?	這還好。我只需要洗一桶衣服。你說這是在哪裡呢？
Front Desk	Take the elevator down to B, turn left off the elevator and follow the hallway. You will pass a vending machine area, a children's play area, and the laundry for guests is on the right. Do you need to get some change for the machines?	乘電梯下到 B，下了電梯左轉，並延著走廊直走。你會經過自動販賣機區，兒童遊樂區，供客人用的洗衣區就在右邊。你需要洗衣機的零錢嗎？
Guest	Yes, but is there a change machine in the laundry room?	是的，洗衣房裡面沒有換零錢機？
Front Desk	No, there isn't. There are machines that will sell you laundry soap, bleach, and softener though, so all you need to take down there is your laundry.	沒有，那裏沒有。有自動販賣機器可以買到洗衣皂、漂白劑和柔軟劑，所以你只需要把你要洗的衣服拿下去就可以了。

Part Ⅲ 旅館英語

Words

單 字

* return /rɪˋtɚn/ *v.* 返回
* basement /ˋbesmənt/ *n.* 地下室
* change /tʃendʒ/ *n.* 改變；零錢
* cost /kɔst/ *v.* 花費
* dry /draɪ/ *adj.* 乾的；乾燥的

Grammar
文法片語

1. to ask you about… 問你有關……的問題
   ★小提點：動詞〈ask〉問，〈ask about〉詢問，可以用〈ask+ 人 +about〉來詢問某人某件事。

   例一：I need to ask you about the schedule for tomorrow. 我要問你有關明天的行程安排。

   例二： The manager wants to ask you about Mr. Lee's reservation tonight. 經理想要問你有關李先生今晚預約的事。

2. You have a place where I can do it myself? 哪裡我可以自己洗衣？
   ★小提點：myself 為反身代名詞。同樣的用法有 himself、herself、yourself、itself、themselves、ourselves、yourselves。是「……自己的」的意思。

   例一：You must take care of yourself. 你必須自己照顧你自己。

   例二：They asked me a few questions about myself. 他們問了一些關於我的問題。

3. It will cost... 這會花費……
   ★小提點：動詞〈cost〉花費，通常是指金錢上的費用。

   例一：It will cost a little extra for hotel weekend rate. 飯店週末房價會有額外的費用。

   例二：The high quality tea will cost a lot of money. 高品質的茶葉是不便宜的。

   ★小提點：〈cost〉也可用來形容所付出的無形的時間，勞力或代價。

   例三：It you don't act now, it will cost you later. 如果你現在不採取行動，你以後會付出代價。

4. That's not bad. 這是不錯的
   ★小提點：形容詞〈bad〉不好的，〈not bad〉是負負得正，就是「不錯的」，有點比預期還好的意思。

   例一：The receptionist's English is not bad. 接待員的英語講的很不錯。

例二：This dish is not bad and I might order it again next time. 這菜不錯，我可能下次還會再點。

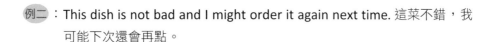

Short Sentences
不尷尬短句

❶ You can get ice from the ice machine on the 3rd floor.
在三樓你可以在製冰機裡拿到冰塊。

❷ The vending machine is not working right now.
自動販賣機現在壞了。

❸ There is a safe box in the room.
房間裡有保險箱。

❹ Everything in the small refrigerator in the room is free.
房間裡冰箱的東西都是免費的。

❺ As soon as you go into the room, you will see some fruits on the table. That's our welcoming gift for our guests.
你進房間後會看到桌上有水果，那是我們的迎賓禮。

❻ The tea on the table is famous Taiwan Alishan Oolong tea and you can brew it with hot water to drink.
桌面上的茶是台灣有名的阿里山烏龍茶，你可以用熱水沖泡來喝。

❼ There is a Keurig Coffee Machine in the room that you can use.
房間有膠囊咖啡機可以使用。

❽ There is a computer room on the second floor of the hotel and there is a printer you can use.
飯店二樓有電腦室可以上網。電腦室有印表機。

❾ There is one vending machine for drinks and another one for snacks at the end of the hallway.
在走廊的盡頭有一個飲料機和一個零食機。

❿ There is a self-help coffee area in the guest hall on the B2 floor at the hotel.
飯店 B2 樓層的貴賓廊裡面有自用咖啡區。

Speak Up!
說出來！ MP3 086

Dialogue 01 對話

Guest: I know you have laundry service, but do you also have a laundry area for guest to do their own laundry?

顧客：我知道你有洗衣服務，但你是否有可以供客人自己洗衣服的洗衣區？

Concierge: We do have a little laundry room for guests. Let me tell you where it is.

禮賓服務人員：我們是有一個供客人使用的小小洗衣房。讓我告訴你是在哪裡。

Dialogue 02 對話

Guest: I was wondering where the vending and ice machines are. I can't find one on our floor.

顧客：我想知道自動販賣機和製冰機在哪裡。我在我們的樓層無法找到。

Front Desk: They are on every other floor- on the even numbers.

櫃檯：自動販賣機和製冰機每隔一層樓都有，也就是在偶數號碼的層樓。

Dialogue 03 對話

Housekeeper: A guest told me the ice machine on the fifth floor wasn't giving her any ice. Have you tried it recently?

房務人員：有一位客人告訴我，在五樓的製冰機沒有給她任何的冰。你最近有試了嗎？

Head Housekeeper: I will check it out. In the meantime, can you deliver some ice to her room?

房務部主管：我會查查看。在此期間，你能把一些冰塊送到她的房間嗎？

Housekeeper: Yes.

房務人員：我會的。

Ice machines, vending machines, and laundry areas seem to be either hidden away in hard to find spots or malfunctioning and no one knows who's responsible for fixing them. Most of the time the malfunctioning is user error; meaning the guest couldn't figure out from the directions how to make them work. Using large poster size images demonstrating how to use the machines transcends languages and will decrease the problems guests have with them. Make sure the laundry area is clean and inviting instead of a place you don't want to sit for an hour or two while a load of wash is completed. Put books, magazines, and a few toys in the area and provide seating. Keep laundry supplies stocked and the machines spotless. It's difficult enough to have to give up some of your work time or vacation time to do laundry without being stuck in a dreary place! You may not be the person responsible for the design of public areas, but you can help keep it inviting and pleasant by checking it frequently. If a vending machine is empty, tell a supervisor so they can call and have it filled. If the ice machine is broken, report it.

製冰機、自動販賣機、洗衣區似乎都是在比較隱藏的地方，如果有髒的地方或故障都是不太明顯，也沒有人知道誰要負責修復。大多數的故障原因是用戶的操作錯誤，這意味著客人弄不清楚如何操作。如果能使用大海報這樣大的圖像來顯示如何使用機器是可以超越語言的說明，並會減少客人使用上的問題。你要確保洗衣區是乾淨和溫馨，而不是一個你在等待洗衣的時候也不想坐上一兩個小時的地方。把書籍、雜誌和幾個玩具擺放在該區域，並提供座位。保持洗衣物用品的庫存，也要讓洗衣機一塵不染。要放棄一些工作時間或休假時間來洗衣服本來就是讓人感到很難做到的事，所以客人更不希望卡在一個沉悶的地方！你可能不是負責公共區域的設計的人，但你可以經常檢查這些小地方來讓這裡保持令人感到溫馨及舒適。如果自動販賣機是空的，你可以告訴上司讓人填補庫存，如果製冰機壞了，也應該要立即報告。

Unit 02 Facilities / Housekeeping 設施 / 房務部

3.2.3 Complimentary Breakfast / 早餐服務

Conversations 不停住對話 MP3 087

A guest appears at the breakfast **buffet**, but has lost her breakfast **coupon**.
一位客人出現在自助早餐，但丟了她的早餐券。

Mother	I know I had in my hand when I left my room, but I can't find it now. I'm sorry!	我知道，我離開房間時早餐券是在我的手上的，但我現在無法找到它。對不起！
Host	No problem, Ma'am. What is your room number?	沒問題的，夫人。你的房間號碼是幾號？
Mother	I can't remember. Either #345 or #346. I'm in one and my **daughter** is in the other. There she is now. (to daughter approaching her). What room am I in, dear?	我記不起來了。不是 # 345 就是 # 346 。我住一間，我的女兒住另一間。她來了。（女兒正在走近她）。哪個房間是我的，親愛的？
Daughter	You're in room # 356, mom, why?	媽媽，你住 356 號房，為什麼這麼問？

Mother	I lost my breakfast coupon and the boy asked me what room I was in and I couldn't remember.	我丟了我的早餐券，這個男孩問我是在哪個房間，我就是記不起來。
Host	Here is another coupon with your room number written on it. Leave it on the table when you are finished and someone will pick it up when they clean the table. Do you need another coupon for tomorrow?	這裡是另外的早餐券，上面有寫你的房間號碼。當你用完餐後，請把早餐券放在桌子上時，當工作人員清桌子時，他們會收早餐券。你明天需要另外的早餐券麼？
Mother	Oh no, I'm sure the rest of the week's coupons are in my room.	哦，不需要的，我很肯定這週其餘的優惠券都是在我的房間。
Host	You can either notify the front desk or me if you find they are lost as well. Is this your first time having breakfast with us? We have both Western and Asian breakfast items on the buffet.	如果你發現其餘的優惠券也丟了，你可以通知櫃檯或我。這是你第一次吃我們的早餐嗎？我們的自助餐有西式和亞洲風味的早餐項目。

Part II 旅館英語

Words
單 字

* buffet /ˈbʌfət/   *n.* 自助餐
* coupon /ˈkupɑn/   *n.* 贈券
* daughter /ˈdɔtɚ/   *n.* 女兒
* leave /liv/   *v.* 離開
* notify /ˈnotəˌfaɪ/   *v.* 通告；通知

Grammar
文法片語

1. I lost my... 我遺失了我的……
   ★小提點：過去式動詞〈lost〉遺失，原形動詞是〈lose〉，因為是過去發生所以用過去式。〈I lost my wallet.〉「我遺失了我的錢包」，如果用現在式則表示「常態性」的事情。〈She loses her car keys all the time.〉「她常常遺失她的車鑰匙。」
   ★小提點：〈lost〉也可以當形容詞，〈I am lost.〉這句可以有很多的解釋，「我迷路了」、「我搞不清楚」、「我迷失（人生的）方向」。

2. Leave it on the table 留在桌子上
   ★小提點：動詞〈leave〉離開，請對方把東西留在某個地方就可以用「leave something on somewhere」。
   例一：Just leave it as it is. The housekeeping will clean it. 就放著吧，房務部會來清理。
   例二：I will leave it up to the manager to make the decision. 我會讓經理來做決定。
   ★小提點：〈Leave it.〉也可以用在非物品的形容，當對話時，你要對方「不要再講了」或「不要再提某件事時」，也可以用〈Leave it.〉，例〈Please leave it. I don't want to talk about it anymore.〉「不要再提了，我不想再談這件事」。

3. pick it up 把東西撿起來
   ★小提點：當中間用代名詞時片語是〈pick it up〉，如果用名詞，可以有兩種形態「pick the trash up」或「pick up the trash」，意思完全一樣。
   例一：Can you pick up the toy? 你可以把玩具撿起來嗎？
   例二：We need to pick up the luggage in the morning. 我們需要在早上去拿行李。

275 Unit 2 Facilities / Housekeeping 設施 / 房務部

不尷尬短句

❶ Breakfast is included in the hotel price.
早餐包括在房間的價格內。

❷ The breakfast time is from 5:30 AM to 11:00 AM.
早餐時間是早上 5:30 到 11:00。

❸ I am sorry, but if you lost your breakfast coupon, we have to have charge you.
很抱歉，早餐券不見了，需要收取費用。

❹ I'm sorry. The breakfast time is over.
對不起，早餐供應已經結束了。

❺ I am sorry. We are completely out of fried eggs and bacon.
很抱歉，我們的荷包蛋與培根目前已經完全沒有了。

❻ We have Japanese, Chinese and continental style breakfast.
我們有日式、中式、歐式早餐。

❼ We offer American style breakfast.
我們提供美式早餐。

❽ We can made fresh waffles for you.
我們可以幫你做新鮮的鬆餅。

❾ The coffee is freshly brewed every morning.
咖啡都是每天早上新鮮現煮的。

❿ The hotel's restaurant offers afternoon tea time.
這個飯店的餐廳有提供下午茶。

Speak Up!
說出來！
MP3 088

Dialogue 01 對話

Waitress: Would you like some coffee? We have a complete coffee bar to the left of the fresh fruit. Do you see where it is?

服務員：你想喝點咖啡？在新鮮水果的左側我們有一個完整的咖啡吧。你有看到它在哪裡嗎？

Guest: I'd really like some tea.

顧客：我真的很希望能喝茶。

Waitress: There is an assortment of tea bags next to the coffee and I will bring a pot of hot water to the table for you.

服務員：在咖啡的旁邊還有不同的茶包，我會幫你帶來一壺熱水。

Dialogue 02 對話

Guest: I can't find the pancakes. You have syrup and French toast, but no pancakes.

顧客：我找不到煎餅。你有糖漿和法式吐司，但沒有煎餅。

Waitress: I'm sorry but we aren't serving pancakes today. They are on the menu for tomorrow and the French toast is delicious. The chef just delivered a fresh pan full of them a few minutes ago.

服務員：對不起，但我們今天不提供煎餅。他們是在明天的菜單上，但是法式吐司很好吃。廚師在幾分鐘前剛剛送上新鮮做好的法式吐司。

Dialogue 03 對話

Guest: How much longer are you serving breakfast?

顧客：你們早餐時間還剩下多久？

Host: We serve until 9:30 and it's 9 o'clock now. On the weekends we serve until 10 o'clock, but on weekdays we finish at 9:30.

接待員：我們是服務到 9:30，現在是 9 點。在週末我們是服務到 10 點，但是在平日是在 9:30 結束。

Job Wisdom
職業補給站

Soup and rice for breakfast? For Westerners, certain foods are breakfast foods only and aren't something you'd eat outside of breakfast times. While things are changing slowly, they still think that scrambled eggs, toast, and bacon are only breakfast food. Many will need explanations of the food found on the breakfast buffet that they don't consider breakfast food. Learning the English names for traditional Chinese food will help you explain to guests what the food is and what it's made of. Having that knowledge may encourage them to take risks and try new foods.

As a server at a breakfast buffet, clean plates off the table before they pile up and make suggestions of new items they might want to try next time. If the line for omelets, fresh waffles, or something else is short, let your guests know. Keep the coffee flowing and the water glasses full as well.

早餐喝湯和吃飯？對於西方人來說，某些食物就是早餐的食品，而不是在早餐時間之外你會想要吃的。雖然情況有在慢慢的變化，他們仍然認為炒雞蛋，烤麵包和培根才是早餐食品。有許多人會需要知道什麼原因飯店所提供的自助早餐是他們不認為是早餐的食品。如果你有學習中國傳統食品的英文名稱，這會有助於你解釋給客人知道這是什麼食物以及是什麼做的。當你有了這樣的知識，你就有可能鼓勵他們大膽來嘗試新的食物。

作為自助早餐的服務員，在髒盤子疊得太多之前，你就要把桌子的盤子拿開，你也可以建議他們下一次可能想要嘗試的東西。如果蛋餅，新鮮鬆餅，或其他什麼東西的排隊是短的，你可以讓你的客人知道。你也要同時注意倒滿咖啡與水。

3.2.4 The Room Service 客房服務

Conversations

不停住對話 🍷 MP3 089

Guest is ordering room service for a late night snack.
顧客在點客房服務的宵夜。

Guest	This is Room #765. Is it too late to order room service? I don't need a full dinner, but I am hungry.	這是房間 # 765。現在點客房服務是不是太晚呢？我並不需要一個全套的晚餐，但我肚子餓了。
Room Service	Our kitchen is open until **midnight** and we have <u>a variety of</u> late night snacks available. Do you see the copy of our menu on the desk in your room?	我們的廚房是開放至午夜，我們是有提供多種宵夜。你在你的房間的桌子有看到菜單嗎？
Guest	Can I still order a club sandwich?	我還可以點一份俱樂部三明治嗎？
Room Service	Yes sir. <u>It comes with</u> chips and pickle.	是的，先生。這是有配備了洋芋片和醃製小黃瓜。
Guest	Perfect. <u>Leave off</u> the **avocado** and don't toast the bread as well. I'd like a **domestic** beer with that too.	太棒了。請不要放酪梨，麵包也不要烤。我也想點國內品牌啤酒。

Room Service	That is a club sandwich without an avocado on untoasted bread with a domestic beer for Room #765. Correct?	你點的是一個俱樂部三明治，不要有酪梨，麵包也不要烤，還有一瓶國內品牌啤酒送到房間 # 765。這樣對嗎？
Guest	Yes, and I see you have homemade cookies and milk. What kind of cookies are they?	是的，我看到你們有自製的餅乾和牛奶。是什麼樣的餅乾呢？
Room Service	Chocolate chip with **walnuts**.	巧克力片與核桃。
Guest	Can you send up the cookies without the milk?	可以只要餅乾但不要牛奶嗎？
Room Service	Of course. Are you going to be wanting room service in the morning? If you give me your order now and tell me what time you'd like, it will be **delivered** within 15 minutes of the order time-guaranteed.	當然。早上需要客房服務嗎？如果你現在給我你的訂單，告訴我你什麼時候想吃早餐，保證在預定時間不超過 15 分鐘就可以送到。

Part Ⅲ 旅館英語

Words
單　字

* midnight /ˋmɪdˏnaɪt/　*n.* 午夜；半夜
* avocado /ˏævəˋkɑdo/　*n.* 酪梨
* domestic /dəˋmɛstɪk/　*adj.* 國內的
* walnut /ˋwɔlnət/　*n.* 核桃
* deliver /dɪˋlɪvə/　*v.* 送達

Grammar
文法片語

1. a variety of⋯ 各種各樣的⋯⋯

★小提點：名詞〈variety〉多種類，〈a variety of 〉後面加名詞，〈all sorts of 〉各種，〈all kinds of〉各種，後面都是可以加名詞，這三個片語程度的用法都差不多。

例一：The store sells a variety of toys. 這家商店出售各種不同的玩具。

例二：The gift shop in the hotel sells a variety of local souvenirs. 這個禮品店酒店出售各種當地紀念品。

例三：The city offers a variety of day trips to visit tourist locations. 這個城市有提供各種不同參觀旅遊點的一日遊。

2. It comes with⋯ 附有⋯⋯

★小提點：片語〈come with〉通常用在商品附帶有另外的東西或主要的東西具備有的配件，這也常用在點餐時所附加的東西如沙拉、飲料。

例一：The meal comes with a hamburger, fries and drink. 這個套餐是包括有漢堡、薯條和飲料。

例二：Does that order come with salad? 這個點餐是否有配沙拉？

例三：The vacation package comes with two tickets to the museum. 這個度假套票含有兩張博物館的票。

3. leave off 除掉

★小提點：〈leave off〉除掉某件事，常用在從列表裡除掉某件東西。

例一：Leave off the ball room from the cleaning list since it was cleaned last night. 請不需要清潔舞廳，因為昨天晚上就清理好了。

例二：Please leave off the onion. 請不要放洋蔥。

★小提點：〈leave out〉省略或排除，這個片語有阻止要做的行為，不給予對方考慮的機會。

例三：Leave out the cinnamon next time you make cookies. 下次你做餅乾時請不要放肉桂粉。

例四：Leave out the meat to thaw before dinner time. 晚餐前請把肉拿出來退冰。

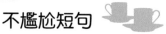

不尷尬短句

❶ The order will take 30 minutes to prepare and deliver to your room.
你所點的東西會在 30 分鐘後會準備好送到你的房間。

❷ Please call down when you are finished and I will come fetch the dirty dishes immediately.
當你用完餐後請打電話下來，我會立刻去取髒盤子。

❸ You can call for a breakfast order the night before, so you won't have to wait so long in the morning.
你可以在前一天晚上點早餐的食物，這樣你在早上就不會等太久。

❹ You can order breakfast from room service.
你可以透過客房服務點早餐。

❺ Would you like to see what's on the menu today?
你想看看今天菜單上有什麼嗎？

❻ There is a menu on the phone table in each guest room.
在每間客房的電話桌上都有菜單。

❼ You can order room service in the morning.
你可以在早晨請求服務。

❽ Please give us an hour's notice about room service so that you get it on time.
請於預定的客房服務時間前一小時通知，這樣我們可以把你需要的東西準時送達給你。

❾ Please make sure you call in the morning if you decide you need room service.
如果你決定你需要什麼客房服務，請確定你在早晨打電話來。

❿ You can just leave your tray in the room. The housekeeping will take it in the morning.
用完餐點放在房間就好，隔天一早會有清潔人員來處理。

Part III 旅館英語

Speak Up!

說出來！　　MP3 090

Dialogue 01 對話

Guest: I would like to order breakfast for tomorrow.
顧客：我想訂購明天的早餐。

Room Service: Very good. What would you like?
客房服務：好的。你想要什麼？

Guest: The smoked salmon bagel and the power smoothie.
顧客：煙燻鮭魚貝果和能量冰沙。

Room Service: And what time would you like your order delivered?
客房服務：你要你所點的食物什麼時候送到呢？

Guest: About 7:30 am.
顧客：約早上 7:30。

Dialogue 02 對話

Guest: I would like a bottle of Pinot and a platter of cheese and fruit for two delivered to room #598 tonight.
顧客：我今晚想要一瓶黑比諾和兩人份的奶酪和水果拼盤送到房間 # 598。

Room Service: Very good, sir. Any specific time you'd like it?
客房服務：好的，先生。哪一個任何特定的時間是你希望的呢？

Guest: Around 8 o'clock would be good. Can you include some chocolates with that order? It's our anniversary.
顧客：8 點會是好時間。你可以包括一些巧克力嗎？這是我們的結婚紀念日。

Dialogue 03 對話

Room Service: (Knocking on door) Room Service! Where would you like me to set up your order?
客房服務：（在敲門）這是客房服務！你要我把你所訂的食物放在哪裡呢？

Guest: How about the small table by the arm chair. I'll move the papers off it.
顧客：就放在扶手椅旁邊的小桌子如何？我會把這些文件拿開。

Working room service will keep you very busy taking orders, delivering orders, and retrieving dirty dishes. You will report to the Room Service manager who will tell you which floors you are working as well as any needed restocking. Keep the food cart well stocked so that if a guest requests more napkins, condiments, or extra glasses you have them available instantly. When delivering the food, go over the order with the guest verifying that it is correct. If it is wrong, fix it right away. Be professional at all times. If a guest's pet dog jumps on you and licks your hands, remember to change your clothes and wash your hands before preparing to deliver the next meal so that allergens won't be transferred to your next guest. If there is no room to place the food in the room, ask permission before moving any of the guest's items. When taking the order, be quick but also listen carefully to any requests so that you deliver the food in a manner the guest wanted. If a guest can't find the menu, offer to run one up to her and take her order in person.

在客房餐飲服務的工作會讓你非常忙碌，因為你要接受訂單、交付訂單、以及收髒盤子。你會向客房服務經理報告狀況，客房服務經理會告訴你要在哪一樓工作，以及任何需要補充的庫存。你要保持推車有充足的庫存，這樣如果客人要求更多的餐巾，調味品，或額外的杯子，你就可以馬上給他們。當你在提供食物時，你要和客人再確認訂單是正確的。如果是錯誤的，你就要馬上解決。你要在任何時候都表現出專業的態度。如果客人的寵物狗跳上你的身上或舔你的手，你要記得換你的衣服，並在準備下一個訂單時之前要洗手，這樣過敏原才不會由你轉移傳染給下一個客人。如果在房間裡沒有足夠的空間來放置食物，在移動任何客人的物品之前，要先徵得同意。當你在接受訂單時，你的動作要很快，也要認真聽取任何的要求，這樣你才會用客人要的方式來提供他們所點的東西。如果客人無法找到菜單，你要提供給她另一個菜單，也要親自寫下她要點的東西。

Conversations
不停住對話 MP3 091

Guests are speaking to Concierge at the Resort.
顧客在度假飯店與禮賓人員說話。

Guest 1	We are here for three days. Is there anything we need to schedule ahead of time in order to do it?	我們會在這裡三天。有什麼活動是我們需要先提前安排才可以做的呢？
Guest 2	I really want to do scuba diving and sail a Hobie cat.	我真的很想潛水，和來一趟霍比式帆船航行。
Concierge	Let's book the events you know you want to do now so that you can **fit** everything in. How about scuba diving Tuesday morning at 10?	讓我們現在就預訂你所知道的活動，這樣你就可以做好一切的計劃。你覺得週二上午 10 點潛水的活動如何呢？
Guest 2	Do you have a later slot. I'm planning on sleeping!	你有沒有比較晚一點的空缺。我是打算要先睡覺！
Concierge	We do, but you want to scuba dive early in the day to see all the different kinds of fish.	我們是有，但是如果你早一點潛水的話，那就能看到所有不同種類的魚。

Guest 1	We'll take it! What about sailing?	我們就訂下了！帆船呢？
Concierge	I can reserve a boat for you for Wednesday afternoon. Is 3 o'clock fine?	我可以為你在週三下午保留一條小船。3 點好嗎？
Guest 2	Perfect. What about renting a **scooter**?	很棒。租一輛摩托車如何？
Concierge	You need to have an international driver's license to rent scooters, but we have plenty of bikes available.	你需要有一個國際駕照才能租摩托車，但我們有很多的自行車可供你選擇。
Guest 2	Next time I'll have the **license**!	下一次我會帶駕照來的！
Concierge	Have you used your free tea coupons yet? If not, I suggest you go to one of the coffee shops today and try it. There will be live music on the **veranda** from 2 to 4 o'clock today and I think you will enjoy the music.	你用了你的免費茶券了嗎？如果沒有，我建議你今天去其中一個咖啡館。今天 2 至 4 點在陽台會有現場音樂，我想你會喜歡那樣的音樂。

Part Ⅲ 旅館英語

Words
單 字

* fit /fɪt/   *v.* 合適

* scooter /ˈskutɚ/   *n.* 摩托車

* license /ˈlaɪsəns/   *n.* 駕照

* veranda /vəˈrændə/   *n.* 陽台；走廊

* enjoy /ɛnˈdʒɔɪ/   *v.* 享樂；喜歡

Grammar 文法片語

1. in order to 為了……

★小提點：名詞〈order〉秩序，〈in order to〉後面加原形動詞，這個片語可以在句子的前面，也可以在句子的後面。這個片語的用法通常聽起來是比較正式的。

例一：In order to catch the train on time, we have to leave the hotel earlier.
為了要趕坐到火車的時候，我們不得不提早離開飯店。

例二：We should call early in order to get the reservation for the summer.
我們應該要早一點打電話才能預約到夏天時的房間。

2. I'm planning on sleeping! 我是打算要先睡覺！

★小提點：〈plan〉動詞，計畫。也可以當名詞使用。此句型為〈plan on doing something〉計畫做某事。

例一：When do you plan on going to Taiwan? 你計畫什麼時候去台灣呀？

例二：The wedding was fine and everything went as planned. 婚禮一切依照預定計畫內進行。

3. plenty of… 很多……

★小提點：名詞〈plenty〉豐富，〈plenty of〉後面可以加可數名詞，也可以加不可數名詞。

例一：Taiwan has plenty of natural resources. 台灣有很多的自然資源。

例二：They have plenty of time to get ready. 他們有很多的時間可以做準備。

★小提點：形容詞〈plentiful〉「很多的」，通常是修飾事物。

例三：Tomatoes are plentiful in the summer. 在夏天有很多的番茄。

4. you will enjoy… 你會喜歡……

★小提點：動詞〈enjoy〉享樂，這個動詞後面可以直接加名詞和動名詞。

例一：I hope you enjoy your time in Taiwan. 我希望你喜歡在台灣的時間。

例二：The two American tourists really enjoyed their trip to Taipei. 那兩個美國觀光客真的很喜歡去臺北的旅程。

Short Sentences

不尷尬短句

❶ Our resort is an ideal location.
我們的度假飯店是位在一個理想的位置。

❷ You can rent a holiday villa in Kenting.
你可以在墾丁租度假別墅。

❸ Our reservations for the villa by the sea are all full.
我們在海邊的度假飯店的預訂全部都爆滿。

❹ We offer a vacation package for the Green Island with three nights of villa stay.
我們提供綠島的度假套票包括住三晚的別墅。

❺ You can consider renting a holiday villa in the mountains.
你也可以考慮在山上租一個度假別墅。

❻ Our villa is rated number 1 by a famous domestic traveler's magazine.
我們的度假飯店由國內知名雜誌評選為第一名。

❼ When you come to our villa, you must join the special SPA we have here.
當你來我們的度假飯店時，你一定要參加我們特別的 SPA。

❽ The weekday for the villa is 20 % off but the weekend rate is 20 % more of the regular price.
平日打 8 折。假日會比平常日貴 20%。

❾ We have several individual buildings so you can enjoy complete privacy.
我們有獨棟的建築物，你可享受完全的隱密。

❿ In our resort, we have a huge garden with flowers and trees, as well as swimming pool for adults and play pool for children.
在我們的度假飯店裡，我們有一個很大的花園，花園裡有花和樹、我們也有成人游泳池和兒童戲水池。

說出來！ MP3 092

Dialogue 01 對話

Guest: Is it easy to get to your resort by the public bus?
顧客：乘坐公共巴士可以容易到你的度假飯店嗎？

Front Desk: Well, the bus only comes here twice a day. It is easier to take the taxi to the resort.
櫃檯：還好，巴士一天只到這裡兩次。坐計程車會比較容易到達度假飯店。

Guest: Okay. Thanks.
顧客：好的。謝謝。

Dialogue 02 對話

Guest: I heard you have a children's play area in this resort, but I can't find it.
顧客：我聽說你在這個度假飯店有一個兒童遊樂區，但我找不到它。

Front Desk: It's in the basement of the second building. Go to the yellow building and take the elevator all the way to the bottom. I'm sure you'll find it once you're in the right building.
櫃檯：這是在第二大樓的地下室。你到黃色樓，乘電梯一路到底。我敢肯定，一旦你在正確的建築物裡你就會發現它。

When you say resort, people think luxury. They are willing to pay more for a vacation to a resort because they are expecting to be pampered and to have time to relax or try new things. A resort offers a variety of activities from planting a small flower, arts and crafts for the children, and physical outdoor experiences. The important thing for your guests is that they create beautiful new memories with their families and friends. When something disrupts that positive experience, they will get frustrated and feel cheated. Whether it is illness or poor service, the feelings they leave with are the feelings they will share with everyone they meet. If they are having a bad time and you can help them cope with the things out of your control, they will remember your kindness. It will color a bad day with warmth. If an activity is cancelled, offer them a choice of different activities to do instead. You can't control the weather on a day trip day, but you can suggest they have a spa day instead of a hiking day. You can make a difference in the memories they take home.

當你說是度假飯店時，一般人會有奢侈的聯想。有些人願意花費更多的錢去度假飯店，因為他們期待被寵愛，並有時間來放鬆身心，或嘗試新事物。度假飯店會提供多種活動包括種植小花，為孩子設計的美勞活動，和戶外體驗。對你的客人重要的是，他們要與他們的家人和朋友創造美好的回憶。如果有事情發生而擾亂了這樣正面的經驗，他們會感到沮喪，也感覺被騙了。無論是客人自己生病或惡劣的服務，他們離開度假飯店時的感覺就是他們以後會和所見到的每一個人分享的感覺。如果他們有不好的時光，在你不能的控制情況下你還是可以幫助他們應付，他們會記得你的好意。如此，你就像用一個溫暖心把客人不好的一天增添色彩。如果活動被取消，你可以為他們提供不同的活動做代替。你不能控制一日遊的天氣，但是你可以建議他們去水療中心來替代健行。你可以幫助他們把不同的回憶帶回家。

Part II 旅館英語

Unit 03 Handling Special Situations
特殊情況處理

3.3.1 Deal with Guests' Complaints 處理房客抱怨

Conversations

不停住對話 MP3 093

Angry guest confronts the front desk.
憤怒的客人向櫃檯抗議。

Guest	This is the worst hotel I've ever stayed at. Not only are there kids running and yelling in the halls on my floor, but the room is **filthy**.	這是我住過的最差的酒店。在我住的層樓的走廊不僅有孩子跑來跑去並大聲喊叫,而且房間很髒。
Front Desk	What room number are you in, sir? Let me call **security** and send him up to quiet the children <u>right away</u>.	先生,你的房間號碼是幾號?讓我呼叫保全讓他馬上去叫孩子安靜。
Guest	Room 732, but that doesn't **solve** the dirty room. There are spots on my sheets- SPOTS! <u>Didn't you bother to put clean sheets on the bed?</u>	房間 732,但這樣還是沒有解決房間骯髒的問題。我的床單上有斑點!你們就不會把乾淨的床單鋪在床上嗎?

Front Desk	Security is on the way to quiet down the children and I'm sending up housekeeping immediately. I don't know what happened, but dirty sheets are NOT acceptable. I'm sorry. Is there anything we can do to make you happy?	保全正要去平息孩子的嬉鬧聲，我也馬上請清潔部上去看看。我不知道發生了什麼事，但我們不允許給客人髒的床單。對不起。有什麼我們可以做到讓你高興的嗎？
Guest	Send maintenance while you're at it. I can't get the heater to turn on and it's freezing in here.	如果可以的話，馬上請維修來。暖氣無法打開，房間裡好冷。
Front Desk	I'll make sure Housekeeping checks on it when they get there.	我會確保客房部到那裡時也做一下檢查。
Guest	I hope they hurry.	我希望他們快點來。

Part Ⅲ 旅館英語

Words 單　字

* filthy /ˈfɪlθi/　*adj.* 髒亂的
* security /sɪˈkjʊrəti/　*n.* 保全；安全；保證金
* solve /sɑlv/　*v.* 解決
* acceptable /əkˈsɛptəbəl/　*adj.* 可接受的

Grammar 文法片語

1. right away 馬上

★小提點：副詞片語〈right away〉強調動作迅速，一點時間都沒耽誤到。

例一：The manager will be here right away to help you. 經理會馬上來幫你。

例二：We are leaving right away. 我們馬上就離開。

例三：The bus should be here shortly. 巴士應該很快就會來這裡了。

2. Didn't you bother to put clean sheets on the bed? 你們就不會把乾淨的床單鋪在床上嗎？（把乾淨的床單鋪在床上有很麻煩你嗎？）

★小提點：bother 是一個很常見又常用的動詞。意思為打擾別人。

例一：Are the children bothering you? 小孩打擾到你了嗎？

★小提點：也可以解釋為「使人困擾、不開心」。

例二：Does it bother you that people think you're the older sister? 別人把你當成姐姐有帶給你困擾嗎？

3. what happened 發生了什麼事

★小提點：原形動詞〈happen〉發生，過去式是〈happened〉，通常事情已經發生了才會導致這樣的說法，所以比較常用的會是過去式的用法〈what happened〉。

例一：We need to tell the police what happened in the night market. 我們需要告訴警方在夜市發生了什麼事。

例二：I don't know what happened, but I lost my luggage. 我不知道發生了什麼，但我失去了我的行李。

例三：Do you know what happened to him? 你知道他發生什麼事嗎？

4. Not acceptable. 不能接受

★小提點：形容詞〈acceptable〉令人接受的，〈not acceptable〉通常是在指不能被接受的行為或狀況

例一：Your loud noise is not acceptable in the lobby. 你在大廳大聲講話是不能被接受的。

例二：The room condition is not acceptable. 房間的狀況是不能接受的。

★小提點：相反的說法就是〈It is acceptable.〉「可以被接受的。」，也可以加強語氣地說〈It is very acceptable.〉「非常可以被接受的。」，其他常用的有〈culturally acceptable〉文化上可以被接受的，〈socially acceptable〉社交上可以被接受的，〈perfectly acceptable〉完全可以被接受的。

Short Sentences

不尷尬短句

❶ The music is too loud. Do you know when they will quit?
音樂太大聲。你知道他們什麼時候會停止？

❷ The lobby is a bit noisy because a group of high school athletes just are checking in the hotel.
大廳有點吵，因為有一群高中運動員剛剛住進飯店。

❸ The front desk has called the electrician to fix the air conditioner.
櫃檯已經叫電工來修理空調。

❹ The TV remote is not working, but we can replace it with a new one right away.
電視機遙控器壞了，但我們可以馬上更換一個新的。

❺ The guest complained that the hair dryer is making a strange noise.
客人抱怨說，吹風機會發出奇怪的聲音。

❻ We are sorry that the bed sheets have spots. I will call the housekeeper to replace it with a new one.
我們對床單有斑點感到很抱歉。我會請房務部更換一個新的。

❼ The rooms have four cockroaches. We need to change to a different hotel so please return our deposit.
房間有四隻蟑螂，我們需要換旅館所以請退我們訂金。

❽ The toilet in the room is broken, but we already asked someone to fix it.
房間廁所的馬桶壞掉了，但我們已經請人修理了。

❾ There is no water from the faucet, but we will send someone to repair it.
水龍頭沒有水，但我們會派人去修理。

❿ We have a team of technicians and they can fix anything in the hotel.
我們有一個修理技師的團隊，他們可以修理飯店內的任何東西。

Part III 旅館英語

Speak Up! 說出來！　MP3 094

Dialogue 01 對話

Lead Housekeeper: Room # 454 complained that the room was dirty yesterday. He said that the floor hadn't been mopped in the bathroom and that the counter tops were dirty as well. What happened?

房務部主管：房間 # 454 投訴說昨天房間很髒。他說，浴室的地板沒有擦，而檯面也是很髒。發生了什麼事呢？

Housekeeper: Room # 454? Let me think. Is that the room where the air conditioner wouldn't come on? I think so. I was in the middle of cleaning it when maintenance arrived and made me leave while they worked on it.

房務部人員：房間 # 454 嗎？讓我想想。那是房間裡的空調壞的那間嗎？我想是的。我在清潔的時候剛好修理部的人到達，在他們修理時要我出去。

Dialogue 02 對話

Guest: The people next to me are playing their TV too loud. I can hear everything the actors are saying.

顧客：住在我旁邊的人看電視的聲音太大。我可以聽到演員講話的所有一切內容。

Front Desk: What room are you in?

櫃檯：你是在什麼房間呢？

Guest: Room # 844 and it's the people to the left of me.

顧客：房間 # 844，那些人是住在我的左邊。

Front Desk: I will ask them to turn it down immediately.

櫃檯：我會要求他們立即將電視關小聲。

Dialogue 03 對話

Guest: The heater in my room is very noisy. It rattled all night long and kept me up.

顧客：房間裡的電暖器非常吵雜。它整個晚上都嘎嘎作響，讓我無法睡覺。

Front Desk: I'm sorry. I will send maintenance up right away to look at it so it won't bother you tonight.

顧客：對不起。我會馬上派維修人員去看一下，這樣今晚它就不會打擾你。

Even if you disagree with the guest's concern, don't be defensive. That response may make the guest more frustrated and angry. When approached by a guest with a difficult situation, try the following technique: LEAF

L- Listen. Listen carefully to the complaint and ask questions to clarify the issue.

E- Empathize. Reflect back to the guest how you'd feel if you were in their situation. Apologize for the situation and let them know that you aren't fine with them feeling upset.

A- Action. Turn a negative into a positive. Ask the guest what solution they want and work with them to resolve it. Give them several solutions and let them figure out which one works for them.

F- Follow-up. When the situation is resolved, check in with your guests and see how they're feeling about the situation now.

Not everything will go well every day, but when something does go wrong — fix it!

即使你不同意客人的問題也不要有防守的態度。你這樣的反應可能使客人會更加沮喪和憤怒。當客人有困難的情況下來找你時，你可以嘗試以下的方法：簡稱為 LEAF

L-Listen 聆聽：認真聽取投訴的問題也要問問題來澄清對方的問題。

E-Empathize 感同身受：你要想想，如果你是在他們的情況下，你會有如何的感受。對當時的問題來道歉，並讓他們知道你也不願意他們有生氣的感覺。

A-Action 行動：將消極變為積極。問客人他們會想要什麼樣的解決方案，並與他們一起合作來解決。給他們幾個解決方案的選擇，讓他們找出哪一個解決方案會是適合他們的。

F-Follow-up 後續檢查：當問題解決之後，與你的客人檢查一下看看他們對情況的感受是如何。

不是一切都會天天順利，但是當事情有出差錯時——就要解決問題！

Handling Special Situations
特殊狀況處理

3.3.2　Charge Additional Fee 向旅客收取額外費用

Conversations
不停住對話 　MP3 095

A New Housekeeper is talking to the Head Housekeeper about the policies of the hotel.
一位新進房務部人員正在與房務部主管談論有關飯店的政策。

Lead House-keeper	Make sure you **label** <u>lost and found</u> items with the room number and **submit** it to Lost and Found at your first **opportunity**. Often our guests will return for their items and we want to <u>make it easy for them to</u> get them back.	請確保你有記下失物招領和房間號碼，一馬上有機會時，就把資料提交給失物招領部。我們的客人往往都會回來找，所以我們希望他們能夠很容易的找回失物。
New House-keeper	What if I find something broken or stolen from the room?	如果我在房間內有看到東西壞了或被偷呢？
Lead House-keeper	Report it to me **immediately** and I will file the **maintenance** or a stolen property report. It is important that you tell me before the new guests arrive.	要立即向我報告，我會提交一份維修單或財產偷竊報告。很重要的是你要在新的客人到達之前告訴我這件事。

New House-keeper	What happens if things are stolen?	如果東西是被偷竊怎麼辦？
Lead House-keeper	All the guest sign a form saying they are <u>responsible for</u> everything being in the room that was there when they arrived and if it isn't, the hotel can charge their account for the missing items. So if the hair dryer is missing from room #328, we mark it on the room sheet and the hotel will <u>charge them for</u> the cost of replacing the hair dryer.	所有客人都有簽署一份表格，這是要確認他們到達房間時對房間內的東西是要負責的，如果不是的話，飯店可以對丟失的物品向客人的賬戶收取費用。因此，如果吹風機在房間 # 328 不見了，我們就會在房間表內做記號，飯店將可以向他們收取更換了吹風機的成本。
New House-keeper	Does that reduce the amount of theft?	這樣是否有減少盜竊案件？
Lead House-keeper	Our hotel offers an option for the guests to buy our products and have it charged to their bill so that reduces a lot of theft as well.	我們的飯店有提供了一個選項可以讓客人購買我們的產品，我們可以把費用加在賬單裡，這樣是有減少了很多的盜竊案件。

Part Ⅱ 旅館英語

Words
單 字

* label /ˈlebəl/   *v.* 標記
* submit /səbˈmɪt/   *v.* 提出
* opportunity /ˌɑpɚˈtunətɪ/   *n.* 機會
* immediately /ɪˈmidɪətlɪ/   *adv.* 馬上
* maintenance /ˈmentənəns/   *n.* 維護；維修

Grammar
文法片語

1. lost and found 失物招領

★小提點：〈lose〉遺失，〈lost〉是過去分詞，〈find〉找到，〈found〉是過去分詞，在這裡加起來就是「失物招領」。

> 例一：This is the phone number for the Lost and Found. 這是失物招領的電話號碼。

> 例二：I am looking for the Lost and Found. 我在尋找失物招領。

2. make it easy for ...to 讓……比較容易做……

★小提點：〈make it easy for ...to...〉通常指因為什麼事讓對方感到比較容易做某件事，也可以用〈make it easier for...〉。後面通常會加代名詞或名詞如〈make it easy for me〉「對我來說會比較容易」〈make it easy for Amy〉「對愛咪來說會比較容易」〈make it easy for the dog〉「對那隻狗來說會比較容易」。

> 例一：Our online hotel website makes it easier for you to make a reservation. 我們的網站預約系統可以讓你更容易進行預約。

> 例二：The self check-in at the airport makes it easier for travelers. 在機場的自助通關讓旅客感到很方便。

3. responsible for... 對……有責任

★小提點：形容詞〈responsible〉負責任的，對什麼負責任會用〈responsible for〉後面接名詞或子句。

> 例一：Who is responsible for the hotel reservation? 誰是負責飯店的預訂？

★小提點：類似的片語有〈in charge of〉「負責，照料」。

> 例二：The manager is in charge of the hotel management. 經理是負責飯店的管理。

4. charge them for.... 向他們索價為了……

★小提點：動詞〈charge〉索價，通常用在買賣的動作。如果買者覺得東西太貴不合理，可以用〈overcharge〉索價過高。

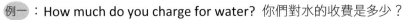

例一：How much do you charge for water? 你們對水的收費是多少？

例二：Do you charge for a bowl of rice? 你們對一碗飯的收費是多少？

★小提點：〈charge〉也可以當名詞「價錢」，介係詞是用〈for〉。

例三：There is no charge for cancellation. 不收取任何取消費用。

Short Sentences
不尷尬短句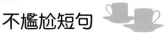

❶ The coffee pot in this room is missing.
這個房間裡的咖啡壺不見了。

❷ The housekeeper thinks the guest either broke the glass or stole it.
房務部認為客人要不是打破就是偷走玻璃杯。

❸ I just checked into room #495 and there is no ironing board or iron.
我剛住進房間＃ 495 但並沒有看到燙衣板或熨斗。

❹ The housekeeper checks everywhere in the room but can't find the remote control.
房務部在房間內到處找遍了，但找不到遙控器。

❺ There is an additional fee if you break any item in the room.
如果你在房間裡打破任何東西，你是要額外付費。

❻ The hotel has a policy about how to handle theft in the hotel.
本飯店有一個關於如何處理盜竊的策略。

❼ It is very possible that the guest damaged the flat screen TV.
很有可能是顧客破壞那個平面電視。

❽ The guest insisted that he did not break the window.
顧客堅持說他沒有破壞那個窗戶。

❾ The head housekeeper asks the housekeeping staff to carefully make sure nothing is stolen in each guest room.
房務部的主管要求房務部人員要小心地確定每一個房間都沒有東西被偷。

❿ The hotel has a security camera in each floor hall.
本飯店每一個層樓的走廊都有監視器。

Speak Up!
說出來！ MP3 096

Dialogue 01 對話

Housekeeper: There are no towels in Room # 523 today. No bathrobes either.
清潔人員：今天在房間 # 523 內沒有毛巾。也沒有浴袍。

Lead Housekeeper: Make sure you note that on your room card so that management can charge the guests who stayed in that room.
房務部主管：請確保你在你的房務卡內有寫下來，這樣管理部就可以向住在那個房間的客人收取費用。

Dialogue 02 對話

Housekeeper: There is supposed to a coffee pot in this room but it's missing. Do you think they broke it or stole it?
房務部人員：這個房間裡應該有一個咖啡壺，但卻不見了。你認為他們把它弄壞了或偷走了？

Lead Housekeeper: It doesn't matter. Fill out the missing appliance report and we will turn it in. The charge for it will be placed on their bill.
房務部主管：沒關係。填寫丟失的設備報告，我們會拿給櫃檯。我們會把這個東西的收費加在他們的賬單裡。

Dialogue 03 對話

Guest: What's this charge on my bill?
顧客：這是什麼費用加在我的帳單裡？

Front Desk: That's for items from the mini bar- for a soda and a beer.
櫃檯：這是迷你酒吧的項目，一瓶蘇打水和啤酒。

Job Wisdom
職業補給站

The Housekeeping team is a critical component of a hotel's success. If a guest walks into a room that isn't clean or has missing items, she will automatically rate the hotel lower. If it's missing items like a coffee pot, a hair dryer, or an ironing board, it's annoying to have to call housekeeping to request items that belong in the room. Plus, if your hotel charges their guests for missing items, they don't want to be charged for things that weren't in the room when they checked in. The mini bar needs to be checked at check in and check out with all items missing charged to the room and the bar restocked for the next guest.

　　房務部團隊是飯店成功的一個關鍵組成部分。如果客人走進一個房間是不乾淨或有遺失物品，她的腦海裡就會自動降低這個飯店的品質。如果是缺少像咖啡壺、吹風機、或燙衣板，讓客人要求清潔部把這些本來就應該屬於在房間裡的東西會讓客人覺得煩。另外，如果你的飯店對客人把物品遺失有收取費用時，他們不希望被收取的費用是他們在住入房間時本來就沒有的東西，迷你酒吧要當他們住入和辦理退房時就做好檢查，如果有什麼不見了，飯店可以收取所有不見的項目，而迷你酒吧也要馬上就放好存貨準備給下一位入住的客人。

Part Ⅱ　旅館英語

Appendix 附錄
Common Words 常見單字

1. Meat and Seafood　肉類海鮮　　　　　　　　　　　MP3 097

chicken/ˈtʃɪkən/ 雞肉

drumstick/ˈdrʌmstɪk/ 雞腿

wing/wɪŋ/ 雞翅

liver/ˈlɪvɚ/ 肝

gizzard/ˈgɪzəd/ 雞腱

pork/pɔrk/ 豬肉

ground pork/graʊnd/ /pɔrk/ 豬絞肉

beef/bif/ 牛肉

ground beef/graʊnd/ /bif/ 牛絞肉

steak/stek/ 牛排

lamb/læm/ 羊肉

turkey/ˈtɚki/ 火雞肉

duck/dʌk/ 鴨肉

shrimp/ʃrɪmp/ 蝦子

fish /fɪʃ/ 魚

clam/klæm/ 蛤

scallop/ˈskæləp/ 扇貝

trout/traʊt/ 鱒魚

salmon/ˈsæmən/ 鮭魚

crab/kræb/ 螃蟹

lobster/ˈlɑbstɚ/ 龍蝦

mussel/ˈmʌsəl/ 淡菜

oyster/ˈɔɪstɚ/ 牡蠣

cod/kɑd/ 鱈魚

eel/il/ 鰻魚

herring/ˈhɛrɪŋ/ 鯡魚

mackerel/ˈmækəəl/ 鯖魚

octopus/ˈɑktəpʊs/ 章魚

squid/skwɪd/ 魷魚

tuna/ˈtunə/ 鮪魚

2. Fruits and Vegetables 水果蔬菜　　　　　　　　MP3 098

banana/bəˈnænə/ 香蕉

strawberry/ˈstrɔˌbɛri/ 草莓

blueberry/ˈbluˌbɛri/ 藍莓

raspberry/ˈræzˌbɛri/ 紅莓

apple/ˈæpəl/ 蘋果

orange/ˈɔrəndʒ/ 橘子

watermelon/ˈwɔtɚˌmɛlən/ 西瓜

lemon/ˈlɛmən/ 檸檬

lime/laɪm/ 萊姆

pineapple/ˈpaɪnˌæpəl/ 鳳梨

grapefruit/ˈgrepˌfrut/ 葡萄柚

grape/grep/ 葡萄

kiwi/ˈkiwi/ 奇異果

plum/plʌm/ 李子

onion/ˈʌnjən/ 洋蔥

green onion /grin/ /ˈʌnjən/ 蔥

cabbage/ˈkæbədʒ/ 高麗菜

radish/ˈrædɪʃ/ 蘿蔔

potato/pəˈteto/ 馬鈴薯

carrot/ˈkærət/ 紅蘿蔔

celery/ˈsɛləri/ 芹菜

tomato/təˈmeto/ 番茄

coriander/sɪˈlæntro/ 香菜

cucumber /ˈkjukəmbɚ/ 小黃瓜

squash/skwɑʃ/ 節瓜

pumpkin/ˈpʌmpkɪn/ 南瓜

corn/kɔrn/ 玉米

okra/ˈokrə/ 秋葵

mushroom/ˈmʌʃrum/ 蘑菇

bell pepper/bɛl/ /ˈpɛpɚ/ 紅椒

3. Breakfast Menus　早餐

ham/hæm/ 火腿

toast/tost/ 吐司

wheat bread/wit/ /brɛd/ 全麥麵包

egg/ɛg/ 蛋

cheese/tʃiz/ 起司

sausage/ˈsɔsədʒ/ 香腸

sandwich/ˈsændwɪtʃ/ 三明治

bun/bʌn/ 餐包

porridge/ˈpɔrədʒ/ 稀飯

coffee/ˈkɔfi/ 咖啡

milk/mɪlk/ 牛奶

skim milk/skɪm/ /mɪlk/ 脫脂牛奶

whole milk/hol/ /mɪlk/ 全脂牛奶

cream/krim/ 奶油；奶精

chocolate milk /ˈtʃɔklət/ /mɪlk/ 巧克力牛奶

butter/ˈbʌtɚ/ 奶油

steamed bun /stimd/ /bʌn/ 包子

croissant /kwɑˈsɑn/ 牛角餐包

biscuit/ˈbɪskɪt/ 英式餅乾

cereal/ˈsɪrɪəl/ 麥片

hash-brown/hæʃ/ /braʊn/ 馬鈴薯餅

scrambled egg 炒蛋 /ˈskræmbəld/ /ɛgs/

jelly/ˈdʒɛli/ 果凍

jam/dʒæm/ 果醬

pancake/ˈpænˌkek/ 煎餅

waffle/ˈwɑfəl/ 鬆餅

bagel/ˈbegəl/ 貝果

hot cocoa/hɑt//ˈkoko/ 熱可可

oatmeal/ˈotmil/ 燕麥片

yogurt/ˈjogɚt/ 優格

peanut butter /ˈpinət/ /ˈbʌtɚ/ 花生醬

4. Tablewares　餐具　　　　　　　　　　　　　　MP3 100

casserole /ˈkæsəˌrol/ 西式砂鍋

cookware /ˈkʊkˌwɛr/ 餐具

mixer /ˈmɪksə/ 攪拌器

oven /ˈʌvən/ 烤箱

timer /ˈtaɪmə/ 計時器

baking pan /ˈbekɪŋ/ /pæn/ 烤盤

microwave /mˈaɪkrəwˌev/ 微波爐

toaster /ˈtostə/ 烤麵包機

dishwasher /ˈdɪʃˌwɑʃə/ 洗碗機

bread machine /brɛd/ /məˈʃin/ 麵包機

chopper /ˈtʃɑpə/ 大菜刀

stove /stov/ 爐灶

egg slicer /ˈɛg/ /ˈslaɪsə/ 切蛋器

cutting board /ˈkʌtɪŋ/ /bɔrd/ 砧板

blender /ˈblɛndə/ 果汁機

steamer /ˈstimə/ 蒸器

fork /fɔrk/ 叉子

spoon /spun/ 湯匙

knife /naɪf/ 刀子

napkin /ˈnæpkɪn/ 餐巾紙

salad bowl /ˈsæləd/ /bol/ 沙拉碗

bowl /bol/ 碗

plate /ˈplet/ 盤子

5. Coffee, Liquor and Alcohol　咖啡與酒類　　　　MP3 101

Cappuccino/ˌkɑˌpətʃino/ 卡布其諾
Café Americano/kæˋfe/ /əˌmerıˋkɑnəʊ/ 美式咖啡
espresso/ɛkˋspɛso/ 濃縮咖啡
Café latte/kæˋfe/ /ˋlɑˌte/ 拿鐵
Café mocha/kæˋfe/ /ˋmokə/ 摩卡拿鐵
decaffeinate/diˋkæfəˌnet/ 低咖啡因
caffeine/kæˋfin/ 咖啡因
sweetener/ˋswitənɚ/ 糖精
hot chocolate/hɑt/ /ˋtʃɔklət/ 熱巧克力
vanilla/vəˋnılə/ 香草
vodka/ˋvɑdkə/ 伏特加酒
cream soda/krim/ /ˋsodə/ 奶油蘇打水
rum/rʌm/ 甜酒
tequila/təˋkilə/ 龍舌蘭酒
cocktail/ˋkɑkˌtel/ 雞尾酒
whisky/ˋwıski/ 威士忌酒
cognac/ˋkonˌjæk/ 干邑白蘭地
brandy/ˋbrændi/ 白蘭地
orange liqueur/ˋɔrəndʒ/ /lıˋkɝ/ 橙利口酒
almond liqueur/ˋɑmənd/ /lıˋkɝ/ 杏仁利口酒
champagne/ʃæmˋpen/ 香檳酒
chardonnay/tʃɑrˋdɑne/ 夏多內白酒
Riesling/ˋrizlıŋ/ 雷司令白酒
Bourbon/ˋbɚbən/ 波旁酒
Martini/mɑrˋtini/ 馬丁尼
Ice Wine/ˋaıs/ /waın/ 冰酒
Raisin Wine /ˋrezın/ /waın/ 葡萄乾酒
Gin/dʒın/ 琴酒

6. Cooking Methods and Egg Cookings　烹調手法與雞蛋煮法　MP3 102

deep fry/dip/ /fraɪ/ 炸

stir fry/stɚ/ /fraɪ/ 炒

steam/stim/ 蒸

bake/bek/ 烤

pressure-cook/ˈprɛʃɚ/ /kʊk/ 壓力鍋煮法

marinate/ˈmɛrəˌnet/ 醃

caramelize/ˈkɛrəməˌlaɪz/ 焦化

clarify/ˈklɛrəˌfaɪ/ 提煉

dice/daɪs/ 切塊

drizzle/ˈdrɪzəl/ 淋上

ferment/fɚˈmɛnt/ 發酵

glaze/glez/ 淋在糕點上增加光澤的蛋漿

peel /pil/ 削皮

preserve/prəˈzɚv/ 醃製

mix/mɪks/ 混合

melt/mɛlt/ 融化

smoke/smok/ 熏烤

stew /stu/ 燉

boiled egg/bɔɪld/ /ɛg/ 水煮蛋

scrambled egg/ˈskræmbəld/ /ɛg/ 炒蛋

7. Seasoning and Salad Dressing　調味料與沙拉醬　　MP3 103

salad dressing/ˈsæləd/ /ˈdrɛsɪŋ/ 沙拉醬

sauce/sɔs/ 醬

black paper/ˈblæk/ /pepɚ/ 黑胡椒

white paper/ˈhwaɪt/ /pepɚ/ 白胡椒

salt/sɔlt/ 鹽

soup/sup/ 湯

condiment/ˈkɑndəmənt/ 調味品

cream/krim/ 奶精

seasoning/ˈsizənɪŋ/ 調味料

spice/ˈspaɪs/ 調味粉

topping/ˈtɑpɪŋ/ 配料

soy sauce/sɔɪ/ /sɔs/ 醬油

steak sauce/stek/ /sɔs/ 牛排醬

Tabasco sauce/təˈbæsko/ /sɔs/ 塔巴斯科辣椒醬

mayonnaise/ˌmeɚnez/ 美乃滋

mustard /ˈmʌstɚd/ 芥末醬

ketchup/ˈkɛtʃəp/ 番茄醬

pickle/ˈpɪkəl/ 醃製小黃瓜

Ranch dressing/ˈræntʃ/ /ˈdrɛsɪŋ/ 鄉村醬

Thousand Island dressing/ˈθaʊzənd/ /ˈaɪlənd/ /ˈdrɛsɪŋ/ 千島沙拉醬

Caesar dressing /ˈsizɚ/ /ˈdrɛsɪŋ/ 凱薩沙拉醬

8. Chinese Cusine　中餐菜名　　　　　　　MP3 104

Stir fry vegetables 炒菜
steamed dumplings 蒸餃
salted goose 鹹水鴨
braised pig's intestine with garlic sauce 蒜泥肥腸
sliced poached chicken 白切雞
beef shank with five spices 五香滷牛腱
braised bean curd 滷豆腐
egg omelet with dried turnip 菜脯蛋
stir friend spinach 炒菠菜
Kale with oyster sauce 蠔油芥蘭
porridge 清粥
Steamed turnip cake 蘿蔔糕
spring roll 春卷
pineapple shortbread 鳳梨酥
Steamed bun with red bean paste 豆沙包
Aiyu jelly 愛玉
steamed rice 白飯
hot pot 火鍋
fried rice 炒飯
fish ball soup 魚丸湯
chicken ball soup 雞肉丸湯
rice with shredded turkey 火雞肉飯
rice with shredded chicken 雞肉飯
rice with braised beef 牛肉飯
steamed bun with pork 豬肉包
cold noodle with shredded egg cucumber and carrot 涼麵
pan fry dumplings 煎餃
rice noodle soup 米粉湯
noodle without soup 乾麵
sweet and sour soup 酸辣湯

9. Hospitality Staff　從業人員職稱　　　　　　　　　　　MP3 105

Valet /væˋle/ 泊車專員

Chauffeur /ʃoˋfɚ/ 司機

Concierge /ˌkɑnsıˋɛrʒ/ 禮賓接待員

Receptionist /rıˋsɛpʃənıst/ 接待員

Chef /ʃɛf/ 廚師

Housekeeper /ˋhaʊsˏkipɚ/ 客房服務員

Conference Coordinator /ˋkɑnfəəns/ /koˋɔrdəˏnetɚ/ 會議協調員

Convention Services Manager /kənˋvɛnʃən/ /ˋsəvəsəz/ /ˋmænədʒɚ/ 大型會議服務經理

Promotion Specialist /prəˋmoʃən/ /ˋspɛʃələst/ 促銷專員

Banquet Coordinator /ˋbæŋkwət/ /koɔrdəˏnetɚ/ 宴會支援員

Systems Analyst /ˋsıstəmz/ /ˋænələst/ 系統分析員

General Manager /ˋdʒɛnəəl/ /ˋmænədʒɚ/ 經理

Personnel Manager /ˏpəsəˋnɛl/ /ˋmænədʒɚ/ 人事經理

Director /dəˋɛktɚ/ 主任

Lobby Duty Manager /ˋlɑbı/ /ˋduti/ /ˋmænədʒɚ/ 大廳經理

Assistant Manager /əˋsıstənt/ /ˋmænədʒɚ/ 副經理

Receptionist /rıˋsɛpʃənıst/ 接待員

Head Housekeeper /hɛd/ /ˋhaʊsˏkipɚ/ 清潔部主管

Room Maid /rum/ /med/ 客房服務員

Cleaner /ˋklinɚ/ 清潔員

Restaurant Manager /ˋrɛstərənt/ /ˋmænədʒɚ/ 餐廳經理

Host /host/ 接待員

Hostess /ˋhostəs/ 女接待員

Bartender /ˋbɑrˏtɛndɚ/ 酒吧員

Switchboard Manager /ˋswıtʃˏbɔrd/ /ˋmænədʒɚ/ 總機經理

Security /sıˋkjʊrətı/ 安全人員

Service Manager /ˋsəvəs/ /ˋmænədʒɚ/ 服務中心經理

Chinese Chef /tʃaıˋniz/ /ʃɛf/ 中餐廚師

Western Chef /ˋwɛstən/ /ʃɛf/ 西餐廚師

Line Cook /ˋlaın/ /ʃɛf/ 廚房助理

Pastry Chef /ˋpestri/ /ʃɛf/ 糕點師傅

Executive Chef /ıgˋzɛkjətıv/ /ʃɛf/ 總廚

Cashier /kæˋʃır/ 前檯出納

Operator /ˋɑpəˏretɚ/ 總機

Marketing/ˈmɑrkətɪŋ/ 行銷部
Public Relation Specialist/ˈpʌblɪk/ /rɪˈleʃən/ /ˈspɛʃələst/ 公關部專員
Maintenance/ˈmentənəns/ 工務部

10. Floor plans and Space　樓層與空間　　MP3 106

escalator/ˈɛskəˌletə/ 電梯
entrance/ˈɛntrəns/ 入口
lounge/ˈlɑʊndʒ/ 休息室
housekeeping/ˈhɑʊsˌkipɪŋ/ 房務部
main kitchen/men/ /ˈkɪtʃən/ 主廚房
restaurant/ˈrɛstəənt/ 餐廳
machine room/məˈʃin/ /rum/ 機房
guest room/gɛst/ /rum/ 客房
ballroom/ˈbɔlˌrum/ 正式舞廳
banquet room/ˈbæŋkwət/ /rˈum/ 宴會廳
bar/bˈɑr/ 酒吧
business center/ˈbɪznəs/ /ˈsɛntə/ 商務中心
conference center/ˈkɑnfəəns/ /sɛntə/ 會議中心
fitness and recreation/ˈfɪtnɪs/ /ænd/ /ˌrɛkrɪˈeʃən/ 健身和娛樂中心
front desk/frʌnt/ /dɛsk/ 櫃檯
garage/gəˈɑʒ/ 車庫
gift shop/gɪft/ /ʃɑp/ 禮品店
hospitality suite/ˌhɑspəˈtæləti/ /swit/ 多功能款待房
laundry room/ˈlɔndri/ /rum/ 洗衣房
lobby/ˈlɑbi/ 大廳
restroom/ˈrɛstˌrum/ 廁所
spa/spɑ/ 水療

五星級餐旅英語

作 者	林昭菁、Jeri Fay Maynard（梅潔理）
封 面 設 計	高鍾琪
內 頁 構 成	華漢電腦排版有限公司
發 行 人	周瑞德
企 劃 編 輯	徐瑞璞
校 對	劉俞青、陳欣慧
印 製	世和印製企業有限公司
初 版	2014年6月
定 價	新台幣369元
出 版	倍斯特出版事業有限公司
電 話	（02）2351-2007
傳 真	（02）2351-0887
地 址	100 台北市中正區福州街1號10樓之2
E m a i l	best.books.service@gmail.com
港澳地區總經銷	泛華發行代理有限公司
地 址	香港筲箕灣東旺道3號星島新聞集團大廈3樓
電 話	（852）2798-2323
傳 真	（852）2796-5471

國家圖書館出版品預行編目（CIP）資料

五星級餐旅英語／林昭菁，梅潔理（Jeri Fay Maynard）著
. -- 初版 . -- 臺北市：倍斯特, 2014.06
面；　公分
ISBN：978-986-90331-8-3（平裝）
1. 英語　2. 餐旅業　3. 會話
805.188　　　　　　　　　　　　　　103009760